MOMOTARO

XANDER AND THE
LOST ISLAND OF MONSTERS

C.1

MOMOTARO

XANDER AND THE
LOST ISLAND OF MONSTERS

MARGARET DILLOWAY

with illustrations by Choong Yoon

𝒟𝒾𝒮𝒩𝔼𝒴 • HYPERION

Los Angeles   New York

First Edition, April 2016
1 3 5 7 9 10 8 6 4 2
FAC-020093-16015
Printed in the United States of America

Library of Congress Cataloging-in-Publication Data
Dilloway, Margaret.
Momotaro : Xander and the lost island of monsters /
by Margaret Dilloway.—First hardcover edition.
pages cm
Summary: Twelve-year-old Xander discovers and learns to use the fantastic powers
that are his birthright in order to save his father. Based on Japanese mythology.
ISBN 978-1-4847-2487-3
[1. Fathers and sons—Fiction. 2. Mythology, Japanese—Fiction. 3. Friendship—
Fiction. 4. Racially mixed people—Fiction. 5. Fantasy.] I. Title.
PZ7.1.D563Mom 2016
[Fic]—dc23   2015004970

Reinforced binding
Visit www.DisneyBooks.com

For Elyse, Ethan, and Kaiya

"See first with your mind, then with your eyes, and finally with your body."

—Yagyū Munenori,

A Hereditary Book on the Art of War, 1632

The pale old man stands in the middle of the rainy street and watches the boy through the school windows. The classroom faces the road, but it's hard to get a clear view inside. That's fine. He doesn't want the boy to notice him. Not yet.

The boy is in front of the class, one hand fidgeting with papers, the other dipping into his pocket to jingle imaginary coins, then combing through his hair. The whiteboard behind him seems to engulf him, each word on it at least the length of the boy's arm. The old man's used-to-be heart drops in sympathy. He's supposed to be twelve, this boy, but he's no bigger than a seven-year-old.

That's him, all right, the man thinks. Blue eyes, straight black hair. Like his father and his grandfather. But this boy is frightfully weak. The pale man shakes his head. Can the boy handle this?

The old man limps toward the school, hoping for a better view. A monster-size pickup truck passes through him. Neither the pale man nor the driver notices.

The man presses his transparent face to the windowpane. That's better. Now he can see *and* hear. But none of the students see

1

him—the rain sluices through the old man's face, making it look like a puddle gathered on the glass.

The boy is back at his desk now, supposedly paying attention to the lecture. Which he most definitely isn't. He's drawing. Like he always does. The pale man shimmers in the rain like a waving piece of plastic wrap.

That teacher sounds like a robot. Why, the old man almost drops off just listening, and *he's* already dead. So the old man can't blame (What is his English name? So hard for him to remember . . .) Xander for being bored. Xander Musashi Miyamoto. The boy's named after Musashi Miyamoto, one of the greatest samurai and artists who ever lived. The old man calls the boy Musashi in his head. Always has, ever since Xander was born.

We have no choice. He is the one. He must rise. The pale man exhales a breath that would have sounded like a sigh, had he any lungs.

He goes back to sit on the bench again, waiting for his grandson to notice him.

CHAPTER ONE

shuffle through my notes once, twice, three times, feeling sweat starting to trickle down my sides and from my palms. I'm standing in front of twenty-five of my fellow sixth graders, in the middle of giving my report, "Snow in Ecuador: How Climate Change Affects the Rain Forests," which is a really great title, if I do say so myself.

But I've lost my place. Not just a little bit. Completely. I can't remember the last thing I said or what I'm supposed to say next. It doesn't help that I basically copied and pasted my entire report out of Wikipedia and some random guy's blog without reading any of it. I meant to go over it this morning, but I forgot because my friend Peyton got a new app on his phone and we were playing it right up until the bell rang. The worst part is, the app—*Xoru, Master of Magic*—wasn't even very good. What a waste of time. Whoops. This project is for extra credit, which I desperately, desperately need in social studies, and I'm about to blow it.

I cough and clear my throat. Rain beats in a steady *thumthumthum* against the windows. The whole class shifts around, impatient, starting to whisper. *Clickclickclick.* Someone's taking cell phone photos. I look up, and, sure enough, it's Lovey, the most misnamed person on the face of the planet. The forbidden phone peeks up over the top of her textbook. She didn't even bother to turn off the sound. Sheesh. She looks straight at me and giggles. Fantastic.

Mr. Stedman doesn't seem to notice. He lets out a sigh. "Xander, please continue or sit down. We have a lesson to do."

I feel like I'm standing in front of the class in my underwear. I look down at my legs, just to make sure. Yup, pants are on. I put my hand in my pocket and rock back and forth in my Converse, stare at the white toe caps. *Come on.*

Finally, inspiration hits.

"Four score and seven years ago, our fathers brought forth the subject of climate change." I sweep my hand around like I'm Abraham Lincoln. The whole class jerks upright, suddenly awake. Peyton flashes me a thumbs-up from his seat in the back. "They kept talking. Nothing much happened. We still drive cars and make smog, and now there's, like, a ton of snow in Ecuador. So, basically, that's it. Let's all stop climate change. Together. Stop using plastic, people. Wake up!"

The class applauds, and I take a little bow and run back to my seat with a grin plastered across my face. There. I've done it. Score. I mean, I might not have gotten full points, but that was good for at least five, right?

Mr. Stedman rolls his eyes. "Thank you, Mr. Miyamoto." He shakes his head so I can be sure he doesn't mean it. "Everyone, turn to page one hundred and fifty in your textbooks."

Page 150 again? We've been on this page for a week. I flip open the book and start making a list in my head. *Things I'd Rather Be Doing*, in order of preference:

1. Playing computer games
2. Drawing
3. Drawing pictures of computer games
4. Getting a cavity drilled
5. Walking down the street with no pants on
6. Watching that wedding-dress show with my grandma

And then I tick off the minutes, like this. Like I'm a freaking prisoner in a medieval dungeon cell serving a two-million-year sentence, scratching the years into the wall with my bare fingernail:

Five minutes of class, done! Ten, done! And I'll keep going on and on and on, until I have twelve sets—it's a block day, which means that some classes are double periods. Today Mr. Stedman has the Social Studies block.

And then the bell rings, and the torture starts all over again.

For some reason, Social Studies seems twice as long as, say, my computer class, the one class I actually enjoy. Why is that? Why do things you love seem to take a shorter time? Seems like the opposite should be true.

Mr. Stedman has started his lecture, but it's the day before spring break, and, therefore, nobody's paying a bit of attention. Everyone's dreaming about sunshine and ice cream and warm beaches and Easter candy. But does Mr. Stedman care? Heck no. And we're all just staring at him, counting the black hairs coming out of his zombie-white forehead (he doesn't have that many hairs—they look like my number countdown, kind of) and dodging the spit flying off his lips (never sit in the front row of Mr. Stedman's class).

"*Blah blah blah* global warming. *Blah blah blah* fire at the South Pole. *Blah blah blah* tropical hurricane in Maine. *Blah blah blah* super hurricane-blizzard in New York."

I feel my brain quiver in my skull, probably wishing it could break out and run free. I yawn and stare out the window at the road. Rain's pouring down in sheets, and I hope it lets up before school ends.

The best thing about Social Studies is where the classroom is located—the windows look out onto the street. Sometimes a car goes by, but that's about it. Today just one old man sits at the bus stop. More boringness. What else is new? This place where we live, Oak

Grove, is a one-horse town, way out in the boonies of San Diego, so horribly far away from the actual city of San Diego that nobody even calls this San Diego anymore. They call it "backcountry." Or the mountains, where people go when they want to see some snow and pretend they have a real winter, even though they live in Southern California. It's so small that grades K–8 are all at the same lower school, and the entire sixth grade is in this classroom with me.

The old man outside doesn't seem to mind the rain. Which is good, because it's raining big, fat drops, more like a waterfall. It's supposed to rain for the next three days, on and on. So much for sunshine and warm beaches.

It hasn't rained like this in years. Not since . . . well, maybe back when I was just a little kid. When I'd tried to run away from home.

Most four-year-olds wouldn't be ambitious enough to take off down a mountain road, looking for their mom. Especially not on a day when cartoons got interrupted with the loud squeal of an emergency signal. "Flash flood warning in the mountains," a bored robotic female voice had said. "Severe weather threat until five o'clock." I had shrugged and turned off the TV, not knowing what a flash flood was. Just that it was raining a lot, which was no big deal to me. My grandmother had talked about how it was the wettest day the county had seen in two decades, during an already wet El Niño rainstorm year, when everything in California stayed green through the summer instead of turning into brown tinder.

But I was a super-sneaky four-year-old, the kind who'd climb the cupboards to steal a cookie while my grandma was in the bathroom. The kind who could blame the cookie theft on the dog and get away with it. The kind who knew which floorboards squeaked like wounded rats when you stepped on them. The kind who knew to turn the doorknob forty-five degrees to the left, then pull it hard so it opened smooth and quick. My grandma hadn't known I was gone for hours.

Mom had left us only about a month earlier, and it felt like two years. All Dad said was, "She had to go on a trip." But when your mom takes a hundred percent of her clothes with her *and* removes her entire Precious Moments figurine collection from the glass curio cabinet, you can kind of figure out what the truth is. Even if you are only a little kid.

The day I ran away, the ditch by the street had filled with roaring water, and the sidewalk was nothing but a muddy bank. I watched the water carry sticks and bits of trash downhill. *This way, Xander,* the ditch river seemed to say. *Follow me and you'll find your mother.* So I starting slogging through the mud, my shoes making a *squinch-squinch* sound.

I guess I was thinking that Mom would magically drive up in her green car, her red-gold hair shining in the sunless afternoon, and take me back home. I didn't know then how long a walk it was down the mountain, and I was shivering because I hadn't remembered a jacket. (Even though I was Sherlock Holmes sneaky, I was still only four.)

I wanted Mom back for a lot of reasons, but the main one was so she could sing me my bedtime song. She was the only one who knew the words to my favorite, "All I Ask of You," from *Phantom of the Opera*. (Hey, it's not my fault—she got me hooked on it by singing it to me when I was a baby. I haven't listened to that soundtrack in years.) My dad only sang me "Twinkle, Twinkle," and my grandma only knew songs from the 1940s. I wanted my regular bedtime song. When you're a tiny kid, that kind of thing is as important as looking for Santa Claus on Christmas Eve.

I had followed the ditch river for what seemed like hours. The rain was falling so hard I could barely see. The runoff stream grew wider and wider and rose until it filled the whole road and stole away bigger things, like trash can lids and a bike tire and branches.

Finally, I reached a driveway at the bottom of a hill, my short legs feeling like overcooked noodles. The ankle-deep water stole one of my shoes. As I watched it get swept away, I got a little scared for the first time. I climbed to the mailbox and sat on a boulder next to it, feeling as soggy as a book dropped into a bathtub, and started waiting.

I'd just sit right there until Mom came by. No matter how long it took. Like the story of that dog in Japan who hung out at the train station waiting for his dead master that they made into a really sad movie I'll never watch, because I hate sad movies.

A woman with short blond hair, in T-shirt and jeans, had walked down the hillside, I guess to get the mail. She jumped about a mile into the air when she spotted me. "I thought you were a rock!" She bent to peer into my face. Her eyes were the shade of new grass, with smile lines fanning out around the edges. "Aren't you the Miyamoto boy from next door? What are you doing here?"

"Waiting for my mom," I said.

"Your mother?" The woman bit her lip, and I knew that she knew my mother was gone. "I'm Mrs. Phasis. Why don't you come on inside, and we'll call your grandmother?" The woman held out her hand. She seemed nice enough, but she wasn't my mother, so I said no.

"No?" Mrs. Phasis looked as if she couldn't believe I'd defied her.

"No," I repeated.

"Okay, then." She picked me up like a sack of rice.

"Nooooo!" I screamed, and I kicked her and scratched her arms, but she didn't drop me. She just hurried into the warm house. Then she plunked me down in front of the TV and wrapped a fluffy blanket around my shoulders to stop my shivering. "Wait here, okay? Peyton, be nice to this little boy." The lady disappeared.

"Hi."

A boy about my size was perched on the floor, a big purple bowl in front of him. His golden hair stood up from his scalp in a crescent—sort of a natural Mohawk—and his eyes were a bright blue in the cloudy light. He cocked his head at me as he looked me up and down. Then he grinned and dipped his face into the bowl, his pointy nose and pointy chin disappearing behind the purple.

At first I didn't understand what he was doing. Then he straightened up, cheeks bulging, white kernels of popcorn sticking out of his mouth. "Want some?"

"Yes, please." If Peyton shoved his face into a bowl like that nowadays, I'd be too grossed out to share, but we were only four back then.

He pushed the bowl toward me, and I grabbed a handful. We watched the rest of the show in easy silence. It was some program about the jungle, and I felt calmer than I had in a long time. And then my grandmother showed up to haul me back home, apologizing profusely to Mrs. Phasis.

So something good came out of that experience. That was the day I met Peyton. It was probably also the last day we were the same height.

I'm still sorry I tried to kick his mom. But how was I supposed to know she was helping me?

And, no, my mom hasn't come back. We haven't heard from her in eight years. Not a phone call or a letter or an e-mail or a carrier pigeon. I never tried to look for her again.

I glare at the clouds outside my classroom. Rain, rain, go away, I think at them. Come again some other day, when I don't have to walk home from school.

CHAPTER 2

I open my notebook stealthily, because Mr. Stedman is known for freaking out if he thinks you're not worshipping him. Especially me. Just because I once forgot to take a test because I was watching big pieces of hail hit a parked car outside and wondering if the windshield would break and how fast the ice would have to be falling for that to happen.

Do you want to know what my brain looks like? A browser with twenty-five different pages open at once. I flip back and forth between them and open even more before I'm done reading what I meant to read. And then I forget what it was I was looking for.

My teachers have tried to get Dad to medicate me. Every year since first grade, and I'm in sixth now. My report cards say stuff like

Unfocused. Daydreams. Draws on his math papers. It makes me feel like I'm broken somehow. A computer with a virus in it. And you know what? Knowing that my teachers think I'm broken does not make me want to come to school more.

I don't think I'm broken. I just prefer to do my own thing instead of the lame things the teachers want me to do.

Dad says that's just how I am, a freaking creative genius (well, he doesn't actually use the word *freaking*, which he would call "a non-academic term"), and they all can just deal with it. "I know medication benefits many children," Dad always tells them, "but Xander doesn't need it. It is not medically necessary. He behaves appropriately at home. The difficulties arise only in certain classes, and so he does not meet the criteria for diagnosis."

Earlier this year, when Mr. Stedman pressed the issue, sending home note after note and making Dad come in multiple times, my father finally got angry during a conference. He stood up to his full height, and his eyes turned into polar ice caps. "You want these kids to grow up into unthinking cubicle monkeys. But that's not going to happen to Xander, I can tell you that much," Dad had said. "You bring this up one more time, and you'll be very sorry."

I was sort of impressed. I'd never seen Dad threaten anyone. The worst thing he ever did was write a slightly annoyed letter to the newspaper for misspelling something. *You folks really need to invest in a copy editor,* he wrote. I wondered how Dad would make

Mr. Stedman sorry. Probably sit him down and lecture him *so hard*. Maybe even wag his finger at him.

For a second I wondered what my mother would have done about Mr. Stedman, if she were here. She had a real temper—Dad said it came with the red hair and the Irishness. I remember her curls flying all around her head, like a flaming halo of doom, when she got mad. Mom got angry about a lot of stuff—one of my last memories of her is Mom yelling at Dad about how he made a peanut butter and jelly sandwich. "You put the peanut butter on *after* the jelly, not before! Otherwise, the peanut butter sticks on the knife and gets in the jelly jar!"

It seemed like a really funny thing to get so worked up about. I asked Dad about it once, and he said she wasn't mad, just passionate. "Passionate about peanut butter and jelly?" I asked. "It's only a sandwich!"

"Passionate about everything." Dad got a big smile on his face. "Besides, it wasn't the sandwich she was angry about." He shook his head and looked gloomy. I changed the subject.

That makes me think that my mother would have given Mr. Stedman more than a lecture. She probably would have given him a solid right hook to the jaw.

Anyway, the threat worked. Mr. Stedman's nostrils flared as he sputtered and combed his fingers through his balding hair. Dad's glare bored holes into my teacher until Mr. Stedman finally looked away.

This whole school pretty much hates my family now. Especially Mr. Stedman.

I strategically place my thick textbook in front of my notebook and start drawing while I stare at Mr. Stedman like he's the most fascinating thing I've ever seen. If I don't draw, I will literally fall asleep, because Mr. Stedman's voice is like Ambien. And if that happened, he would truly go nuts.

I consider what to draw. Self-portrait? Too boring. Just straight black hair in a style that's almost a bowl cut, because Grandma, Obāchan, cuts it for me. (Dad keeps promising to take me to a real barber, but I'm not holding my breath.) Gray-blue eyes. Skin I can never find the right crayon color for anyway, even in Crayola's "Multicultural" collection. It's a shade with too many pink undertones to be yellow and too much yellow to be pink.

A mix. A blend. A mutt. That's me.

"Yesterday, a volcano in Hawaii froze," Mr. Stedman says.

I pause. Huh. Now *that's* interesting. Idly, I draw sharks ice-skating on frozen lava covering the ocean. Weird climate things have been happening for the past two years. Pretty much every day, some news anchor interrupts my grandma's *Wheel of Fortune* show to tell us about snakes fleeing a rain forest, or enormous tuna jumping out of hot ocean water, or people in Florida having to buy ski jackets for a sudden blizzard.

Climate change. I guess maybe it is a problem. But it's all happening far away. Too far away for me to worry about.

On my left, Clarissa taps my arm. She grins, showing two rows of braces with hot pink rubber bands. She points to my notebook. "You should put that into the game," she whispers.

I shrug quick, feeling my face go all hot. My hands start sweating. She tucks her long, curly black hair behind her ear and wiggles her eyebrows at me. I've known Clarissa since kindergarten. We've watched each other pick our noses. I don't know why I'm so nervous around her now. Once, I called her a hobbit—I meant it as a compliment, because hobbits are the coolest creatures ever and she's the only girl still shorter than I am—but she socked my arm so hard it left a purple bruise for two whole weeks.

The game she's talking about is what we're working on in computer class. We play this game called *CraftWorlds*, where you can build your own, well, worlds. Anything you can make with pixels. Since you actually have to know some coding to change the game, the teacher's letting us use it in class.

Not to brag, but I'm the king of the computer class. It's the one place where I pretty much rule over all the other kids. The characters I program look better, jump higher, and can do more than anyone else's. I'm famous for it around here.

Clarissa smiles at me again and I smile back, and Mr. Stedman shoots a glare at me. What, it's illegal to smile now? *Mind police.* Mr. Stedman sticks a pencil behind his ear, near the ring of hair around his bald spot. "Find two articles about global warming and summarize them." He writes the assignment on the whiteboard like we're morons. Summarizing is the most boringest thing in the free world. Why do I have to tell you exactly what I read? *I* know what I read; *you* know what I read. I want to tell you what I *think* about it.

I look down at my notebook.

I blink.

My sharks aren't there anymore. In their place there's a drawing of an ape and a human mixed together, except it has a long lizard tail studded with spikes, like a dinosaur's, waving in a muscular curve. His skin is hairy but wet-looking, in shades of red and purple and iridescent green.

I suck in a quick breath and look at my black-ink pen, then back down at the colorful drawing. What the heck?

I put my fingertips on the drawing. I could be wrong, but it kind of feels like the ink is rising up from the paper. . . .

I yank back my hand and shake my head to clear it.

The creature's eyes stare back at mine. They're like a shark's—no white, no iris, just all black pupil.

I have the urge to set the notebook on fire. Or bury it someplace. I'm frozen. I can't take my eyes off it.

The creature's smiling at me with serrated yellow teeth, and I know there's all kinds of gross bacteria on them, like a Komodo dragon who poisons his prey. A pink-red tongue forks into three snakes at the tip. The tiny snakes hiss their displeasure. *SSSsssssss.*

Hissing?

It's a drawing. It can't make noise.

But I *hear* it, the same way I can hear Mom calling, "Xander," sometimes as I'm waking from a deep sleep.

The hair on my neck stands straight up, and my stomach drops like I'm falling into a pitch-black and cold endless pit. Then my stomach feels like I've been hit by a really hard ball. I gasp, trying to get air into my lungs.

"Are you okay?" Clarissa whispers.

I nod once and shut my notebook fast.

Suddenly Mr. Stedman's forearms, covered in wiry black hair, appear by my face. *SMACK!* He hits the desk with his metal ruler so hard the fillings in my teeth rattle. "Xander! This is not art class."

I shrug, trying to hide how much he startled me. "Of course it's not art class. This school doesn't *have* an art class."

Clarissa giggles softly. Mr. Stedman's nostrils flare. He yanks my notebook away, turns to a blank page, and puts it back on my desk. He narrows his eyes. "You're on thin ice, Mr. Miyamoto."

"Like sharks by the frozen volcano?" I ask before I can help myself. Whoops.

This time both Clarissa and Peyton, who's sitting a few rows back, snort.

Mr. Stedman bares his teeth like he's in some teen werewolf show. I sigh and nod. "Sorry." I manage to sound like I really mean it. And I do. I know he's going to spend the rest of class time watching me, and I hate that.

He stalks to his desk. "Get into your groups. I don't want to hear too much noise, or this exercise will be over."

The good news is, five more minutes have passed. I make more hash marks. Only thirty more to go and we're on spring break. Freedom. I can't wait.

We move around to do our group work. Peyton throws four newspapers on the table. "You look through two; I'll look through two." He sits in his chair backward, the way teachers always tell you not to do. But Peyton's Peyton, so nobody corrects him. His blond-brown hair sticks up in the middle, and he smooths it down, which only works for a second before it springs back up again in a feathery plume.

Peyton's taller than most people's dads, though he's not thirteen yet. He plays a ton of sports, and his size is an advantage for him, which is why somebody on the other team always demands to see Peyton's birth certificate. Last year I went to his Little League play-off game, and a loudmouthed mother from the opposing team shouted, "No way that kid's only eleven. Lookit them long arms and legs! Chicken legs!" (I thought that was pretty funny, but Peyton didn't.) Also, under his pointy nose, Peyton has a mouthful of naturally straight white teeth. Oh, and he has a great voice as well. In class he isn't too loud or too quiet, he stays on task, and he makes girls and teachers laugh instead of annoying them. He's pretty much the mayor of Oak Grove Lower School.

It's a good thing I met Peyton when we were only four. Because if we'd met in sixth grade, I'm not sure the Number One Jock and the Number One Nerd would be such good friends.

Allow me to demonstrate how well Peyton and I know each other.

Phone rings. One of us answers. "Dude."

"Dude."

"7-Eleven. Ten minutes."

"Yup."

Hang up.

Boom. Done. That's all we need.

And most of the time, it doesn't matter that I'm smaller than Peyton. If I can't do something physical, my friend will do it for me.

Like the time, back when we were seven, I thought it'd be fun to design a parachute out of bedsheets and clothesline and jump off the garage roof onto a pile of garbage bags stuffed with leaves and pine needles. If I'd been just a few inches taller, I could have climbed the wooden fence next to the building and pulled myself onto the roof.

I could imagine how cool it would have been to leap from those gray asphalt shingles, the parachute billowing behind me. "Whatcha think?" I asked Peyton. Before I even got the words out of my mouth, Peyton had the parachute strapped to his back and was scrambling up the fence.

My grandmother had emerged from the house just in time to see Peyton launching himself off the roof, his arms spread and his eyes closed, like he had every confidence in the world that those flimsy garbage bags would cushion his leap. And there I was, yelling, "Fly, Peyton!" and being more than a little bit jealous of what he could do.

My eardrums still hurt from the sound of Obāchan's scream.

Oh, and by the way, the bags *mostly* held. Peyton only got one little fracture in his ankle and had to wear a small cast for six weeks.

It was a while before Peyton's parents let him come over again.

Now, in Mr. Stedman's class, Peyton goes off to get the scissors. Clarissa and Lovey move their desks near ours. They are besties. I wish Lovey would sit somewhere else. Like in the middle of the frozen volcano about two thousand miles away from me.

Lovey's supposedly the prettiest middle-schooler in town, because she more or less looks like Barbie. But I've known her since second grade, and she's got the worst personality ever. That makes anybody ugly. I wouldn't want to run into her in a dark alley.

Plus, Lovey wears so much makeup—in frosted pale colors, over sunburned skin—that she doesn't even look like a girl to me anymore. She looks like a baboon wearing clown makeup. I don't know why Clarissa bothers being friends with her.

Clarissa smiles up at me. "Hey, do you have time after school to help me with my modding in Scratch? I can't get my DreamShine characters to look like they're dancing."

Scratch is an animation program. Is she asking because she likes me, or because her code won't work? Is the computer lab open today?

How do I get the characters to dance? I frown, thinking about all this stuff.

"DreamShine . . ." I say out loud, picturing the code, what those characters would look like.

Clarissa's smile fades. "DreamShine is a band."

"I know who DreamShine is. That boy group." I blush again. Clarissa and Lovey both giggle. *Masculinity, minus 1,000 points.* "The most annoying band in the history of time, that is."

"DreamShine?" Peyton puts some scissors down on the table. "I like that one song, 'Blame It on the Heart.'" With that, he breaks into an accomplished falsetto, notes trilling up and down. *"Blame it on my heart/it's not so smart/and when you sleep it's an art. . . ."* The girls smile up at him. *"And then you rip a big fart."* This whole side of the classroom laughs. He shuts his mouth and spins around. "Darn. Forgot the glue."

Mr. Stedman glances up at Peyton but says nothing about the musical interlude. That, ladies and gentleman, is my friend Peyton. He could wear a pink tutu to school and not lose any masculinity points.

"You know what, Xander? You don't need to help me. I probably just made a typo in the code." Clarissa turns pink and opens her newspaper.

Oh. She thinks I don't want to help her. Just because I was frowning? I'm so dumb. "No, I'll help you. Meet after school?"

Clarissa shrugs. "I think the computer lab's probably not open today. We can do it after spring break." She sounds a lot less enthusiastic now. She gets up and crosses the classroom to sharpen her pencil.

Oh well. I inhale a huge breath. I will dazzle her with my mad modding skills after break. Then we'll be friends again. I open up a newspaper and scan the headlines. "Earthquake in Kansas Topples Houses."

Strange, but (a) do earthquakes count as climate change? and (b) who cares about earthquakes? We have them all the time here. Let other places experience our joy, too.

I look through the newspaper, praying Lovey will keep quiet. She's one of those people who finds out what bugs you the most, then pokes at it over and over. Just because she's bored as well as mean.

"Hey, Xander." Lovey wrinkles her perfect little nose at me. "I thought Asians were supposed to be smart. Why are you so dumb? You totally failed that report."

This isn't the first time she's said this. I'm the only half-Asian—or any-Asian—in the whole school. Plus, I'm not in GATE—that's *Gifted and Talented Education*—a program that you get into by scoring high on an intelligence test. The GATE kids have a special math teacher and go to some kind of fun enrichment class a few times a week, leaving the rest of us behind to stew in social studies purgatory. Peyton's in the program. So is Clarissa. And Lovey.

She's not the type of person to let you forget.

Dad says it's not Lovey's fault; it's her parents'. "Parents can infect their children with their own backward thinking," Dad once said. "You should feel sorry for her."

I glare at Lovey, and I don't feel sorry at all. I feel like I want to punch her right in her clown face. "How many Asians do you even know?"

Lovey leans forward, her head cocked to one side, squinting at me like I'm a pile of roadside trash. "You know you're ugly, right? You're like the bad parts of white people and Asian people mixed together. And I've never seen such an ugly color of blue eyes before. Like dirty water."

My cheeks go hot, but I keep my cool. I raise an eyebrow at her. "Have you looked in a mirror lately? You're not exactly supermodel material yourself."

She opens and closes her mouth like a brainless fish.

I doodle in my notebook, my pen pressing down hard into the paper as I draw cubes. Yes, my family has blue eyes—it goes back a long way, my dad says. We have some ancestors from Russia who migrated to Japan and became the Ainu. Besides, my mom is— was—as Irish as they come, with blue eyes and red hair. Of course that's what color my eyes are.

Peyton puts down the glue. "Find any articles yet?"

"Hi, Peyton," Lovey sings, and I swear she bats her eyes at him. Her mascara's so thick it falls on her cheeks in little clumps. "I saw your baseball game last week. You did awesome."

"Stalker," I mutter. Now I know she's the dumbest person in

town. If you're in love with Batman, you don't go around harassing Robin.

"Thanks." Peyton glances at me. He knows what Lovey's like. I doodle another cube, probably looking as upset as I feel. He sits down. "You should go somewhere else, Lovey. You're not in our group."

"Mr. Stedman said to sit here." Lovey smiles at Peyton. "We won't bother you."

Peyton angles his head at me and I shrug. If I make a scene, Stedman will bug me even more. "It's fine," I mumble. Clarissa returns, and she and Lovey are actually quiet for a change as they cut out their articles.

I look out the window. The old man at the bus stop stands up and walks across the street, toward the school. Even from here his skin looks pale, papery. Must not get much sun in the old folks' home. I wonder how he escaped. Maybe he hitchhiked all the way up here. Should I call the cops or something?

He comes up to the classroom window and looks straight at me.

Our eyes meet. I have this strange feeling that I know him, or should know him.

We stare each other for a second. Then he winks. A ridiculous, dramatic, slow wink, like a stage actor making sure the last row can see it.

I slide down in my seat and look at my desk again. Where have I seen that man before?

Oh. He must look familiar because he's Asian, like my grand-mother and father. That's why. You don't see many Asians around here.

"That old guy must be from out of town," I say to Peyton.

"What guy?" Peyton pastes his article onto his paper.

I look out the window. The old man is gone. "Huh. Nobody, I guess."

And now, suddenly, the sun is out. Not only has the rain stopped, but there's not a cloud in the sky. I grin. Maybe it's an omen that spring break is going to be awesome.

"Have you actually done any work?" Peyton takes the notebook out of my hand. His eyes go Frisbee-wide. He looks up at Lovey and snorts. "Dude. Ha. Good likeness." He shuts the notebook, shaking his head with a wide grin. He whispers, "You better hide it, though. You'll be in a load of trouble if Stedman sees it."

What is he talking about? The cubes? The beastly man? I flip open to my drawing.

It's Mean Girl Number One, Lovey. As a baboon. Wearing clown makeup and a clown suit, her nostrils huge, her hairy knuckles dragging on the ground.

Not only did I make her look horribly—and awesomely—ugly, she is also doing something not so polite. If you've seen apes or mon-keys at the zoo, you might have experienced this: sometimes they poop and then throw it. They hurl it at the people gawking at them through the glass, and even though it just hits the window, everybody screams and ducks as it slides down in front of their faces. It's completely disgusting—and completely hilarious.

That's what Lovey was doing in my picture. Pooping into her hand. Getting ready to throw it.

I make a weird squeaking noise and slap my hand over my mouth. It is the grossest, most spectacular caricature I've ever seen. The only thing is, I have no memory of drawing it.

How did it get into my notebook?

I'm about to put it away, but I just have to admire it for another minute. It's really, really good. County-fair-blue-ribbon quality. She looks alive. You can almost *smell* the stench.

I gaze at the drawing for another minute, this strange sort of excitement building inside of me. I feel like I did last year, when I asked my father for a Nintendo 3DS for my birthday and he said they were too expensive, but then he handed me this perfectly shaped box and I tore away a little corner of the wrapping paper and I recognized it.

Yessss! I want to yell. I want to wave the drawing around the classroom, shout about it to the town, publish it in the local newspaper. *Look at how great this is!* I grin and swallow the giggles that want to come out. I've never, ever felt this way about a drawing I've made before.

Then I make a fatal error. A laugh escapes from my gut. If you can call it a laugh. It's more like an elephant trumpet. Deafening, echoing around the room, reaching every single ear. I can't control it. My hand falls away from my face, and I bend over, laughing my head off.

Peyton and Clarissa start laughing at my laugh. That makes me laugh even harder—so hard that tears come out and splash on the page. The colors don't smear. Peyton's guffawing so much he turns bright red and can't breathe; he just slaps the table over and over with his palm.

"What's so funny?" Lovey yanks the notebook from my hands.

"No!" I leap forward to get it back. My stomach lands on Clarissa's desk, on top of the glue. I hit my chin on the edge of Lovey's desk and bite my tongue. "Ow," I say, tasting blood.

"Xander!" Clarissa shrieks. "My project!"

Lovey's face turns bright pink. She juts out her chin, and her hair fans out as if she's been electrocuted. She hops up and down, her mouth moving and a string of drool coming out, too mad to talk anymore.

Just like a baboon.

I'm lying stomach-down on Clarissa's desk, and Mr. Stedman's leaping across the room, and quite possibly I'm bleeding to death, but still I can't stop laughing. I point at Lovey and just let it out. That excited feeling stays with me. Finally, I am conquering Lovey.

Then Lovey gets her voice back. "WHAAAAAT IS THIS? I'll KILL YOU!" I've never heard a girl bellow like that before. She sounds like Peyton's dad.

I try to get up and away. Too late. She flings the notebook down, grabs me by the shoulders, and twists me off the desk. I fall on my back, the newspaper sticking to my chest. She's over me, raising her fist, and I close my eyes, waiting for the punch.

And still I can't stop giggling.

CHAPTER 3

wo whole hours after spring break began, I'm still at school.
Torture in the first degree. This is against the Geneva
Convention, I think.

I must be exceptional. I never really thought so before today. But
it turns out I am.

I'm the first kid in the history of time to get detention the day
that spring break starts.

Yay, me.

Peyton pulled Lovey off me before she could break my face.
Getting beat up by a girl: *masculinity, minus 2,000 more points.* Having to be rescued by your best friend: *masculinity, minus another 50
points.*

And somehow, though she's the one who attacked me, I'm the one who's in trouble.

Mr. Stedman's being a jerk, making me wait around until he's good and ready to let me go. No book to read, no paper to write on, no nothing. Just me sitting here while he cleans up his classroom and does stuff on his computer—I don't know what. Probably playing solitaire, or writing to all his imaginary girlfriends.

Finally, he types a note in boldface addressed to my *Parent and/ or Guardian*, prints it out, and hands it to me. "That drawing you created is a form of bullying, Xander. It shall not be tolerated."

"I didn't draw it," I say, but I know that sounds like a lie. "And she bullied *me*. She called me ugly and made a crack about Asians. What about that?"

The slightest frown crosses his face. "Well. I didn't hear that, so I can't punish her." Mr. Stedman crosses his arms. "Anyway, Xander, you're not allowed to punish her yourself, no matter what she says. It's not an eye for an eye around here."

I just nod. What else can I do? He won't believe me.

I don't even believe me. How can somebody draw something and not remember doing it?

"Xander, I don't know why everything has to be so difficult with you," Mr. Stedman says with a sigh. "Go on home."

I don't hesitate. I stick the letter into my back pocket, grab my stuff, and run out.

I find Peyton sitting at the bus stop. It's warm and breezy, just like spring break is supposed to be. So much for the weather forecast. This makes me feel better. I grin. "Aren't you supposed to be at baseball practice or something?"

He shrugs and holds out a bag of Flamin' Hot Cheetos. His blue-green eyes squint up at me from under his ball cap. His skin is a permanent goldenish tan from all the time he spends in the sun. "Don't tell my dad."

I won't. Peyton's dad is basically bent on turning his son into some kind of super Olympic athlete. Water polo in the fall. Basketball in the winter. Baseball in the spring. Summer's for training camps in at least two sports. Extra time is designated for long-distance running. Or mountain biking down hills so steep and rocky I have a panic attack just looking at them.

Mr. Phasis is a navy pilot, and he wants Peyton to follow in his footsteps. If he found out Peyton skipped practice, he'd ground him for two weeks, easy.

"I'll throw some dirt on you so it looks like you went." I kick a cloud toward his shins. The thought of his father makes bubbles churn in my stomach. He would rather Peyton find a new best friend. One who could mountain-bike or ski or even play driveway hoops with him.

The day after my birthday last year, I went over to Peyton's house, my Nintendo 3DS in my hand and a brand-new game loaded up.

I knocked five times fast and three times slow, our special

Hey-it's-me-I'm-coming-in code, and put my hand on the doorknob. Mr. Phasis threw open the front door, a smile settling over his face like one of those clear plastic Halloween masks. His blond-red hair bristled like a rooster comb on top of his head. "Peyton's busy, Xander. Come back another day." He began to close the door.

I stuck my foot into the doorway without thinking. Mr. Phasis was supposed to be gone for a few days, flying people to Florida. "Hey, Mr. Phasis, erm . . ." I tried to think of a reason why I had to speak to Peyton. Besides the video game. "I . . . the teacher . . . Mr. Stedman . . ." I was babbling, as I always did when I spoke to Mr. Phasis. "He gave me some work for Peyton."

Mr. Phasis leaned against the door frame and considered me the way my grandmother considers mushy brown bananas when she's deciding whether to make some banana bread or just throw them away. "Why didn't Peyton get it at school?" He crossed his massive arms over his barrel chest.

I shrugged. "Mr., um, Stedman, like, forgot."

Mr. Phasis looked down his long nose at me. The same nose Peyton has. Peyton says it's an aquiline nose, which means it's like an eagle's. "Two minutes. No more." He moved aside. I leaped through before he could change his mind, and ran upstairs.

In his bedroom, Peyton stood at the far corner of his bed, struggling with the upended mattress. Grunting, he pulled a blue fitted sheet over the corner, then pushed the mattress back down onto the bed frame.

Immediately the sheet slid off the corner. "ARRRGH!" Peyton squawked. "IT. WON'T. STAY. DOWN!" He sat on the bed, put his hands in his feathery hair, and tousled it until it was as wild as a tangle of weeds.

"Hey."

Peyton looked up and wiped his eyes with the back of his hand. Was he crying? "Now is not a good time, Xander."

I gulped, feeling my own cheeks go hot. Maybe I could cheer him up. I held up the 3DS. "Look what I got for my birthday."

"Good for you." Peyton stood up again and turned his back to me. "I can't hang out. I've got chores to do. I've been working on this stupid bed for more than an hour." He lowered his voice into an imitation of his father's. "'There's a wrinkle here, son. Redo it.'" He kicked the bed frame, then screeched and grabbed his foot. "OOWWWWW!"

"Hey, what'd the bed ever do to you?" I put the 3DS in my pocket and shut the door. "Didn't he show you how to do it?"

"Yeah, but only once, and I didn't think it would be so hard." Peyton sniffled, his brows knitting together. "Who cares if there's a wrinkle? Why does it have to be so perfect? I'm not in his stupid military." Peyton flopped on the bed again.

"Leave it to me." Finally, I could prove to Mr. Phasis that I knew something. "My grandmother showed me how to do this."

"But doesn't she do it some weird Japanese way or something?"

"No, she doesn't do it some weird Japanese way or something. She does it better than a military guy," I retorted. "Just you watch."

Peyton had missed one key step—you have to put one corner of the fitted sheet on first, then the opposite diagonal corner, pulling it taut. After I did the other two corners, I put the flat sheet on, folding the top part down like a tight envelope. Finally, I showed him the special secret. I slid under Peyton's bed and pulled the corners as snug as possible so there wasn't a single wrinkle on the surface.

"Thanks, Xander." Peyton sounded relieved. I saw his bare feet hopping back and forth. "It looks one hundred percent perfect now."

"No prob." I gave the sheet one final tug.

Directly below me, I heard Peyton's dad moving around on the first floor. "Ha," I said. "Your dad sure is loud."

"Tell me something I don't know." Peyton threw a blanket over the bed.

"Do the corners like I showed you, and I'll pull this tight, too." I fixed up the blanket.

Downstairs, Mr. Phasis's voice rumbled. I could catch some of the words. "I better go see . . . little ne'er-do-well . . . distracting Peyton."

Did he just call me a "ne'er do well"? Indignation rose in my throat like a scream.

Mrs. Phasis said something I couldn't quite make out. I thought I heard my name.

Mr. Phasis kept going. ". . . real troublemaker . . . lazy . . . not even in . . . GATE program."

Something like a cold, hard stone materialized in my gut.

"Phillip!" Mrs. Phasis said in a loud, stern voice. "I will not have you picking on him. That poor child. His mother—"

"It's not like I . . . to his face. Hey, PEYTON!" Mr. Phasis bellowed suddenly. These words went right into my eardrum, loud as a firecracker. "YOU DONE YET?"

"Almost!" Peyton shouted back.

Peyton's father clomped out of the kitchen, with one last comment to his wife. "I can't wait . . . Peyton . . . Army and Navy Academy . . . away from bad influences."

The Army and Navy Academy? I sat up. Ouch. Bad idea. Wooden board, meet forehead. I slid out from under the bed. "Peyton," I said breathlessly, "your dad's sending you to military school!"

Peyton snapped his quilt high up over the bed and let it float down. "Yeah. For high school."

"Yeah?" I echoed. "You know?"

Peyton shrugged. "Yeah. It's a good school. They have excellent sports programs, and their graduates go to top colleges." He said it like he was reading from a brochure. "It'll be fine," he mumbled.

My chest clenched. High school without Peyton? That would be impossible. Like, utterly impossible. Everyone from around here had to be bussed to Valley Mountain High. Nine hundred teenagers and one little me. I would perish.

And Peyton—Peyton was not the military type. He couldn't even make his bed.

Peyton's dad flung open the door, his eyes darting around the room. "What are you boys up to?"

Irritation shot up my spine. I had a sudden, self-destructive impulse to tell him, *Making your son's IQ points go down, as usual,* but, thankfully, I managed to say nothing.

Peyton stood up as if pulled by a wire in the ceiling. "I'm all finished, sir."

Yes, Peyton calls his dad "sir."

Peyton's dad glanced sideways at me, and I felt a blush spread over my face. *Little ne'er-do-well. Not even in GATE.* I'd never forget that as long as I lived. I wanted to run out of there, but I couldn't abandon Peyton.

Mr. Phasis pulled back the quilt and blanket and inspected the sheet. He took a quarter out of his pocket and threw it down on the bed. Peyton and I held our breaths. It bounced up, high. Mr. Phasis smiled and clapped his son on the back. "Finally. This is how a bed should look. I knew you could do it, son. Like I say, all you have to do is put your mind to something. Not give up. Not cry about it."

I sighed inside. Great. He was getting ready for a good long lecture.

Peyton opened his mouth. "Xander actually . . ."

Helped. He was about to say *helped.* "I've got to go," I said quickly. "Peyton really did a good job on that bed, huh, Mr. P?"

Peyton closed his mouth and shot me a grateful look.

Mr. Phasis's face relaxed into a real smile for once. "Peyton, I think you've earned a couple of hours of R and R. You can stay, Xander." He turned and left the room.

Anyway, that's why I can't let Mr. Phasis find out that Peyton is ditching practice today. Especially not to spend time with me.

Peyton tips the bag of Cheetos into his mouth and we walk up to my house. It sits on top of a hill, set back a half acre from the road. Behind us is the Laguna mountain range, rolling hills of pine stretching out like a sea of trees. Above it is a sky so blue that I've mistaken it for ocean. We're about forty minutes outside of the actual city of San Diego, and one of the few places in the county that actually has seasons—and snow.

There isn't very much to the town of Oak Grove, which suits some people, like my grandmother, just fine. Me, not so much. It's boring to have to visit the same three places over and over again (school, library, convenience store). There's no movie theater or bowling alley or anything like that. There are two churches, where most social events take place, but we only go on major holidays. And besides, Lovey goes to our church, too, and I'd rather not have to see her in youth group on top of seeing her at school.

Peyton pokes my shoulder and points at my house. Up in the living room window, I see my *obāchan* watching us. Her X-ray trouble-sensing vision can probably read the note crumpled in my pocket. Shoot. "There she is," I say under my breath. "Maybe if I ignore her she'll go away."

Peyton and I pause and eat the last of the Cheeto crumbs. The bright orange powder makes my lips sting. "I have my laptop." Peyton pats his bag. "We can play *CraftWorlds*."

"You mean we can take turns watching each other play." My dad's a laptop hog. I hardly ever get to play on it.

"It's better than nothing." Peyton starts walking up the hill.

My grandmother bangs on the window with her palm, gestures *Hurry up*.

"Think she knows?" Peyton asks.

I shrug. "Yeah." My stomach flutters, but I'm ready to meet my doom. Knowing Obāchan, she'll use it as an excuse to make me stay inside.

We walk up the steep driveway, past the many plastic jugs of water Obāchan stores by the garage, next to the black trash cans crammed with canned food and medicine.

My grandmother's what they call a "prepper." If she could, she'd build us an underground bunker. She says the world's going to end soon. "Look at the climate change. The earthquakes. The floods. The wars and evilness," she says. "It's coming."

She's been saying this since I was four, when she left Japan to come live with us.

Not that I mind her, most of the time. She's a really good cook, and she makes sure I have clean clothes and stuff like that. My dad, the absentminded professor, forgets to bathe half the time. I'd definitely be dead by now if it wasn't for Obāchan.

I don't know how old she is. Her face is still pretty smooth, but her back has a hump in it. She usually says, "Somewhere between seventy-five and two hundred." Then she tells me it's impolite to ask ladies their age.

I open the door. "*Tadaima!*" I yell, though I know my grandma's standing right there. We always say this. It means *I'm home!*

"*Okaeri,*" my grandmother replies. This sounds like "oh-kai-ree" and means *Welcome back.* Obāchan closes the door behind us. "Get inside. Bad weather coming."

I glance out the window at the clear sky. The rain's long gone. "Um, okay, Obāchan."

She locks the door. Double dead bolts. Like anybody's going to bother coming up this steep hill to steal our bottled water.

We kick off our shoes, sliding them to the side of the door. Going shoeless in the house is one of the habits we have that others sometimes find strange. It's Japanese.

"Peyton can eat dinner with us," Obāchan says. "As long as he doesn't complain about my cooking."

"He did that *once*. We were *four*." My grandmother will never let Peyton live that down. "To be fair, you made tofurkey." Tofu-shaped and flavored to taste like turkey that she'd cooked as long as a real turkey. I know some people eat it, but my grandmother made up her own recipe and it was capital-*A* Awful. It tasted like a post-Thanksgiving burp mixed with glue.

"I promise I won't. Thanks for inviting me," Peyton says politely. He takes off his baseball cap before she can remind him to. Obāchan is old-school: gentlemen remove their hats when they come indoors.

She smiles up at him, pats his shoulder. "Good boy." She looks at me. "Your father wants to talk to you. He's in his office." Obāchan disappears into the kitchen.

Great. If anybody's seen an e-mail from Mr. Stedman, it's Dad, since he's been sitting in front of his computer. We go upstairs. Peyton walks ahead to my room. "Good luck," he says.

"I need it." I don't even know what I should say. Yeah, I was mad at Lovey. Yeah, I did laugh. But I honestly don't remember making the drawing. Maybe I need a brain scan. Maybe I'm losing my mind.

This isn't going to go over well with Dad. I'd overheard him talking about me to Obāchan just last night. "I'm worried about Xander," Dad had said in a low voice, in the kitchen, where they think I can't hear them. "He's not working up to his potential."

"It's because his mother left," Obāchan said in an even lower voice. "You were never like that."

"She couldn't help what she did," Dad said sharply. "You know that."

Obāchan changed the subject. She and Dad always did when someone brought up my mother. She sputtered out a long breath.

"Xander is just a daydreamer. He's young. He's not you. Give him time."

Dad had sighed. "That might not be an option."

After that I didn't want to listen anymore.

Now Dad sits behind his beat-up metal desk, tapping away on his laptop. Books are bursting out of the shelves. His office is cluttered, but Dad claims to know where everything is.

Near Dad's feet, our dog, Inu, sees me first and thumps his baseball-bat-size tail. *Inu* means *dog* in Japanese, so yes, we have a dog named Dog. He's a big goldendoodle with maybe some Great Dane mixed in, because he's pretty huge. One hundred-and-forty pounds. Weighs about sixty pounds more than I do. He's got soft, curly golden hair all over, and I can't remember ever not having him around. *Woof,* he says in his deep voice. A doggie hello. He lumbers over, his black lips seeming to smile. Some slobber drips off his beard onto my shoe. "Eww, Inu!" I say, but I don't mind. That's just him. He whines softly, wanting attention. His head comes up to my hip. I rub him between the eyes, the way he likes. He wags his tail madly, wiggling his entire body and sending a few of Dad's papers flying. Inu always greets me like I've been away for a hundred years, even if I've just gone to the bathroom.

I flop into the ancient leather easy chair and brace myself. I really hate the expression Dad has when I do something wrong. Sad, like that one football kicker who lost the Super Bowl because he missed. Dad looks like that every time he sees my report card.

His blue eyes focus on me from behind thick glasses. With his long silver-gray ponytail, he looks like a Japanese hippie. But his body is wiry and as strong as iron from hours of hiking and rock-climbing. "Xander-chan, how was school?" He folds his sinewy brown hands—like tree roots—in front of him.

"Fine." I'm not going to give him any extra information. I pick up a thick leather-bound journal and flip through it. It's filled with Japanese handwriting I can't read, and some rough illustrations of fairy-tale monsters. I'm used to finding stuff like this in his office. He's the professor of folklore at a local college. It's hard to believe somebody can make a living by talking about made-up things. Maybe I can get his job when I grow up. "We're on break now."

"Oh, that's right. I forgot. Well, now that you have some extra time"—he opens his desk drawer and takes out a comic book—"maybe you'd like to read this. Do you know the Momotaro story?"

"Yeah. The peach boy." He hands me the comic, and I check it out. It looks kind of familiar. Maybe I saw this when I was little. It's an old fairy tale about a little boy some old people find in, well, a peach. He grows up and goes to fight some demons. "Isn't that for little kids?"

"Not this one." Dad stares at me, the way he does when he asks me a math question he expects me to know the answer to. I don't know what he's trying to see.

Feeling uncomfortable under his gaze, I fiddle with the framed photo of my mom that he keeps on his desk. In it she's holding me, baby Xander. My mom's red-blond hair poofs around her freckled milk-white face. I remember yanking on her hair when she carried me, because I liked the color. She would grab my hand and say, "Be gentle, Xander," in a soft voice. I don't think she was ever mad at me, come to think of it.

Then why did she leave?

Dad gently removes the frame from my grasp. "You don't have to read it if you don't want to," he says softly.

I shrug. "Maybe I'll read it." I say it just to make him happy. I probably won't have time.

Inu stands up and barks at the window like crazy. There must be a rabbit or something outside.

"Inu, shush," Dad says, and he waves me off.

I roll up the comic and stick it into my back pocket. It's spring break. I'm going to play some video games.

CHAPTER 4

I go into my room and throw the comic book on the bed next to Peyton. He's lying there looking at the drawings I stuck all over my walls. So many drawings that you can't see the actual wall anymore. They flap in the wind coming through my open window. He picks up the comic. "What's this?"

I shrug. "Momotaro. A Japanese fairy tale." I pick up his laptop, which is already open to *CraftWorlds*. I settle down on my stomach. "May I?"

Peyton nods, opens the comic.

I'm in Challenge Mode. That means the computer sends things to attack you at night, and you have to fight them. Werewolves and zombies and feral pigs, oh my.

I've made a farmhouse and have blocky-looking pigs and horses and chickens. I need to feed them their pixelly food. But I don't see my humanoid character, Bob. "Did you change my game?"

"I never log in to your game." Peyton flips open the comic book. *"Mukashi mukashi."*

I squint at him. "You know Japanese?"

"It's written out." He shows me. It's true—it isn't printed with the symbols of the kanji alphabet, which I can't decipher. Huh.

"Mukashi mukashi. It means *Once upon a time*," I say without thinking. I don't know how I know that. My grandma used to read me stories in Japanese. I'm sure she must have told me at one point.

Anyway, I have more important things to worry about. In my game, I still can't find Bob, so I start creating a new figure.

Peyton props the comic on his chest and reads it aloud.

~~~~~

Once upon a time, long ago, Japan was in turmoil. The *oni* demons had taken over the northern island. Along with them came earthquakes and drought and tsunamis. Much of the land was destroyed. Desperate, the people sent army after army to fight the demons, but no one ever returned from the Lost Island of Monsters.

An old man and woman lived poor and hungry on a farm. Their sons had all perished fighting the oni, and there was no one else to help them maintain the animals and the crops. "If only I could have another son," the old woman said. "A big, strong son to assist us. But it is impossible."

One afternoon, the old woman was trying to wash clothes in a stream that was more like a trickle. Dead trees lined the banks. A huge earthquake struck, the ground rolled, and the old woman fell down. Water flooded into the stream, turning it into a river, which swelled until it became as big as an ocean. Then she saw a peach—a huge peach, a peach as big as a house—bobbing down the current toward her. Her mouth watered. She had not tasted a peach in five years, for all the fruit trees were gone. "Look at that," she said to herself. "How delicious! It must have washed down from the mountains."

The peach caught on a branch and stopped moving. The old woman called to her husband, "Hurry! We have a feast here!" Both hobbled over to the peach.

The old woman sliced off a piece. It was the most delicious peach she had ever tasted, like liquid honey. She closed her eyes.

The fruit was so big that they could eat and eat and keep eating long past when they were full. They couldn't help themselves. Finally, their sticky hands reached into the last bit of peach, and they felt the pit.

It didn't feel like the usual prickly peach pit. No, this was smooth under their fingertips.

The old man scraped away the last of the peach flesh.

The pit gleamed gold.

The old man tapped on it. "This is worth a fortune," he said.

"But there are no wealthy people left to buy it," the old woman said.

Suddenly, the pit trembled. The old couple gasped and stepped back, sure that it was going to explode and they were going to be punished for their greed.

The pit split open with a sound like cracking thunder.

A little boy, naked as a newborn, leaped out and landed on the earth in front of them.

"I am Momotaro," the boy said. "I am your son."

The old woman wept and hugged him. Her prayers had been answered!

Inside the peach pit, a samurai sword glittered. The old man pulled it out. Inscribed on the blade was

夢主

The Sword of Yumenushi

It was too big for the boy, so the old man carried it home to keep for him.

Momotaro helped the old people on the farm, and they loved him like a son. They forgot how they had found him, there in the peach with the sword, and they thought of him as any ordinary boy.

Through the years, the land continued to suffer. Earthquakes happened daily. The rains were still sparse. Yet the old couple was happier now than they had ever been, because they had Momotaro to keep them company.

Though the crops barely grew, Momotaro did. He became known throughout the land as the fiercest and strongest boy anyone had ever seen. He could uproot full-grown trees before he was five. When he was eight, he could hold his breath underwater for ten minutes. At age ten, he could shoot an arrow through a knot of wood from half a mile away. The old man burst with pride whenever he spoke of his son.

Momotaro wasn't just the best warrior in the land. When he wasn't preparing his body for battle, he liked to dream. For every tactic he practiced, Momotaro made a painting, until the home of the old people was filled with dozens and dozens of pictures. He had the secret dreaming mind of a poet.

"What good is art in a time of war?" his adopted father complained one day, after Momotaro neglected his chores to make a painting for his adopted mother. "Do not let him waste his talent on such frivolous matters!"

Momotaro bowed his head. He snapped his paintbrushes in half. "I am sorry, honorable Father," Momotaro replied. "I do not know why I dream as much as I do. I will try to be a better son."

Momotaro went outside to do all the chores that the old man found tiresome. The old woman tsked at her husband. "Don't you know," she asked, "that wisdom hides in his heart?" She jabbed at the painting with a bent finger.

The old man looked closely at it for the first time.

It was a picture of Momotaro fighting the oni. He threw the monsters off a craggy cliff. He slashed at their evil with his trusted sword.

Then the old man examined all of Momotaro's art. Picture after picture of the boy fighting. It was as if he was planning his whole battle strategy.

That was when the old man remembered. Momotaro was not his. Their answered prayer had come at a price they had yet to pay.

The old man made his son new paintbrushes and presented them to him with a bow. "Forgive me."

The old man now knew that Momotaro had been sent to Japan for one purpose: to grow up and rid the land of the terrible demons that plagued the North.

One morning, Momotaro awoke early from a dream. In the dream he had traveled through a dark and barren land, alone and lonely and cold. His body shook with dread as his eyes opened. Yet he found himself staring out the window to the

northern mountains, where the oni lorded over his country-
men, and he felt nothing but a determination to go.

It would be easier to stay. To keep living this easy, pleasant life with his elderly parents. But he knew deep inside that
this wasn't the right answer. "It is time," he told his parents
with a heavy heart.

"You are not ready!" his father shouted. "You are too
young."

It was true that Momotaro had not yet grown a whisker
on his face. But he bowed his head. "Please forgive me, honorable Father, but I am called."

"Are you not afraid?" his mother cried, for she was.

"I have never been more afraid," Momotaro said, "but I
must begin. Or I will never finish."

The old man told the boy how to get to the coast and
where he could find a ship to hire. The old woman made him
a basket of food to take, and her tears salted the rice balls.

———

Peyton stops reading and sits up. "*Yumenushi*. What does that mean?"

I look over at the word and shrug. "Dunno. Don't really care."
The laptop fan starts whirring like it's a helicopter about to take off.
"Uh-oh. I hope *CraftWorlds* isn't breaking your computer."

"My dad will kill me." Peyton pokes at the laptop screen. "Did
you download a new skin?"

"No. It's the same one." Skins are layers you can add to make different characters. For example, you can download a skin to give your character scales, and then another to give him a mustache. I haven't downloaded a new one in ages.

My game should look the same as it always does, minus Bob, my missing character. But when I look at the screen, I see something totally different. A warrior in samurai gear swings his sword. His pixelly blue eyes almost jump out at me. "Wow," I say. "I'm an even better coder than I thought. Must be some kind of glitch. Are you sure you didn't log in from your house and do this?" I point.

Peyton snorts. "I don't even know your password." He peers at the screen. "Dude, check you out. You're playing in Hardcore Mode."

"What?" I look. There are a few different modes that the game lets you play in, but all of them let you regenerate or start over except one. This one.

Hardcore Mode means that it's life or death. You die, and your whole world gets destroyed.

I never play in Hardcore Mode. I tried it once and lost. Miserably. It was brutal. I'm not going to lie, I shed a tear that day.

I swore I'd never play in Hardcore Mode again. "No, no, no!" I press ESCAPE, but nothing happens. CONTROL Q to quit, nothing. MENU, nothing. "Abort mission! Peyton, what do I do?"

"I don't know!" Peyton's looking over my shoulder. "Turn it off?"

I press the POWER button. Nothing.

The samurai man walks around, his head moving back and forth like he's looking for something. He stops by my barn. The animals run away, squealing and flapping wings. Huh.

The sun goes down in my game. That means all the bad creatures will be coming out to get him.

He gets into battle stance, knees bent, one foot in front of another, sword held high over his head.

"Zombie attack!" I yell, and get my fingers ready over the buttons.

But it's not a zombie that pops out of the building.

It's the beast-ape-man that I drew earlier today, before the whole Lovey incident. The monster's dinosaur tail whips around, his tongue lashing out.

He doesn't move like the other figures, like a block puppet with hinged joints. No. He moves like he's real, all sinuous and muscular. The scales on his body glisten. Those black-hole eyes are still there, sucking all the life out of everything around him. I shiver.

His head whips around. He looks at me and smiles. At *me*.

Hisssss.

I gape at the screen. The pixels seem to move closer. It's like I'm staring at one of those hidden picture things until suddenly the jumble of colors pops into 3-D. Like my eyeballs are sucking me headfirst into *CraftWorlds*. I see multicolored pixels all around, close enough to touch.

I feel the three snakes' tongues flit across my lashes. Smell garbage-pail breath.

"Ahhhh!" I shut the laptop and leap backward, falling off the bed. My pulse thumps in my mouth, and I realize my eyes are squished closed. I open them and see tufts of Inu fur rolling around under my bed. I was supposed to vacuum here last weekend. I've never been so glad to see dust bunnies. For a second I thought I was *inside* the game.

"Xander?" Peyton looks at me over the edge of the bed. "Are you okay?"

"Yeah." I stay down on the floor for a second. I'm such an idiot. What the heck is wrong with me? It's just a game. The greatest game ever created, yeah, but still a game. I must need some sleep or food. School's getting to me. Mr. Stedman harping about my nonexistent "condition." This is what adults call "burnout."

"I'm fine." I scramble up, my nose itching from the dust. I push the laptop away and sit down on the bed. "I've just never seen that skin before, is all. That samurai character. Or that beast-man. Did you see that thing? It looked so real. It didn't look like it belonged in *CraftWorlds* at all."

"You must have downloaded it. Maybe you don't remember. Maybe it came with another skin." Peyton leafs through the comic with a shrug. "Who knows? Computers do weird stuff all the time."

Peyton's right. In fact, that's probably why I drew the monster in school. I must have seen it while I was playing *CraftWorlds* and I just forgot. Or maybe they stuck him into an ad, as a subliminal message, the way a hamburger chain might stick a picture of a burger in an ad for toys to make kids hungry. My heart calms down.

I open the laptop again. The black screen pops into full color.

My world's deleted. All of it. A year of building, gone. Poof. "Gosh dang it! What the heck?" If my obāchan wasn't in the house, I'd definitely be using stronger language. I restart the game. Still nothing appears.

I shut the cover. I should reboot the whole computer. Maybe that'll help.

"This is some good stuff." Peyton flops the comic book down on top of the laptop. "I swear, one day you're going to be working for Marvel."

"What do you mean?" I pick up the comic. Now I see it's stapled together, a homemade photocopy.

Peyton's finger points to three words on the cover: *By Xander Miyamoto.*

I gasp like I've inhaled a lungful of water. I grab the comic out of his hand.

It's my handwriting, all right. My style of drawing. Mine. All of it.

I fling it across the room like it's a black widow spider. It hits the bookcase and knocks a box off the shelf, I throw it so hard.

"What's the matter with you?" Peyton's giving me the same look my grandma gives me when I fart in her presence.

I open my mouth to tell him. But what? If I tell him the truth, I'll sound so crazy he'll be forced to call 9-1-1 and have me carted away to the nearest hospital. If I don't, he'll know I'm lying. Peyton always knows when I'm hiding stuff. It's his best and worst quality.

"Dinner!" Obāchan yells up the stairs.

Saved by the grandma. Peyton and I get up without another word and run into the bathroom to wash up, knowing that if my grandma doesn't smell the scent of soap coming off us, she'll send us back to redo the job. No more questions from Peyton. An angry obāchan just isn't worth the time.

CHAPTER 5

I f you want Peyton to forget about something, just offer him food. Which is fine by me. I'll think about it later, I decide. Maybe ask Dad. Ask him why he gave me that comic and didn't say, *"Hey, remember drawing this?"* He probably assumes I remember. Which is pretty reasonable.

There must be a logical explanation for all of this. I just don't know what it is yet.

It's only ten till five. Obāchan says her old belly agrees better with an early dinner. Peyton's family eats at seven, so Peyton will have dinner twice tonight. Not that he minds.

Steaming chicken thighs, crackled with sweet glaze, are piled onto a platter, along with sticky white rice from the cooker. We have rice at least once a day. Peyton loves rice like I love chocolate bars.

"Have as much as you like. I made extra." Obāchan heaps a giant spoonful of rice onto Peyton's plate. "You growing boys need it."

He slaps a big glob of butter on it. "Thanks."

Inu and Dad come down. Inu settles next to Dad's chair, his paws politely folded.

Obāchan bows her head and says the blessing in Japanese. It's a Zen Buddhist thing called the "Verse of the Five Contemplations."

> *We reflect on the effort that brought us this food*
> *and consider how it comes to us.*
> *We reflect on our virtue and practice, and whether*
> *we are worthy of this offering.*
> *We regard greed as the obstacle to freedom of mind.*
> *We regard this meal as medicine to sustain our life.*
> *For the sake of enlightenment we now receive this food.*

Her eyes fly open. She thumps her fist on the table. "Dig in before it gets cold."

I won't argue with that. We eat.

Inu sits next to me and gives me his best, saddest look. He puts one paw on my leg.

"No begging, Inu," I say for my grandmother's benefit. I'm not supposed to feed the dog at the table, but I tear off a piece of chicken and secretly toss it onto the floor. Inu eats it, then lies on top of my feet, awaiting the next morsel.

"Delicious dinner, Mrs. Miyamoto," Peyton says.

"I'm glad you like it. Akira," Obāchan says to my father, "pass me the salt."

Dad hands her the crystal saltshaker. "Don't use too much. It's bad for your blood pressure."

She shakes a huge amount over her chicken. "I'm ancient. I do what I want." She stops and squints at Dad. "I heard something today." Then she cuts her eyes at me and edits herself. "Remind me to tell you later."

Dad glances my way, too. He nods.

Uh-oh. She got the phone call from school. My stomach flips. I put my fork down. Good thing Peyton's here—he'll keep them from going crazy. I brace myself for the punishment to come. Worst-case scenario: grounded for all of spring break. With no computer. I will die if that happens, but at least I'm prepared.

I grit my teeth. Maybe I can negotiate. Trade computer privileges for a lifetime of toilet scrubbing. Or digging out a bunker for Obāchan. Something that will make her happy. Watching that bridal reality show with her without complaining, ever. Ugh. Being grounded would be better than that.

Dad smiles at me. "Hey, how about we drive down to the mall in Alpine, get ice cream after dinner? You boys deserve a treat."

This makes me feel worse. My throat closes. My dad's still looking at me with his little smile. It reminds me of Inu. Just—so trusting. I have to tell him the truth. I gulp. "Dad? I kind of got into trouble today."

Peyton kicks me under the table. He never tells his parents anything.

Dad's fork pauses en route to his mouth. "What kind of trouble?"

The house shudders, the windows rattling like pebbles in a tin cup.

The sound stops. We look at each other. Obāchan's face goes white-gray.

Dad wipes his mouth and goes to the window.

"No, Akira," Obāchan whispers. "Sit down."

Dad faces us. His blue eyes seem to melt into his face. He looks like somebody just told him his best friend died.

He takes off his glasses, sticks them in a hard protective case, and puts that on the table. "Everybody," Dad says softly, "no matter what happens, stay inside this house. Got it?"

I swallow hard and nod. "Is it an earthquake?"

Dad's eyes shoot warnings. "I said stay inside. You must do as I say, even if it seems wrong. Do you promise?"

"Why?" I put both hands on the shaking table.

"Promise, Xander!" Dad shouts.

Dad never yells. Unless it's super-maximum serious. Fear leaps into my throat. "I promise."

The old chandelier above the table begins to swing, its lights blinking and the little crystals tinkling, softly at first, then harder and harder, until it sounds like a thousand jackhammers on cement. I cover my ears.

Inu whines and barks.

"Get down here, boys!" Obāchan crawls under the table.

The rumbling sounds again, and the whole house seems to jump. The walls—I'm not kidding—they bulge in and out like they've turned into lungs. The hardwood floor vibrates, the boards rippling across the room. I fall onto my belly, the wind knocked out of me. It feels like I'm riding a boogie board in a stormy ocean.

Something wails—wind, the forest, a person? I don't know. The house seems to brace itself.

The couch rises up, and then, incredibly, it pauses in midair, quivering. Dad's trying to get to the front door, his arms flailing like wind socks. Before he can reach it, he falls to his knees and puts his hands behind his head, bowing with his forehead on the floor. The couch smashes down right in front of him, splintering the hardwood, exposing the empty dirt crawl space underneath.

"Dad!" I scream, but I can't hear myself at all.

Obāchan yanks me underneath the table.

Peyton's already there, clutching Inu. The dog growls and barks. *Woofwoofwoof!* I grab Inu, too, and feel his heart hammering in his rib cage as he pants hard. I don't even care that he's slobbering on me.

A *BOOM!* shoves us back. I hang on to Inu and Peyton. There's a flash of blinding light.

The house bursts open.

My chest slams hard against the floor. I'm deaf and blind from dust. I'm being shaken like ice cubes in a blender. I don't know which end is up.

Finally the shaking stops. I wipe at my eyes. White plaster fogs the air. Shards of glass and china cover the floor. The furniture's tumbled all over the place. I can see sky through the roof. A plane, I think. A plane must have crashed nearby.

The dog bolts from under the table and runs out the open front door.

"Inu!" I shout, but he ignores me.

Peyton gets up slowly. He's still got his napkin clutched in one hand and a bare chicken bone clenched in the other. He spits out a chunk of plaster. "I'm okay. Are you okay?"

"Yeah." I don't see Dad or Obāchan anywhere.

From outside someplace, Inu gives two sharp barks.

Peyton carefully places the chicken bone on the table, as if it matters where his trash goes at this point. "Come on." I follow him outside onto the deck, and we look down at the open meadow leading to the forest.

Everything's covered in a thick, shimmering gray mist. It's as warm as a bathroom after a long hot shower.

It's completely quiet. No bird or cricket sounds. Just a *missing* kind of quiet.

Like nothing exists.

I'm afraid to breathe.

Down at the tree line, a dark shape moves. *Woof, woof!* Inu's warning bark.

"Inu!" I shout.

The deck lurches under us. I fall forward and grab the railing.

Then I see him. My father is standing a few yards inside the pine trees.

"Dad!" I scramble down the steps and head toward where Inu is running back and forth, still barking.

Dad turns. His eyes glitter and wink like stars. *Stay back, Xander!* His mouth doesn't move, but I hear him anyway.

Inu lets out a great moan and lopes over to me. I put my hand on his big head. He whines again. I try to move around him, to get to Dad, but the dog blocks me.

Now the sky is getting dark. Black thunderheads roll in, like someone is pouring chocolate syrup over the forest.

A salty smell pierces the pine air. I sniff. It's familiar, but wrong. It doesn't belong here.

The small hairs on my arms and neck stand up. I'm dreading something, but I don't know what.

Inu barks and growls at the thunder. He whines again. Then he does something strange. He takes my hand in his big, drooly mouth, hard enough so I feel his teeth, and he starts running back toward the house, almost yanking my arm out of my socket, his jaws bearing down hard enough to break my skin if I pull away.

I have no choice but to run, too. More rumbling sounds, drowning out everything else.

I look back once, and Dad's still standing there. Motionless.

Then I see why we're running.

An enormous wall of water, taller than these thousand-year-old pines, taller than any building I've ever seen, swells toward us.

Trees bend and snap like puny toothpicks. A windy spray shoots pine needles at my neck. Within a few seconds, my hair and clothes are soaking wet.

A tsunami, my brain nudges me.

But here? How? We're on top of a mountain, a one-hour drive from the ocean.

My father finally moves. He takes off running.

Toward the tsunami.

"Dad! Stop!" I yell, but the wind's carrying me away from the water and I can't stop no matter how much I want to.

The wave swallows the trees in front of Dad. He doesn't slow down. He puts his hands up, as though he's pushing an invisible wall as he runs.

The wave hits him. Or he hits the wave.

The powerful water splits. It surrounds him like a fog.

The tsunami shrinks. As it rolls toward us, it gets smaller and smaller, until it's no bigger than a tiny ripple in a stream. It reaches where we're standing and licks our toes.

I look around. The mist has cleared. The sky is brightening.

The mountains are gone. They've completely disappeared. Ahead is water for as far as I can see. All the way to a flat, blank horizon.

I'm standing on a beach.

CHAPTER 6

stand and gape. It's so surreal my mind can't catch up to my eyes. I don't realize that my mouth is hanging wide open until a fly buzzes into it and I spit it out.

The grass near my feet, where the water is lapping, is already flattened and turning brown, dying off. The water's totally calm, like a bay. The sky is blinding blue again. A white seagull caws and swoops.

It's as if the forest was never here at all.

And my dad is gone along with it.

"Dad!" I yell. I walk out into the water, up to my knees. "Dad, Dad, DAD!" It's a hundred percent useless.

Peyton puts his hand on my shoulder. "Dude, your dad's gone. He . . ." His voice cracks. "He got washed away."

My ears feel pressure, like I'm ascending in an airplane. But I can hear my grandmother's voice, faint, from inside the house. *"Kita, kita! Come here, quickly!"*

"Obāchan!" I'd lost track of her. Peyton and I rush back into the house.

Inu races in first, barking. We follow him up the partially collapsed stairs to the bedrooms. Why did she go up here?

We run by Dad's office, nothing but a pile of books and lumber. My room's a mess, too. Everything's fallen off the shelves. A gentle breeze now wafts through the broken windows, and my drawings flutter through the air. Not a single one is left on the walls.

Obāchan is wedged under a collapsed metal bed frame, with the heavy solid-wood bookcase on top of that. Blood streaks her forehead. Inu licks her face, and she pushes him away with a grimace. "Stop that, you silly dog."

I run to her, try to move the bookshelf off, but of course I can't budge it. "Help me." Peyton pries up the other end so Obāchan can scoot out.

I pull her to her feet. She brushes off her polyester pants. Her arm's bleeding, too. "Don't worry, I'm fine. Old skin tears easily."

I think of Dad, out there in the forest. Which is now water. I shake my head, trying to clear it of this nightmare. "Obāchan . . ." My throat closes. "Dad's dead."

She puts her hand on my arm, clenches it tight.

"There was . . ." I don't know how to explain the rest to her. ". . . a big wave. We got flooded."

Her small brown eyes lock onto mine, and she lets go of my arm. "Come on. We have to hurry."

"I better go home and check on my mom." Peyton starts for the door. "I'll call 9-1-1, tell them about your dad."

"No." My grandmother grabs my friend's arm in a death grip this time. "Your house is fine for now, Peyton. You must help."

His eyes dart from the door, to the window overlooking the ocean, to me. His tan face is covered in red blotches, the way it gets when Peyton's trying hard not to cry, like the time his cheekbone was cracked by a stray fastball. I'm glad, because if Peyton starts crying, I will, too, and I can't do that. I might not be able to stop.

"I promise. It's all right." Obāchan's tone will not be argued with. She's so sure of herself that Peyton visibly relaxes. She releases him as if she's letting an unruly Inu off leash.

Peyton slumps to the floor, Inu flopping down beside him with a loud doggy sigh.

I turn to help my grandmother, who is now scrabbling through the fallen objects on the floor. "What are you looking for?"

"Here it is." Obāchan picks up a wooden shoe box with Japanese writing on it. It used to hold candy—now it has Japanese stuff my grandpa left to me.

She takes off the lid and dumps it out. *Netsuke*. Little carved figurines, no bigger than a man's thumb, that people used to stick through their kimono ties and attach boxes to. Kind of like super-decorative buttons with dangling boxes that served as pockets. Anyway, they're really old, and people like to collect them now, as my grandfather did.

Obāchan's gnarled hands sift through the figures. She selects three. A tiny sailing ship, made out of dark wood. Second, an ivory octopus, which Obāchan told me was carved out of the tooth of a whale that washed ashore in my grandpa's hometown when he was a child. It has long, curly tentacles with teensy suction cups on each one. And the last is a wooden monkey with a bare-toothed grin. Each of the netsuke have a small lacquered box attached by a golden thread.

Obāchan displays them in her palm. "There's a reason your grandfather wanted you to have these, Xander. How he wished your father would follow him . . ." She trails off and looks right at me. "But your father had a different way of doing things. He liked to take a more peaceful, intellectual approach. He was trying theories of peaceful resistance." She shakes her head. "I don't think that worked very well."

Thoughts rush around in my head. *Liked*. She said *liked*, past tense. He *is* gone, for real. Dad, the absentminded professor. Gentle Dad, barefoot, urging a line of ants out of the house by making a line of sugar water for them to follow. "He studied fairy tales," I argued, feeling defensive.

"He studied historical events." Obāchan goes silent, letting this sink in.

I blink at her. "What do you mean?"

Peyton gets it first. "I'm sorry, what?" Peyton stands up and unfurls his long arms. "Are you saying that fairy tales are historical events? Jack and the Beanstalk? Cinderella?"

"Not all. The ones Xander's father studied." Obāchan points to the ground. "Now, please sit down and let me finish telling."

Peyton scowls and looks at me. I shrug. He shrugs back and returns his bottom to the floor. Obāchan opens the closet and takes out one of my belts. She secures the octopus and monkey netsuke to it before she speaks again. "Did you read your story of Momotaro?"

"My story?" I'm confused. "You mean the comic book Dad gave me?"

Obāchan clucks at me. "*You* made it, Xander."

So it's true. I drew it. But why don't I remember that? I sit down on my bed, feeling dizzy and nauseated. Inu lies down at my feet, puts one huge paw over my toe, and whines as if to tell me not to worry. I scratch his head. Inu always makes me feel better.

Obāchan sighs and closes her eyes for a second. "Xander, this is not how we wanted you to find out. Your father wanted to protect you for as long as we could. Momotaro is a real story."

Inu howls like a werewolf, cracking the air. My stomach knots up even more. What is she talking about? Demons, here? Momotaro, real? Maybe the earthquake gave her a stroke. She is super old, after all. "Okay, Obāchan. Do you know what year it is?"

She ignores the question. "All the bad things in the world today?" Obāchan says. "It's the oni."

"The oni?" Peyton asks.

Obāchan takes a canteen from the closet, goes into the bathroom, and opens the tap. She tastes the water and makes a face. "Eh. No worse than usual." Then she turns back to us. "War? The oni. Disasters? The oni. A fire eating the South Pole?"

I wait for her to say she's kidding.

She doesn't. "You've seen all the horrible tragedies happening around us. That means the oni are very strong indeed. Momotaro is the warrior who keeps them at bay. Your father is a Momotaro. So were your grandfather and your great-grandfather. All the way back to the original, who appeared when the world was in need of him."

I sag, practically collapsing on the bed. At the same time, I note that Obāchan used the present tense when she talked about Dad this time. A small flare of hope heats my chest. Does she think he's still alive? I don't know. I'm so confused. "What? You're telling me I came out of a peach?"

Peyton giggles nervously. "Peach boy. Cute little fuzzy peach boy." If I could reach, I'd sock him.

Obāchan talks fast. "No. You were born from your parents. But when a boy in our line is old enough, or when it's necessary, you become a Momotaro."

Before I have time to process this, my grandmother grabs my hand and turns it over. She pries the lid off the octopus's box and shakes some big grains of salt into my palm. "In Japan, salt is sacred. In the old days, and sometimes still in certain places, we sprinkle salt at our doorways to keep out the oni. It is one weapon."

My head aches. I slump on the floor. "And here I thought it was only good for putting on food." The room feels like it's spinning really fast. "Obāchan, come on. You're saying I'm destined to be some grand warrior. . . ." I search for words. "And you're telling me all this *now*?" My voice squeals. It does that sometimes, unfortunately.

Peyton snorts, his face fading back into its usual tan. "Xander, a warrior? Maybe in a virtual world. Behind a keyboard. Not in real life."

I glare at him. "Why don't you think I could be a fighter?"

"No offense, Xander. But both you and I know that you're not exactly into sports. Or anything physical. Don't you remember the school Jog-A-Thon, when we had to run around the field to raise money? You gave up after one lap." Peyton shrugs. "I did more laps than that with a broken ankle, for goodness' sake."

"It was hot," I say lamely. "I could have done more if I wanted to." Sheesh. Why does he have to be so darn *right* about it? I feel like I'm an inch tall.

Peyton slides next to me. "I'm not trying to be mean, Xander. I'm only telling you what I've observed." He looks at my grandmother. "Are you sure you didn't get banged on the head, Mrs. Miyamoto?"

"I'm not crazy, if that's what you're thinking." Obāchan holds up a hand. "You two boys stop interrupting." She raises an eyebrow at us and we nod. "We were going to take you to Japan next summer, to study all this and more." She presses her hand against her mouth. "They got too strong for your father. Just like they were too strong for my husband."

My grandfather, another person we rarely talk about. I always thought it was because he and my father disagreed about everything. So my grandfather was a warrior, too. I stare at her, not knowing what to think. Obāchan has never once lied to me. Heck, she's never even told me a fairy tale. Instead of stories, she read me encyclopedia entries at bedtime. Could she have developed an active imagination all of a sudden?

But then again, this mountaintop now has its own private beach, so I should probably keep on trusting her.

Obāchan screws the lid on the canteen. "Xander, there's a window of time when your father can make the water recede. Just like it never happened."

"Dad can do that?" I'm still really confused.

"Yes. And save the people. But instead, your father vanished. That means the oni have him. You must rescue him, and you must go now." She gulps. "If you don't, most of the world will be underwater or worse very soon. We must correct this."

I'm still trying to wrap my head around her words. "So you're telling me these demons . . . these oni . . . are so strong they defeated both my father and grandfather, and now it's my turn?" This. Is. Unreal. "What can I do? I'm just a kid!"

"You're different." Obāchan's lips thin into a line. "You have talents."

Peyton stands again, towering over my grandmother. "I'm sorry, Mrs. Miyamoto, but Xander can't be the Mommy-taso."

"MOMOTARO!" I shout at him.

Peyton slaps his hand down over his bouncy hair. His eyes are lit with excitement. "Whatever. He can't be the Momotaro. He'll get killed. Annihilated. Turned into a thousand little pieces of Xander mincemeat."

Wow. He's on a roll. "Exaggerate much, Peyton?" I stick my fingers into the carpet, start picking at it. Peyton's right. I'm no warrior. The idea is really the most ridiculous thing I've ever heard. I think of Dad. He can do push-ups on his knuckles. That's how strong he is. What can I do? Draw funny pictures of people? "What kind of talents?"

"We don't know exactly, Xander. We think it has to do with your drawing. Nobody else in the family did that." Obāchan sits on the bookcase. "Your grandfather and father were of equal strength, but your grandfather focused more on the physical, and your father focuses more on the mind. Then there's you. . . ." She hesitates. "You're the only one with a mother who . . ." I can tell she's choosing her words carefully, trying not to upset me.

"With a mother who what? Abandoned her kid?" Steady, voice.

"Who's not Japanese," Obāchan says softly. "Nobody knows how that will affect a Momotaro. What talents you will gain, or lose. It's genetics."

Fantastic. Another not-right thing about my heritage. Even when I find out I'm some kind of superhero, something's weird about it. "How is that going to help me, Obāchan? How?"

My grandmother shakes her head. "I don't know if it will help or hurt you, Xander. That's the truth."

Peyton moves over next to me and puts his hands on his hips. "Whatever Xander's going to do, Mrs. Miyamoto, I'm going to do it with him. And nobody can stop me."

Obāchan blinks up at him, a look of gratitude on her face. She pats his arm. "Why, Peyton, I wasn't going to stop you. I was just about to ask you to help Xander."

"Oh." Peyton squares his shoulders. "Well, good. Because I'm ready, Mrs. Miyamoto. Just tell me what to do."

I can't believe Peyton's offering to be oni bait with me. If I were him, I'd be running home by now. I grin. "Aw, Peyton, you're volunteering to be my sidekick? Thanks. I knew there was a reason I was keeping you around."

"Watch it, Miyamoto." Peyton kicks at me playfully. "I'm your bodyguard, not your sidekick."

"Whatever." I grab his ankle. He shakes it free like my hand is a cobweb. Further evidence of my weakness. "You're still my sidekick."

"Bodyguard."

"Sidekick."

"Hush, boys. Pay attention." Obāchan opens up the box attached to the monkey. Rice pours out into her palm, a lot more than you'd think could fit in that tiny container. "Rice and salt and water. This is all you need. The building blocks of life." She puts the lid back on the monkey box and ties the belt tight around my waist, around my T-shirt. "Now, come along."

She walks briskly out of my room. Inu gets up and lopes after her. Peyton and I look at each other.

"I guess we better do what she says," Peyton says.

I look out my window at the brand-new ocean and I want to crawl under the bookcase and hide. But then I think of Dad. He's still alive—someplace—and it's up to me to bring him back. "I guess so."

We follow my grandmother. She barrels downstairs and out of the house, a waterproof messenger bag in her hands. I didn't know she could still move half that fast.

The sun's low in the sky, starting to set—at the appropriate hour this time. Obāchan splashes into the water up to her ankles. "Come here."

We obey. She puts the nylon messenger bag over Peyton, cross-wise. "Time is different where you're going. You have five sunsets until your parents will even know you are gone."

Peyton and I exchange another glance—mine alarmed, his gleeful. "Five days away from my parents? I volunteer!" He sloshes into the water, then pauses, shading his eyes against the setting sun. "Okay, what do you mean by where we're going? All I see is a whole lot of water."

"If we have to swim, I'm definitely out." I take off my socks and wade into the warm water. I'm not a great swimmer. I look like a frog having a seizure.

Peyton belly-flops onto the shore. "Get on my back. I'll carry you, sea-turtle style."

I don't want to. Somehow this is even more humiliating than the notion of me not being able to swim alone. Peyton really is my bodyguard, not my sidekick. "You can't carry me. We don't even know where we're going. It might be like ten miles. Then we'll both drown."

"Nope." Peyton's all confidence. "I won't let us."

"What if there's a shark?"

"I'll punch its eye out." Peyton stands up again. "Stop worrying so much."

"I'm not getting on your back, okay? No way."

Obāchan ignores our comments. She takes in a deep breath. Then she hurls the netsuke ship charm into the sea.

It plops like a pebble and disappears.

That was my favorite netsuke. Why'd she do that?

Inu nudges my hand with his cold, wet nose. *Woof, woof!*

"What?" I say. He whines.

I look where my dog's looking. Hear the sound of rushing water, like a very large bathtub filling up.

A great wooden shaft thrusts out of the water. A tree trunk, maybe? I blink, my brain trying to process all this new stuff and failing miserably.

The ocean tries to shove the tree trunk back down, but it fights, bobbing, and finally the water spits the whole thing out.

An enormous wooden ship bursts from the sea, sending a chest-high wave at me.

CHAPTER 7

The wave knocks me off my feet, flips me over. When I finally emerge, hacking, Obāchan is just standing there, smiling serenely, as if she's seeing us off to school. *No big deal. I just threw a tiny charm into an ocean that wasn't there before, and a huge boat appeared.* "Are you ready?" she asks.

"For what? To get on that?" I don't want to move. The ship's a few hundred yards offshore, at least. That's like the length of three Olympic-size pools. I can't even swim one. "Isn't there a little rowboat to take us?"

It looks like a wooden pirate ship. Last year, my class spent the night on the *Star of India*, an old ship moored in San Diego harbor, and we had to learn about this kind of vessel. The first thing they told us is that a ship like this needs a big crew to manage the sails and everything.

The *Star of India* is more than two hundred feet long. I figure this one is about half that size. It has two masts and big white canvas sails. The taller mast has what I think is the Japanese flag flying from the top. Then I see that the giant circle isn't red, but peach-colored.

It's Momotaro's boat.

"Am I asleep?" Peyton whispers.

I punch his arm as hard as I can. He doesn't even flinch. I pinch myself. Ouch. "Nope."

He nods, looking dazed. "All righty, then."

Inu jumps into the water and starts swimming. Peyton shrugs and dives in himself. Of course he would. It's so easy for him, he might as well be crossing the street.

"Obāchan?" I say in the tiniest voice I've ever heard. "I can't do this."

My grandmother's beautiful face beams. "Sometimes, Xander, the best way to start something scary is to just jump in." With that, my tiny, ancient grandma shoves me into the ocean.

"Whoa!" Suddenly I'm in deep water. Flailing my limbs, I manage to keep my head in the air. "Aren't you coming, too?" I call to Obāchan.

"No." Obāchan takes a step backward. "Have faith, Xander. Faith and imagination."

Imagination, yes. Apparently my imagination is so great it works without me, drawing whole comic books and hilarious pictures of my enemies while I'm not paying attention. But the faith part—I have no idea what Obāchan means by that.

Somehow I don't think faith and imagination are going to kill any demons.

I look toward the ship. Peyton and Inu are already there, Peyton helping Inu climb a rope ladder that's dangling into the water. Inu grips each rung with his teeth as he scrambles ever higher.

"Are you sure you can't come with—" I turn back to my grandmother again.

Obāchan's gone.

In fact, everything's gone.

My house is missing.

Where it once stood there's just barren, black, flat rock. A desert of rock. For as far as I can see. Not a single building or hill or stick of tree on it.

I feel like I just porked down an entire large pepperoni pizza and guzzled a liter of root beer on top of it. But I have to start swimming, because I'm already sinking.

I make my way to the boat, slower than a turtle on land. *Woof!* Inu barks at me from the deck.

Peyton sticks his head over the railing. "Just grab the ladder and climb up."

I grip the rope. "Really? I thought I was *not* going to grab it and just drown."

"Ha-ha." Peyton watches me climb. "Just get to where I can reach you, and I'll pull you up."

I grunt and wheeze. Climbing a rope ladder like this looks a lot easier than it actually is. The ladder bangs against the side of the ship, smashing my fingers, and clutching it for dear life is giving me rope burn. I grit my teeth. If I'm this exhausted already, how am I ever going to get to wherever my dad is? I'll be in a wheelchair by then.

Finally, when I'm near the top, Peyton grabs me under the armpits and hoists me all the way onto the deck. I sprawl face-first, my palms splayed on the polished wood. At least there are no splinters. Inu shakes himself dry, getting bits of fur and doggy water all over me. I sit up, breathing hard.

"You made it." Peyton claps my back.

"Barely." If this is Part One of being a warrior, I don't think I'll survive any other part. I still can't catch my breath with the cramp that's knifing my side. Now I wish I'd chosen to jog around the track during PE instead of just walking. If only the coach had yelled, *Xander, run, because one day you might be on a pirate ship searching for your father and fighting demons.* If I'd known that, I definitely would have tried harder in that class.

I look around. It's full-on night now, but a light glows from below. "Are we alone?"

Peyton, on the other hand, appears to be experiencing emotions opposite of mine. "Yeah," he says with a grin. "Totally alone. How awesome is this? No parents. No adults. Nobody telling us what to do!" He climbs six feet up the netting that hugs the mast. "Woo-hoo!"

Well, it's nice that *he's* feeling at home here. But I'm not. How are Peyton and I supposed to sail this thing by ourselves? I've never even rowed a boat. Not even in a video game. And sailing is the one activity Peyton's dad hasn't done with him.

Maybe I don't have to worry about it. The wind flaps through the canvas sails, and there's a creaking noise as the sails shift on their own.

The ship glides away from shore.

CHAPTER 8

We descend a short ladder into the cabin, helping Inu balance on the rungs. There's a small kitchen with a wooden table and a bench built into the side of the ship. *Galley*, I correct myself. That's what a kitchen is called on a ship. No fridge, but there is an old-looking gas stove and cupboards. One lamp glows above the table.

Kerosene sconces on the walls burst into life as soon as our feet touch the floor. Torches with sensors?

Peyton busies himself opening cupboards. "I could eat an elephant. Or at least a large pony." He shakes his head. "Sheesh. Nothing." He slams a door shut.

My gut agrees with him, growling so loud that Inu cocks his head at me. He wags his tail and yips. "You hungry, too, Inu?" I guess the swim settled my stomach. You wouldn't think I'd want to eat after all that has happened, but we hadn't been able to finish our dinner before the world turned upside down. I start looking through the cupboards, too. "If I were food, where would I be hiding?"

Inu sniffs around and points with his snout at the cabinet above a hammered copper sink. *Woof!*

That alone is a really good reason to have a dog around: sense of smell.

I open the cupboard and inside is a lacquered square *bento* box. It's full of rice balls. *Onigiri*, my grandma calls them. Made of steamed white rice, with meat or another treat in the center. I pop one into my mouth and bite down. "Chicken." I sit on the bench at the built-in table. I throw one to Inu, overshooting his head, but Inu stands up and catches it anyway. "Good boy!"

Peyton slides in next to me and puts two rice balls in his mouth so he looks like a chipmunk. "Chicken and . . ." He makes a face and spits a chewed-up mass of soggy rice into his palm. "Ew. Super salty and sour."

I recognize it from Obāchan's arsenal. "That's a salted dried plum. Obāchan gives those to me when my stomach hurts. You can suck on it and you'll feel better."

He makes a face. "Are you kidding? Sucking on this will definitely make me barf." Peyton looks around for a place to throw it away, but Inu eats it out of his hand.

I pluck out a second rice ball. Inu licks his chops, so I throw it to him and take another for myself. Then I hesitate. This is all the food we have. Maybe I should save it for later. But my stomach rumbles, and I take it out anyway. Peyton knows how to fish. We'll be fine.

The ship's course seems steady. "Do you think this thing is pre-programmed to go someplace?"

"Or it's magic," Peyton says. "That's my bet."

Magic. Fairy tales. If you'd asked me before today, before this hour, if I believed in magic, I'd have said no. I'm not a little kid. I don't believe in Santa or the Easter Bunny or the Tooth Fairy or anything like that anymore.

But I can't exactly explain away all this with technology, can I? "Maybe we're in the Matrix and this is all in our heads." I eat yet another rice ball. My stomach begins to feel full.

"Or maybe we're already dead," Peyton says in a way that lets me know he's kidding, but not quite kidding.

Maybe my father's already dead. *No*, something deep inside me whispers. No. My grandmother knows what she's doing. I have to trust her. "We're not."

Peyton glances sideways at me. "Are you sure?"

"Positive."

Peyton opens the food box again. "In that case, I might as well eat another rice ball."

"No! We better save the rest." I clap my hand down on the box.

Peyton pulls it toward himself. "What are you talking about? It's full again." He shows me. Yes, indeed, the box has refilled itself with fat balls of onigiri. For the first time aboard this ship, I smile.

We sit quietly for a minute, staring at each other, the walls, and Inu, who wags his tail. "No TV on board, huh?" I say.

Peyton unzips the messenger bag and takes out the Momotaro comic. "Want to read this?" He slides it over. "Might help pass the time—or give us some clues about what to expect. Your grandma did say it was a real story."

Clues? I gulp. None of this feels real yet. I'm not ready to think about all the nuts and bolts of how I'm going to save my father. My head throbs. For a second, I want to go to sleep and never read the comic at all.

I realize I'm breathing pretty fast for someone who's just sitting down. I feel like I need to run around the ship, yelling. Forget it. I'm much too torqued up to go to sleep.

I might as well read it and get it over with. It's not like there's a computer in here. There's literally nothing else to do.

I look at the cover.

There's a picture of a man in samurai gear, tons of heavy woven-looking old armor, and a huge sword across his back. His hair is so silvery it glints off the page.

Definitely not me.

I flip through to where we left off and read aloud.

~~~~

Momotaro set off toward the ocean. The journey would take three days on foot.

At night he dreamed his terrible dream of the dark and cold place, and it made him shake with fear, but every morning Momotaro still got up and continued. He was determined not to falter.

Along the way, in a barren field, he came across a dog tied to an old fence post. As he cut its rope, he could count its ribs through its thin brown fur.

Though Momotaro had only three rice balls, he gave one to the dog without hesitation. For Momotaro would rather starve himself than let this dog go hungry, too.

The dog gobbled it up. "*Arigato*. I am at your command," the dog said with a bow. "You have saved me. Where you go, I go."

"Where I go is to the Isle of Akumu," Momotaro said. "It is within the Ring of Fire, where all the earthquakes originate. I am headed there to battle monsters and demons and more than likely meet my doom."

"Where you go, I go. You are my master now." Without hesitation, he fell into step beside Momotaro.

"I must tell you," Momotaro said, "I have very little food."

"I do not care, for I will get food for both of us," the dog answered. "You are the only person who has ever helped me, so my life will be spent helping you."

Momotaro thought of his terrible dream and felt his fear

ebb, for he would no longer have to walk the cold and dark place all alone. He patted the dog on its worn head.

On their way to the ocean, the dog and Momotaro saw a pitiful golden pheasant dying in a bare tree. Its feathers drooped, and its skin showed through in spots. "Please help," the pheasant croaked. "The land has dried up. There is no food left for birds."

Momotaro peered into his lunch box. Only two rice balls remained. But he was a good-souled boy, and he could not let this bird starve.

"Go away," said the dog with a growl. "Momotaro has me. He does not need you as well."

"I must help this pheasant as I helped you," Momotaro said, and the dog went silent. Momotaro threw a rice ball to the bird.

The bird gobbled it up. "I will come with you," the pheasant said. "My life is yours."

"I have no food left to give." Momotaro did not know how he would feed both the dog and the pheasant. "It's too dangerous. Both of you should stay here."

"No," the dog and the pheasant answered. "Where you go, we go."

"Very well. But come at your own risk," Momotaro said. Now he had two companions for his desolate adventure. He would find a way to care for them.

In the evening, they passed through a village of empty houses. A monkey sat alone, picking through a pile of dry garbage. "Please," the monkey said. "Food?"

Momotaro sighed a little bit now, for his own stomach rumbled with hunger. But he did not hesitate before reaching into his bento box and bringing out the final rice ball. "Take this, without obligation."

The monkey bowed so low its forehead scraped the hard dirt ground. "I am at your service, Momotaro."

The pheasant flapped its wings. "We have no need of a monkey! Begone!"

The monkey bared its teeth. "I will rip off your wings, useless bird!"

"Enough!" Momotaro held up his hand. "We must work as one if we are to accomplish anything. Now, do as I say, or do not come at all."

Thus chastened, the animals followed Momotaro to the ocean, where they boarded a waiting ship, and sailed for the Isle of Akumu.

〜〜〜

"They're eating rice balls, just like us." Peyton takes the book from me and flips through. "Dun-dun-duun!"

"So what? Everybody in Japan eats those. It's an easy food to pack." And apparently an easy food to regenerate.

"Duh. Xander, we're following in Momotaro's footsteps." Peyton opens up the comic and points at a picture of the dog. "This is Inu."

It's brown with maybe a hint of gold, but not curly like my Inu. "It doesn't look like him exactly. And Inu's never starved a day in his life."

"It doesn't have to be exact, does it?" Peyton frowns at the drawing.

"I don't know. So which character would you be?" It's nuts, just thinking about this. That we're characters from a comic book, come to life.

"The monkey, maybe?" Peyton flips through the comic. " 'Cause I'm good at climbing and I like eating."

"Or maybe you're not in here at all, because, hello, this is a fairy tale." I take the book back from him. "And even if it was real, who was my father's monkey? His pheasant? I don't think he had those. And Inu is with us right now, not with my father like he should be."

"Do you know everything your father did when he was your age?" Peyton takes the book out of my hands again. "Maybe he had those companions."

I pause. I don't know what my father did when he was twelve. What his life was like back then, growing up in Japan. All I know is that he and his own father bickered a lot, and Dad couldn't wait to be an adult so he could move to the United States. He never gave me the details. "The past is past, Xander," he liked to say. "Unchangeable. Everything happens as it is meant to happen."

See? Not helpful at all.

I remember what my grandmother said—her husband was all about fighting the oni with might, and my father was about fighting them with his mind. Maybe that's what they bickered about. But I don't know for sure. It's making my head hurt again. "No, I don't know, Peyton. That's the problem. He never told me anything." A panicky, trapped feeling comes over me. "Even if you're the monkey and Inu helps me, how am I supposed to fight a demon? I want to get my father back, but really . . . they might as well ask me to fly a spaceship."

Peyton slaps the comic book down, his crest of hair bobbing, and gives me a stern look. "It's not just about your father, Xander. It's about getting that water out—my house is in danger, too, you know."

I hadn't thought about that.

"And it's about, I don't know, saving the world from bloodthirsty demons." Peyton stands up on the bench and spreads his arms wide. "Don't you care about humanity? Sheesh, Xander. You have to try. With that attitude, you're dead before you start."

"All right." I shrink down into myself. Peyton's right. "I agree, already. Stop your squawking."

Peyton jumps down onto the floor and points at me. "Finally. I knew you'd see it my way." He does a high kick at an imaginary enemy. "I can't wait to kick some oni butt."

"Calm down, dude." I've only known Peyton to fight one time. Back in fourth grade, I was standing in the cafeteria line and playing with a *temari* ball my grandmother had made. Temari are embroidered balls made out of scraps of silk kimono fabric, sewn together in geometric patterns. This one was green and gold and silver; it looked like a throwing star was sewn onto the fabric. I probably shouldn't have taken it to school.

"Let me see that," a huge eighth grader named Conrad demanded. The kid was the biggest at the school, solid as a boulder.

I ignored him and kept on throwing the ball up and down. I didn't want anyone taking the ball and ruining it. I figured if I said nothing, he'd give up.

"Let me see that thing." Conrad grabbed for it and missed.

I held it up with a smirk. "Look. You're seeing it fine from where you are."

The next thing I knew, Conrad pulled back his fist and punched me right in the face, snapping my neck back. My nose spurted blood. And the next thing I knew after that, Peyton was tackling Conrad around the knees, sending him to the ground.

"I can't calm down," Peyton says now. He does another high kick. *"This is what I'm going to do,"* he sings in his falsetto, another line from the boy group song. *"I'm going to put the hurt on you."* That last part isn't a real lyric.

Inu puts his head on my lap and yawns, a loud deep sound with a yip at the end. Suddenly I'm tired, too. I've been tired this whole time. In fact, I wish I could just go to sleep and forget this ship. Wake up from this nightmare in my own bed. With no beachside access. I never thought I'd miss that mountain, but I do now.

Inu gets up and goes into a dark corner of the room. More lights flicker on, and I see there's another room connected to the galley. I follow.

"Where are you guys going?" Peyton asks.

"I don't know. Why don't you keep on kicking your imaginary friends?"

"They're imaginary oni, not friends." Peyton does yet another high kick. I sigh.

Here, there are bamboo bunks built into the sides of the ship. Four beds. The mattresses are covered in puffy white down quilts. Inu jumps into a bottom one. Peyton climbs above him and burrows into the quilt so only his face peeks out. "Aaaah," he says. "I'm surprisingly tired."

"Surprisingly?" I sit on the bunk opposite, sinking into the comforter. "Dude. Not after the day we've had."

A small bathroom with a toilet and a pull chain sits off to one side. I think it's called a "head" on a ship. Well, at least we aren't stuck using chamber pots. I wonder where the waste goes—probably just shoots into the ocean. I hope we don't make any whales mad.

I frown. "There are four beds. Why?" It feels like someone's missing. Kind of like when I look at the dining table at home and see the empty spot where Mom used to sit.

"It's just an extra." Peyton yawns. "For guests."

"Well . . ." I think of the story. "I have a dog. I don't have a pheasant or a monkey. Maybe you're the extra. Momotaro didn't have a boy sidekick."

Peyton snorts. "Bodyguard."

"Sidekick." I grin.

"Hmmmm." Peyton turns toward the wall. I can tell he's not used to the idea. "Maybe it's more like you're the brains, and I'm the brawn."

"Hey. I'm the peach boy, not you."

Peyton lifts a hand in the air. "Good night, peach boy. Hope you grow some fuzz while you sleep."

I throw my pillow at him.

Before long, Peyton starts snoring, the way he always does, like he's some kind of grizzly bear. I can't sleep. But it's not because of the snoring.

Because I'm the peach boy. Momotaro. The great warrior, who's going to face an island full of demons.

Except I'm not really Momotaro, the kid who can rip a tree out of the ground. All I have are my bare, puny little hands. I don't even have Momotaro's sword. What on earth can I possibly do?

I try to picture me confronting a monster, that beast-man, and throwing salt in its face. He would just laugh at me before he ate my heart, or whatever oni do for fun.

For a moment I get angry at my father and grandmother again, for not telling me anything. I have no idea what these monsters do, or how many different kinds there are. What if each one has a special way it has to be killed? You know, like a silver bullet, or garlic, or chopping off its head? Dad never talked about it. Obviously, I needed to know this stuff a whole lot more than I needed pre-algebra. What a waste of time school was. I always knew it, but now I *really* know it.

I don't have what it takes to save my father. Poor Dad. Peyton should have been his son, not me.

I wonder if my mother knew about my father being Momotaro. Maybe that's why she left. When I asked my father about my mom leaving, all he said was, "You're too young to understand. But she loves you very much." Not a very satisfactory answer, but the only one he'd give. Just this year, I went to Dad and said, "Hey, I think I'm old enough now to handle whatever you need to tell me."

For a second, Dad peered at me as if he agreed. Then he took off his glasses and rubbed his eyes. "Soon, Xander. I promise."

I'd heard Peyton's parents talking about my mother more than once when I was over at their house. One time, Peyton and I were watching a baseball game. We both probably would have preferred to watch an anime, but that would have caused Peyton's father to come in and lecture us about the uselessness of cartoons. Still, the baseball game was tolerable, mostly because we were splitting a bag of BBQ-flavored sunflower seeds. Peyton pecked his out of his hand, eating ten for every one that I ate. I was trying my best to catch up so he wouldn't finish the whole bag before I got my share.

Peyton's parents were in the kitchen, washing dishes or something. "Guess what?" Peyton's mother said to her husband as she ran water in the sink. "I know someone I could introduce Xander's dad to. That new librarian in town."

I sat up straight and spat out a husk. It hit the television screen. I knew who she meant. A pretty, young librarian with long brown hair who smiled at me every time I came in. She'd special-ordered a graphic novel I wanted from a county library on the other side of San Diego. "No!" I yelled.

Peyton reached out and wiped the husk off the screen. "Ew. Be careful. What are you yelling about? Our team is winning. I know you don't care about baseball, but that's a good thing."

"Can't you hear what your mother is saying?" I said. "She wants to set my dad up with the librarian."

He shook his head. "I can't hear her at all." He spat a shell into an empty paper cup and said nothing else.

"I don't want my dad dating some silly librarian." She'd probably bring me brand-new books and comics all the time, or let me have extra minutes on the library computers, or pretend she didn't see when I was eating a snack in there.

Oh no. I couldn't think of a single negative thing about her. But that didn't mean I wanted my dad to date her. Why wouldn't my friend back me up? "That would be totally awful," I said to him.

Peyton cleared his throat and stared into the sunflower seed cup. "Xander. It's been eight years since your mom left."

I slumped back into the couch. "So?"

"So . . ." Peyton sucked a few more seeds into his mouth. "That's more than half your life."

"So?" I sounded angry, even to myself. "What are you saying?"

He crunched the seeds and looked at the television. "So maybe your mom's just not coming back."

My eyes got hot and teary. And right now they get hot and teary all over again, here on the gently rocking Momotaro ship in the middle of the ocean, as they stare up at the empty bunk.

Because I know Peyton is right. My mother's not coming back, and my whole family needs to get over her and move on with our lives.

Well, maybe my mother's gone because she couldn't handle being the wife of a demon-fighting peach man. I kind of want to run away myself.

Maybe Dad tried to tell her all this and she thought he'd lost his mind. But if that was the case, why didn't she take me with her?

The truth is, I just don't know.

The questions churn in my mind like clothes in a big old washing machine. Great. Now I'll never get to sleep.

I turn over and fluff my sweaty pillow. Across the room, Peyton and Inu breathe slowly and deeply. They, of course, have been asleep all this time.

The current knocks into the ship with a gentle *whoosh, whoosh.* Despite myself, lulled by the rocking, I finally doze off.

I'm in a black forest. Not the pine one that used to be by my house. No, this is a different forest, with lots of leafy trees, and dry brush crunching under my feet. Ahead of me is a small clearing, with dusty dirt on the ground. This is the only spot where the sun shines through.

A silver-haired man, shirtless, in a pair of loose white pants, swings a samurai sword in a circle above his head, his back to me. His white skin has a sort of glow to it, like a dim moon. His back muscles bulge as the sword cuts the air. The blade gleams. Ivory peaches decorate the black handle.

"Ie ni kangei suru," the man says in a quiet, deep voice, his back still turned. *Welcome home*, my brain translates instantly.

The man turns and smiles at me, wrinkles forming parentheses beside his mouth. He has a sparse, closely trimmed silvery beard, and his eyes sparkle like blue topaz.

Without thinking, I drop into a bow. When I straighten up, he slides the sword into a scabbard that is stuck through the left side of his *obi* belt, by his hip. He strides toward me. He's tall—tall for anyone, but especially for a Japanese man. Taller than Dad. I only come up to his chest.

I look up into his eyes. They are eerily like mine, except for the

wrinkles fanning out on the sides. I see myself in his pupils. It's like I'm inside of him, too, staring back at myself way down below.

He steps forward and embraces me. He smells exactly like that old wooden box full of netsuke, a faint whiff of powdered sugar mixed with musty wood and fresh green grass.

"Musashi-chan," he whispers, and kisses the top of my head.

I know it's him, even though I've never met him, and he seems way, way younger than my grandmother. But he died old, not young. "Ojīchan," I say, and it's not a question at all. Somehow I'm not surprised to see him here. Of course—it's totally normal to see the ghost of my grandfather. At least when you've had a day like mine.

I look down at the crackling leaves beneath my feet. This is a really detailed dream. "Where's my father?" I ask. I figure he knows. He's a ghost. Can't they see the whole planet or something?

"You must retrieve him." Ojīchan crosses his arms, and his silvery eyebrows slant down in a scowl.

My heart beats really fast. "But I don't know how." Why did he say *retrieve*, instead of *save*?

"You *do* know how." Ojīchan turns away, gets on his knees as if he's praying. "You have powers unknown to the rest of us. The trick is unlocking them."

"You're wrong. I don't have any power." Tears spring into my eyes, and my nose starts to run. I sniffle. I hate crying, but I can't help it. What do they want from me? A few hours ago, the hardest thing I'd ever done was play in an all-day Mario Kart video game battle.

Ojīchan doesn't answer. His body shakes, and I wonder if it's got something to do with the ship moving in real life. I walk over and put my hand on his shuddering shoulder. "Are you all right?"

My grandfather turns. Slime oozes up between my fingers as if he's an amphibian. It burns my skin. "Ouch!" I wipe my hand on my side, but it still hurts like I'm holding a hot lightbulb.

A forked red tongue darts out of his mouth. At the end of each fork is a hissing, fanged snake. I jump backward.

The skin on his face is now red and scaly, covered in a thin coat of shiny goop.

His eyes are coal-black.

"Xander. At last." The creature reaches for me.

"Anata ni wa nani mo nai!" I don't know what I just said. The creature looks as surprised as I feel.

I shout it again. *"Anata ni wa nani mo nai!"* And then I'm just screaming, a long wail, as I feel myself fall.

CHAPTER 9

wake up by falling out of bed. My eyes fly open right before my face hits the extremely wooden, extremely hard, extremely real floor.

But then I land upright, perfectly fine. How did I do that?

In his bunk, Inu lets out a loud yawn-sigh, high-pitched moving to low. *Buh*, he barks in a bored way, knowing I'm all right. He drops his head back down on the pillow.

"Good morning to you, too." I feel my face with my hands, just to make double sure I didn't get hurt. No bruise, no blood. I use the toilet, then go into the galley.

Peyton sticks his head down from the upper deck. "Dude, are you okay? You were screaming like a girl in a horror movie."

I have to laugh. "You mean, I screamed the same way you scream when you see a spider?"

"Something like that." Peyton grins back at me. His hair's sticking straight up like a cockatoo's head feathers. Mine probably is, too. There's no adult here to tell us to comb our hair or brush our teeth. That's kind of cool. "Nightmare?"

I nod. That's all it was. Not a visit from my real grandfather or a real demon creature. *Justadreamjustadream*, I chant silently to myself. "Yeah. Guess I'm not used to the boat."

I go up on deck. "Here." Peyton comes up beside me and hands me something wrapped neatly, like a diamond-shaped origami, in wax paper. "Found these in that box."

Good old Peyton, always pecking around for food. I unfold the paper to find a big, fat buttery croissant stuffed with chocolate. My mouth waters. "Thanks." I bite into it. So good. Obāchan usually makes me eat something disgustingly healthy for breakfast, like oatmeal sprinkled with bran fiber. Maybe this trip's not such a bad thing. "Did you find something for Inu?" Dogs can't have chocolate.

He nods. "A meaty rice ball."

"Cool." We stand there quiet for a minute, gazing out at the horizon. The sky is stained violet, the way it looks at sunset sometimes, only the sun's getting higher and this sky is definitely getting a brighter shade of purple. The color is reflected in the water, crystalline and countless meters deep, dark mauve in some parts and light lilac in others. I inhale sharply, tasting the salt in the back of my throat from the ocean. A school of dolphins leaps in and out of the amethyst water, their sleek gray-green bodies forming perfect half-moons as they squeak merrily to each other. Only, when I lean forward, I see that they're not dolphins, but unfamiliar creatures with green scales and wider eyes. I just hope they're as friendly as dolphins. I don't feel like battling anything this soon after breakfast.

"Wow," is all I can think of to say. Words seem pretty inadequate at this point.

"Yeah," Peyton says in a hushed tone, like he's inside a church.

We stand silently for another moment as the sun turns brilliant on the sea. The dolphin creatures dive and disappear.

I finish the croissant and lick my fingers. "Got any orange juice?"

"I didn't see it. But that doesn't mean there isn't any."

I stand there for a moment, debating whether I want to bother going back to the galley. Then something tickles my side. Like a branch with soft leaves. I laugh. "Peyton, cut it out." I turn and look at him. He's packing a croissant into his mouth, chocolate smeared around his lips.

And then I see. My mind is blown.

"Peyton," I say, my voice barely above a whisper. I point at his back. Now I can't speak at all. I just keep pointing with a quivering finger.

Peyton frowns and tries to see behind him. He turns all the way around. "What? Do I have TP stuck to my butt?"

No.

He has wings.

Big, golden, feathery, soft, honest-to-goodness, eagle-looking wings.

Finally my voice works again. "LOOK AT THOSE THINGS THAT ARE COMING OUT OF YOUR BACK!"

He cranes his neck until he sees what I see. "AAAGH!" He leaps forward like he's trying to get away. The wings spread out, wider than his arms, longer than his whole body.

Peyton starts running. He sprints all the way down the deck to the end of the boat, then back to the prow, then to the stern again.

His wings start flapping, and his body goes horizontal. The wind catches him and hoists him up.

"AAAAUGH!" he yells again as he's borne out over the water like a crazy hang glider. "HELP!"

I run to the prow. "I don't know what to do! Flap them!"

"I don't know how!" he shouts. "They won't flap!"

Inu runs back and forth from the prow to the stern, barking.

Peyton, now high up by the top of the mast, puts his hands together like he's about to dive into a pool. He zooms toward me, plummeting straight down like a cannonball. He's going to go face-first into the wooden deck. "Slow down!" I crouch and wait for the impact.

But then Peyton pulls his shoulders back, making his body vertical. He lands on the deck, his legs windmilling like a cartoon character as he bounces across the wooden planks. He's going too fast to stop. Throwing his body into a base-runner slide, he skitters across the boards and lands in a pile of canvas sacks.

I run over. His body is bent at funny angles, his arms going in a different direction than his legs. "Are you okay?"

Peyton sits up, his hair even messier than it was before. "Dude, that was awesome!"

I almost cry, I'm so relieved. I thought he was going to die and I'd be alone on this ship. "Dude," I say back. "Dude."

"Dude."

We sit and sort of grin at each other for a minute.

"What the *what*. I have wings, dude. Freaking wings." Peyton flaps them. They blow wind into my face.

I reach out and touch one. Underneath the feathers is hollow bone, just like in bird wings, and I'm afraid I'll snap it. The feathers are iridescent, gold from one angle, deep green and blue from others. The tips are emerald green. They're as soft as my grandmother's silky satin kimonos. "Do they hurt?"

"They feel great. Like I can fly to the moon!" He flaps the appendages. A big smile breaks across his face. "I want to go again." He flaps them harder and he rises to the top of the mast. "Woo-hoo!"

I sit back and look up at him. Those glorious wings spreading out against the sun.

My best friend just grew wings.

Demons took my father. A professor who's actually a mythical warrior person.

This ship popped out of a tiny sculpture, and California is now an island.

What's going to happen to me?

CHAPTER 10

Wge continue cruising through the purplish water. I try turning the wheel, which does nothing. The ship just stays on its course. I guess I'll have to trust it.

We hang out on the deck and eat some more of the never-ending supply of croissants. (Hey, we're a couple of sixth-grade boys— eating's our favorite hobby.) Inu lies on his back in the sun, his legs splayed out wide like an enormous goofy cat. I scratch under his left armpit, making his back left leg wiggle uncontrollably and drool drip out of his mouth. His "spot," Dad called it. *Calls* it. I'm going to think about him in the present tense no matter what.

Peyton sits cross-legged, his wings spread out behind him. Occasionally he flaps them, sending my hair blowing back. Show-off.

I bite into my sixth croissant. "How do the wings feel now?" I ask with my mouth full. No grandmother telling me not to do that, either. I wipe my face with the back of my hand.

He unfurls them to their full length. "Like they've always been there. It's weird. I can feel things with them."

"Like they've got nerves?" I gently bend the end of a feather. "Does that hurt?" Uh-oh. I got chocolate on it. I try to wipe it off.

"Nope. They're more like cat whiskers, I guess." Peyton wrinkles his nose at the state of his wing. "Xander! Quit messing up my wings!"

"Sorry." I use the end of my shirt to get most of the offending smears. "It'll wash off."

Inu leaps up and licks the chocolate, sending spit puddling down the feathers.

"Ugh!" Peyton leans away. "Cut it out!"

"Inu, you're not supposed to have chocolate!" I scold him, and he leans back on his haunches and looks guilty. Then he lets out a loud belch.

Peyton guffaws. "Good one, Inu."

"At least he cleaned you up." I consider Peyton's profile. Will he completely transform into a bird, like a man transforms into a werewolf? His hair sticks up like feathers—they always have. His long nose is what my father calls "Roman," with a little hump in it. "You know, I never noticed this before, but your nose kind of looks like a beak."

"Gee, thanks." Peyton shifts his legs.

I hold up my hand. "I didn't mean that in an insulting way."

Peyton snorts. "Yeah, that totally came across."

"But," I continue, "now that I think about it, you *are* kind of like a bird."

Peyton cocks his head to stare at me.

"Like that!" I point at him. "And your hair. And your extremely long arms and legs."

Peyton shakes his head. "So? What are you saying? You saw this coming?"

"No." I examine his face. No feathers there. Unless you count the beginnings of a blond beard on the lower half of his face. Was that there yesterday? I don't think so. "Do you feel any different? Like, don't birds' hearts beat twice as fast as humans'? Is yours? Are you sprouting feathers anywhere else?"

"No feathers so far." Peyton holds out his arms and turns them over. My eyes widen. His arms are as ropy and muscled as an action figure's. He puts his hand on his chest. "Seems normal enough."

I put one of my hands on his chest and the other on mine, feeling the *thump-thump-thump* of our respective hearts. "Yep. They're both about the same." I sit back. It'd be kind of cool if he turned into a real bird. But then again, if he did, he might not be able to talk.

"I do feel stronger, though." Peyton snaps his wings with such force that I, squatting right next to him, fall backward. Oof. I'm splayed out on the deck. I sit up. He laughs. "Told you I was the bodyguard."

"Fine. You're the bodyguard," I mutter. Can someone who's

stronger ever really be a sidekick? I guess not. "How about *protector*?"

"Whatever." Peyton waves his hand around. "It's just a word, Xander."

But I'm still the one in charge. Still Momotaro. I don't say that aloud, though. Peyton won't like the idea of me bossing him around. I reach for another croissant, but my stomach clenches and I decide that I've finally had my fill.

"So, I'm the pheasant." Peyton does take another croissant and shoves the entire thing into his mouth. It's his tenth, I think.

I nod.

"I told you." Peyton slaps my back a little too hard, and I almost choke. "We're the comic! We better finish reading it." Peyton gets up and runs to the ladder.

"It's not a school assignment, you know!" I call after him. Okay, he was right. It sure seems like we're following the plot, with the ship and the dog and the oni and now Peyton. Could it tell me how to fight like Momotaro, too?

I try again to remember drawing the book, but I can't. Was I asleep? In a trance? You would think that even if I blanked on it, I'd wonder where that block of time had gone, like if I started drawing it at noon one day and finished at four.

And how did that happen? Did my father give me paper and tell me to draw it?

I decide I probably did it when I was supposed to be asleep. That's when I do my best work after all.

Peyton returns with the comic in a flash. He's not even out of breath, and his muscles are all ripply, like he's a comic book character himself. It's disgusting, actually. I fold my puny arms, which actually seem like they've shrunk since yesterday. "Let's read it."

A few dark gray clouds begin covering the sky like ice spreading across a giant windshield, and a frigid wind cuts across the deck, numbing my ears. I frown. "Hey, uh, how do you know if a big storm's coming?"

"The wind would be stronger than this." Peyton sticks his finger in his mouth and then holds it up in the air. "And it's coming from the south. That's usually not bad. I think it's just cooling off."

"But do we even know that south is south here?" I examine the clouds. They're feathery, not super dense like thunderheads, so I guess they're okay.

Inu cranes his neck at the sky, too, and then curls up into a warm ball beside me.

"If it starts raining, we'll go inside. What else can we do? Turn this thing into a submarine?" Peyton sits next to me on the deck and arranges his wings so that Inu and I are protected from the wind. Now that is kind of convenient. He opens *Momotaro* and I read it aloud.

~~~~~

The ship took them to an island with a castle sitting on top of a craggy cliff.

The group walked around the perimeter of the castle, searching for an entrance. They could not find a way in.

They stumbled upon a group of young women washing bloody garments in a pond.

Momotaro called out, "Who are you?"

A maiden stood up. The dress she wore was soaked in blood, too. "This was once our island, but the oni have enslaved us," she said pitifully. "They have eaten all our people and will eat us very soon. Go, now, before they eat you, too!"

Momotaro crossed his arms. "No. I am here to help."

"Nobody has helped us for years and years," the girl said warily.

Momotaro planted his feet. "I am here now. Show us a way inside."

The women pointed out a hidden passageway. "But you will die, you know!"

"Thank you for your advice." Momotaro thought for a moment. He recalled the painting he had made for his mother, in which he had painted craggy cliffs very much like these. Perhaps he already knew what to do.

Momotaro sent the pheasant flying up over the ramparts, to distract the oni, and the rest of them went inside.

There they battled the oni with great valor and threw them off the steep cliff. They fought as fiercely as a thousand men.

~~~~~

My blood turns cold. They think I can fight like a thousand men? Try a *thousandth* of a man.

~~~~~

At last, they vanquished the chief oni, and he bowed before Momotaro. "You are the greatest warrior who ever lived. If you spare my life, I shall be forever indebted to you."

"Your life is not mine to spare," Momotaro answered. He put the oni in chains and took him to the emperor of Japan. The emperor was so happy that he invited Momotaro to marry one of his daughters. Momotaro agreed and, in this way, became a prince.

~~~~~

"Is that it?" I grab the comic from him and look at the back. "That's the whole thing? There's nothing in there about how to fight the oni. He just *vanquishes* them. What does that even mean?"

"It means he beat them," Peyton explains patiently. "Also, he threw at least one off a cliff."

"I know that." I feel like throwing the comic book into the ocean. "But how? Does he cut off its head? I can't believe I drew such a useless thing. Some imagination I have." I blow out a frustrated breath.

I remember how Obāchan said that nobody knew how being half-Irish affected a Momotaro's power. Maybe all I can do is draw comics. Maybe in this new, half-Irish Momotaro story, Momotaro is really the sidekick. Maybe the pheasant gets to be the hero this time and I'm just along for the ride.

My stomach clenches. And now the water's getting choppier, thumping the ship up and down. Suddenly all those croissants I porked down don't seem like they were the best idea. I bend in half, trying to quell what I know is coming. "Unnngh," I croak. Also not very herolike.

Peyton's hand grips my arm. "Dude. You're the color of Mountain Dew. You better get to the railing."

I try to get up, but the deck's too wobbly. Or maybe my legs are too wobbly. "I don't think I can."

Peyton helps me to my feet. "Come on, I'll take you."

Leaning on Peyton's solid mass, which seems a lot more solid than it did yesterday, I manage to make my way to the side of the ship. I grip the wood until my knuckles turn white.

"You want me to get one of those salted plums?" Peyton pats my back. I manage to nod. He heads below deck. "Just let it hurl if you have to, dude," he calls back. "You'll feel better."

"'Kay," I murmur. My forehead's clammy. Ohhhh. Why am I such a pig? I lean over the railing. Inu whines and paws at my leg, looking up at me with his big brown eyes. I pat his head. "I know, Inu. Don't worry." I stare at the water, listening to the steady *chop chop chop* of the waves striking the ship and taking deep breaths in and out.

Then I hear something else. Something underneath us.

Swishing. Swimming.

I crane my neck, looking for the source of the sound. Are we going through a bed of seaweed?

For a moment there's just murky water. The ship continues sailing.

I hear the sound again. A creature is down there.

And then, way below us, I spot a light.

A glow, as if someone left on an aquarium bulb way beneath the now calm surface.

I stare. I can see a forest of red-and-white coral spread over the ocean floor, the light coming from somewhere within. Arms of coral stick up, making it look like a fortress, almost, or a palace. Some-place the Little Mermaid would live.

The ship scrapes over a finger of coral and slows. Somewhere very close I can also still hear the creature moving—a whale? It sounds like it could be that huge. I tense, wondering what I should do. Run below deck? Fight—and with what? Is this the first monster?

A shadowy form glides above the light, and I blink.

It's a long sea snake, with green and gold scales on its back, long whiskers on its doglike snout, long golden claws—

Claws? Wait. That's not a snake. That's a dragon. I may never have seen a dragon in real life, but Dad has shown me enough pic-tures of Japanese dragons that I know one when I see one.

My nausea is completely forgotten as I watch the undulating, powerful form of the sea dragon weave through the coral stacks.

He rolls on his back and shows me his shiny red-and-gold belly, his claws spread out to the sides, sort of like Inu when he was lying on the deck. But this thing is huge, bigger than an orca, bigger even than the fifty-foot-long humpbacks I saw on a whale watch once. I can't even see the end of its curling tail.

I shiver. It is a beautiful and terrible sight.

His golden eyes dart up just then and lock onto mine. I gasp.

I expect to be afraid, like I was in my dream with the beast-man, but I'm not. I feel like I'm waiting for something. Not something bad. Like after I've taken a spelling test when I know I've gotten all of the answers right, and I'm waiting for it to be handed back with *100%* written on top.

I hear something that reminds me of bubbles in a swimming pool. Kids, talking underwater. Are they words? If they are, I can't understand them.

The dragon bows his head ever so slightly and closes his eyes.

Without thinking, I bow back, my eyes closed, too. A sense of calm enfolds me. The sun reappears, hot on my skin, and the cold wind dissipates.

When I open my eyes again, the dragon and his palace have disappeared.

The ship changes direction slightly. Inu runs to the prow and barks. I run up there and look at what he's barking at.

Land. To the right (Is that starboard? I can't remember), a mountain peak looms. A big, dark triangle emerging from the ocean. "Land ho, Peyton!" I yell. "Or whatever you're supposed to say."

Inu barks twice sharply, staring down at the water.

The dragon again? I peer over the railing.

No. An undulating cloud of silvery white hovers in the water, in front of the ship.

Peyton comes up beside me. "Here's that salted plum. I ate the rice that was around it."

I take the plum but don't eat it. "Hey, Peyton. Look in the water. What is that?"

"Feeling better, I see." Peyton leans over next to me. "Can't tell from here." Peyton hops up onto the railing, his toes clutching it like a perch. He spreads his wings and jumps off.

"What are you doing?" I shout, startled.

"I'm cool," Peyton shouts back. He glides down next to the water, his wings flapping as if they've always been on his back. It didn't take long for him to get used to those. He jerks his head up at me and climbs the air back up to the deck. "Jellyfish. There are thousands of jellyfish pulling us."

I look again. Now that I know what they are, I can make sense of their forms. All the jellyfish in the ocean must be assembled here, towing this ship toward the island. "Wow. I wonder if they have anything to do with the dragon."

"Xander." Peyton lands next to me, his hands on his hips. He stares hard at my head, above my right ear, then my left. He reaches out and touches the hair. "Man. This trip has been hard on you. You're going gray!"

CHAPTER 11

"What?" I touch my hair. I run down to the bathroom and peer into the small hazy mirror above the sink.

Two long streaks of silver hang at my temples, like someone clipped on a couple pieces of jewelry or something. I clap my hands over them. "Great. Just great." The thought of Clarissa's reaction when she next sees me makes me blush. Like I don't have enough problems already. Now I have to look like my grandfather, too. And my dad.

Wait a second.

The locks are definitely shiny silver, not plain old gray. Yes. Just like my father's and grandfather's.

Just like a Momotaro.

In the mirror, my reflection's face stretches into a wide grin. I go back up to tell Peyton and Inu.

When the sun is directly overhead, it's about noon. I know that much. We're approaching the land. I expect to see a castle, like in the story, but instead there's just a black mountain. An old volcano, I think—I can see pockmarks in the rock. Lava rocks are razor sharp if you touch them the wrong way, and that's what the whole island is made of. You can't climb it unless you want to bleed a lot.

The chunk of rock juts high into the violet sky, which is now streaked with pink and cobalt blue. Peyton climbs the mast and sits on the crow's nest, his wings flapping every so often to keep him balanced as he examines the mountain.

"See anything?" I yell up to him.

"Just a whole lotta rock," he yells back.

The ship's heading toward a little cove cut out of the base of the mountain, bordered by a small wedge of dark sand. From there I don't see any way to get off the beach. I hope there is real land, maybe a nice city with warm houses and comfy beds tucked just past this towering black mass. But there's probably just a barrel of demons instead.

Peyton calls down. "There's a little cave. That must be the entrance."

Inu moves to the prow and makes three short *woof*s.

"Just that way. Maybe." Peyton points in the direction Inu is barking.

The cave opening is about four and a half feet tall, and maybe three feet across. Small. Where does it lead? I look up and down the boulders, searching for any other crevasse in this peak.

Nope. The cave is the only way into the mountain.

I've never been inside an actual cave. All I know about them is that bats live in them and poop enormous amounts of guano; and if there aren't bats, there are bears or tigers or eyeless transparent centipedes or other grotesque creatures that want a taste of you; and caves have drop-offs and collapses and underground rivers and bottomless lakes; and people get lost in them all the time; and you're supposed to wear a helmet with a flashlight on the front when you go in one.

Yeah, um, I'd rather not go in there.

On a cliff above the cave, something catches my eye. Two spheres, a darker black than the rock, seem to shimmer. Something scarlet flashes in and out of the crags. I hold my breath, waiting for it to reappear.

It's gone.

You imagined it, I tell myself. The oni from my drawing and my computer game and my dream is just on my mind. I shake my head, hard, to get rid of the red image.

Peyton spirals down from the crow's nest and lands next to me. Inu woofs and runs around him in a happy circle.

"I bet there's a way to sail around the mountain." My hands tremble, and I stick them under my armpits. I hate being such a coward.

"Maybe there's a good spot on the other side. Let's check it out."

"The ship dropped anchor here," Peyton points out.

It's true. I hadn't even noticed we'd stopped moving.

"I'll just fly up and take a look," Peyton continues. "See how big the island is."

Before I can say anything, he's off, his wings flaring into gliders above the white-capped waves. For a second he looks shaky, dipping too close to the water, but then he flaps harder and manages to soar upward, circling higher and higher until he's above the mountain. I hope he can see what's beyond. Then he swoops back down and heads toward the cave.

Inu barks hard and runs to the prow. He stands there growling, the ruff of his neck standing up and his enormous teeth showing.

"What is it, Inu?" I look where he's looking, at the cave.

A woman in a long white dress stands on the black beach. She's wearing a fur cape over her shoulders and holding something in her hand, like a staff.

Inu dives off the boat and comes up paddling and barking. *Woof-woofwoof!* He's going crazy, growling and snarling.

"Hey!" Peyton shouts at the woman from the air. "Hello. We come in peace! We have a question. How do you get through—"

Suddenly he drops out of the sky like a stone, his left wing streaking blood behind him. He clutches the wing with his right hand and spins out of control. He hits the shallow water shoulder-first.

My heart jumps into my mouth. "Peyton!" I look toward the woman. Now I can see that it's not a staff she's holding, it's a bow and arrow. "Run! Get out of there!"

Peyton drags himself onto the beach. The woman runs toward him, an arrow pointed again. At his chest.

CHAPTER 12

look down at the water, which seems really, really far away. I've jumped into swimming pools before, but truthfully I hate going deep. My ears can't take the pressure change, and they bleed. But I have to get to Peyton. I'll hold my breath; I'll swim up. I picture it in my head for a second, then jump in. Quick, before I can imagine sharks and whirlpools and poisonous jellyfish.

The water closes around me. My feet hit the sandy bottom and my eardrums bulge with pain, and I push myself back up to the air. It's so cold I can barely move. I'm going to turn into a Xander-pop, like those people on the *Titanic*. *Move*, I tell my legs and arms, and reluctantly, they start churning through the water.

I swim as quickly as I can, and finally I make it to the beach.

Inu's already there, circling Peyton and barking wildly at the woman but not attacking.

I stumble over to Peyton. The woman kneels beside him, dabbing the wound with a white cloth that's turning pink. Fat tears stream down her face. "I'm so sorry! I'm so sorry! I thought he was a pheasant. I didn't know."

The woman is beautiful. Or girl—she looks maybe sixteen. Not that I'm in love with her. No matter who you are, if you saw her, you'd have to admit she was beautiful, just like you'd have to admit the sun rises in the east. Because it's a fact.

Her marble skin glows as if there's a light inside her head. She has long hair the color of the mahogany dining table after my grandma polishes it with lemon Pledge. Her hair swirls in the wind like she's on a magazine cover. Her eyes are large and gray, rimmed with thick black lashes. She smells like apples. Really, it's almost ridiculous how pretty she is—she looks unreal, like she just escaped a portrait painted by some Renaissance guy.

She's sobbing as she swabs the wound. Doing no good. I think about the time Dad accidentally ran over a neighbor's cat—it darted out in front of him—and he cried more than the neighbor did, he felt so bad. Inu licks the woman's hand sympathetically.

Peyton's injury is a clean hole in his wing the size of a dime. Blood's whooshing out. "Give me your thing." I point at the fur around her shoulders.

She touches it. "My mantle?"

"Mantle. Cape. Thing. Whatever." I put the fur over Peyton to keep him warm. I take the cloth out of her hand. "Don't worry." I don't know if I'm talking to her or to my friend. So I look at Peyton. "You'll be okay. It's just a flesh wound." I think that's what it is. That's what they say in movies. I try to remember the first-aid training Obāchan put me through in case The End of the World happened. Press down. Keep pressure on it until the bleeding stops.

Maybe my grandma did know what she was doing after all.

The woman wrings her hands. I've never seen anyone do that in real life before. "Oh my. Please, don't die. I wouldn't be able to forgive myself. Ever."

Even Peyton, though he's obviously in pain, thrashing in a pool of water that looks like cherry Kool-Aid, tries to make the woman feel better. He also says, "It's okay. I'm okay. Don't worry."

She smiles then, wiping away pearly tears with the back of her hand. Once the bleeding has slowed to a trickle, she says, "Come inside. I have bandages. Let me help you."

When she stands I see that she is only a little bit taller than me, which means she's pretty darn short. The woman takes me by one hand and Peyton by the other and leads us into the cave. Her skin is cool and a lot more leathery and rough than I would have imagined. I thought girls had soft hands. I also never thought the first girl I held hands with would be someone who, you know, *shot* my best friend.

I duck as we go inside. "Be careful," she says. "Don't hit your heads. I wouldn't want to be responsible for that, too."

"Wow," Peyton breathes.

At first I think he's sighing in pain, but then I see what he's seeing. The cave ceiling stretches up and up and up, for hundreds of feet. But that's not even what's impressive.

Everything is jeweled.

Instead of stalagmites and stalactites made of regular, boring-looking minerals, these are covered with emeralds and rubies and diamonds, like in a dragon's treasure cave. It's at least thirty degrees colder inside, and Peyton and I begin to shiver. The ceiling above the jewels is white ice, and the floor is black ice. We walk slowly, my bare feet slipping and going numb.

I let go of the woman's hand and check Peyton's wound. It has stopped bleeding.

"I'm good. Much better," he says through chattering teeth. He flaps his wings experimentally. "It didn't go through a muscle, so I think I can still fly."

The woman smiles. "Just a little farther inside. It's warmer there, I promise."

We make our way through a maze of jeweled stalagmites taller than we are until we get to an open spot. I hear water spattering and look to the right.

A wall of rain is coming down in a circle. Like a waterfall, only the water's moving quite slowly.

In the center of the circle, I can barely make out a figure behind the wavering curtain of liquid.

"Get out!" a girl's voice screams. "Get out now!"

"Oh, don't mind her," the woman says with another lovely smile. "That's my little sister. She was naughty, so she has to stay in time-out."

"You're too ugly to be my sister!" the girl shouts back.

Suddenly the woman snarls, and her entire face transforms into something monstrous. Her lips curl back, revealing teeth as sharp and white as Inu's. "Shut up, before I come in there and eat you!"

Too late, I realize we've made a really big mistake. I try to move my frozen feet.

"Run!" the girl in the water cries out. She's been trying to warn us. "Don't be stupid."

But before I can move, the woman grabs my arm and twists it backward, her nails digging into my forearm like ten small daggers. I try to pull away, but she digs in deeper. Blood runs down my arm. I kick her and pain shoots up my leg. It's like kicking a block of ice.

All the woman's teeth are out now, in a gummy, wolflike snout. She yanks me close, wraps her icy arm around my neck. Her cold breath prickles my scalp. I can't breathe.

Inu attacks with a growl, going for her neck. It sounds like his teeth clamp down on stone, and he bounces off. He tries again, and she knocks him away. He falls down with a yelp. Peyton tackles her, too, and Inu joins in. This time she slips and slides on the icy floor. I manage to stagger out of her reach. The woman hisses and grabs my other arm.

With my free hand, I fumble to open the octopus's box and dip my fingertips in. *Salt is a weapon.* Could that really be true? Desperate, I throw it at her. *Disappear,* I think. *Melt.*

For a long second, nothing happens. She stares at me with her soulless eyes. Then her bones dissolve, and she falls into a heap of white, bubbling and sizzling. Like a ginormous slug.

It worked! I did it! I'm not totally useless after all.

No time to celebrate. Peyton grabs my shoulder. "Let's go."

But the human girl—she's still in her watery cage. Inu paces around the perimeter, whining, trying to figure out how to get to her.

"It's no good," the girl says, her voice fainter now. "Go out through the back."

"We can't leave her there," I say. "She helped us."

Peyton sighs and slaps his hand to his forehead as he shifts back and forth on his feet. His wings flutter nervously. "Well, why doesn't she just step out already?"

Good question. We stand in front of the girl's water cage. The waterfall drops are bigger now, and falling faster than before. The girl is just on the other side, close enough to touch. She's like a blurred photograph. Brown hair, big terrified eyes. Taller than me. I reach my bloodied hand toward the water. Maybe the water's falling too hard. . . .

Honestly, though, it looks like a shower. Harmless.

"It'll burn you to the bone." The girl's voice is hoarse. "Acid."

I look down at the black ice where the liquid is hitting. A deep ring has been carved into the stone underneath. I believe her.

I see a stick lying on the ground. It has a piece of meat stuck to it; I try not to think about what kind of meat it was and how the stick is probably actually a bone.

I pick it up and push it through the acid, to see what will happen.

The tip of the stick melts away. I drop it quickly.

I find another, smaller stick. I have an idea. I take the salt out. I need to make it stay on the stick. I spit on the stick over and over, and sprinkle the salt over my saliva.

For some reason, I remember a science lesson about outer space. If you pour water in space, it turns into a gel. I imagine this acid turning into a gel, like water in space. As if it's a fact that I'm recalling and not something I'm making up.

"What are you doing?" Peyton says. "I'm going to try to find an off switch." He looks around the perimeter.

The white mound that was the woman bubbles and steams, getting bigger.

"Hurry!" Peyton says.

I take a quick breath. Without thinking any more about it, I push the salt-covered stick into the acid rain.

The liquid courses along the stick, solidifying into a quivering, solid clear gel. It runs along the hilt, then stops right before it hits my hand, the excess dripping off and bouncing on the ground like a Super Ball.

I grin. I was right! I don't know how, but I was right. "We need something bigger than this stick," I say to Peyton. "Anything."

Peyton hunts around. He grips an amethyst-colored stalagmite—a newer one about the size of my arm. Grimacing like a mini-Hulk, he breaks it free with a twist of his torso. He hands the frozen jewel to me. "Here."

This stalagmite is wet and sweating cold. I sprinkle salt on it and push it through the flowing curtain. The amethyst repels the acid like an umbrella, turning water drops into quivering jelly. "Come on out," I say to the girl. "Step under this."

But she just stands there, looking at us. I can see now that she's wearing old, torn blue jeans, red Converse, and a white T-shirt with THE MISFITS printed on it in red letters. My dad listened to their music—punk rock from the eighties. Her hair is long and brown, so dirty it's almost dreadlocked, hanging mostly over her face.

"Come on!" I shout. "Hurry!"

She stares at me for a second, like she doesn't understand English. Finally, she seems to shake herself awake, and she steps through. Maybe she's all weirded-out from being held prisoner.

Carefully, I remove the amethyst from the waterfall. Liquid crashes down again, hissing against the ice. A drop splashes on my shorts and eats a hole in the fabric. Wow. Close.

The girl pushes her dirty hair out of her face. Her eyes are hazel and shaped like mine. I recognize what she is, like I'd know a member of my family. Half-Asian.

"Let's go," she says. But instead of heading to the front of the cave, toward the beach, she bounds deeper inside the mountain.

The whole cavern shakes as though we're on a really turbulent jet. The ceiling trembles and big, boulder-size pieces of snow thump down behind us. Great. An avalanche.

"Our boat's the other direction," Peyton tells her.

"Can't go that way." The girl doesn't stop, and we have no choice but to follow her as the clumps of snow fall more quickly and tumble toward us. The air is now swirling with snowflakes, making it difficult to see.

"Run faster!" I yell to Peyton as I slip and slide. "We're going to get buried!"

The snow reaches us and it's not snow at all. The white flurries are little white bats.

CHAPTER 13

've never heard of white bats. I peer up at them, trying to make out their features.

Red eyes glow, and sharp red claws flex and reach. They make a high-pitched, almost electronic sound.

Those aren't bats—they're white *rats*. With wings.

They swoop down, hissing and clawing, and we duck. I try throwing salt at them, but it doesn't make contact.

The tunnel forks, and the girl chooses left, a narrow and low opening. I go in after her, bent nearly in half. Behind me are the sounds of Peyton's heavy, even breathing and Inu's claws clacking on the hard ground. Only a few rat bats are willing to follow us, and most of those hit the walls and ceiling and drop away. Inu grabs a wing and hurls one against the other, knocking them out of the air like bowling pins.

The girl's awfully quick for somebody who just escaped captivity. The tunnel forks again, and she goes right this time, leading up a slick and steep path. We scramble after her. Not even Inu can keep up.

We zigzag right and left until finally we reach another cave. The ceiling's probably twenty feet high. A dull circle of daylight is visible above. "Up here. Come on." She begins climbing one of the slick walls. She must have found little nooks and crannies for her hands and feet, but I see none. Maybe she's part insect.

I don't know how the heck I am going to get to the top. I try to follow her lead, but to me the walls feel as smooth as a countertop. I give up and just stand there. Inu leans against me and whines.

Peyton screws up his face. Sweat droplets stand out on his forehead, and he's breathing almost as hard as I am. "I'll go up first and see if we can lower something down for you."

"What about the hole in your wing?" I point to it.

Peyton shrugs. "Only one way to find out if I'm okay." He squats, then jumps straight like he's pushing to the surface from underwater. His wings flap twice, then go flat against his back as he shoots up.

The girl's already at the top. Inu and I stand waiting, looking skyward, Inu wagging his tail. I wonder how on earth we're going to get him out. I'm sure not going to leave my dog here.

"Just a sec!" Peyton shouts.

A thick rope of twisted vines studded with trumpet-shaped purple flowers snakes toward me. "Climb up." Peyton wiggles the vine. "It's secure."

"Okay." I try to remember how to scale a rope. We only did it once in PE—we were supposed to climb twelve feet and touch a ceiling beam in the gymnasium. If we couldn't do it, we had to run a mile instead. Yeah. Guess who ran a mile? I can't even do a pull-up.

"Hurry!" the girl yells. "That salt won't last forever on her."

"Give him a minute. Sheesh," I hear Peyton say. The vine goes taut. "I'm trying to pull you up, Xander."

Inu whines. He's got no hands. He can't do this without me. I get an idea. "Here, boy." I wrap the vines around his chest, making a sort of harness, then tie it and tug. "He's ready!"

Inu rises slowly to the top, and then they toss the vines back down. I try to tie them around me, but the flowers are all stripped from them now and the vines are slippery. My knot loosens every time they try to pull me. "What do I do?" I call up.

"Can you climb it?" Peyton's voice sounds doubtful.

"Yeah, sure. Why couldn't I grow wings, too?" I loop the vines around my left foot, then grab the slimy green rope with both hands. *Three points of contact at all times*, the gym teacher's voice says in my head. See, I *did* pay attention.

I pause for a second, trying to figure out what I should do to avoid falling off.

The girl's face appears in the opening above me. "Come on! I don't have all day."

"What, do you have an appointment or something?" Peyton's scowling head is next to hers.

"He's not going to make it up here by himself. I'll have to go down and help." The girl sighs. "Oh. My. GOSH. Could you be any lamer?"

"I most certainly could be," I say. "You've only seen half of my potential lameness. Seventy-five percent at most."

She shuts up. Thank goodness. I reach higher with my hands, pull my knees toward my stomach, and unloop my left foot. Then I rewrap my foot, reach up, curl, and unloop. It's a slow, painful process as I crawl up the vine like an inchworm. Finally, just when I think my arm muscles are going to give out, I reach the opening. Peyton hooks his hands in my armpits and pulls me forward on my belly. I flop there for a few minutes like a dying fish.

When I catch my breath, I see we're in some kind of tropical forest. It's hot and humid and filled with the sounds of buzzing insects and whooping animals.

"Where are we?" I ask the girl.

She stares down at me. "You're bleeding. And you appear to be turning into a zombie. Are you undead?"

Now I notice warm liquid dripping to the ground. I turn my arms over. My left arm has caked blood on it, and my right arm has a fresh new slice from my wrist to my elbow. On top of that, my arms are covered in an angry red rash. An itchy rash.

"If he was a zombie, he wouldn't be bleeding," Peyton says practically. "You can only bleed if your heart's still pumping blood."

"But if your blood's just sitting in your body, it'll come out anyway." The girl doesn't sound at all disgusted, the way I'd expect her to. Most girls I know would be grossed out. Not that I know many girls. "Haven't you ever skinned an animal?"

Peyton wrinkles his nose. "Ew. No."

She rolls her eyes. "Then keep your mouth shut."

"Well, I've skinned a fish." Peyton puts his hands on his hips, and his wings unfurl for a second. "It was a big fish, too."

She shakes her head. "Cold-blooded animals don't count."

"Whaddya mean, they don't count?" The hair on top of Peyton's head rises like a cresting wave.

She shrugs. "They just don't."

He stamps a foot. "That makes zero sense."

While they bicker, I touch my new cut gingerly, trying not to panic at the sight of all that blood. It's not deep—this must be a part of the body that bleeds easily. My ears feel like they're filling up with sand. I gulp and sit down.

"Don't pass out," Peyton says.

"Dude, so helpful. Thank you." I try to stop the bleeding by putting pressure on the cut with my hand. To get my mind off of it, I look up. We're definitely in a tropical rain forest, with a canopy so high I can't see the tops of the trees. I've never been in a real rain forest, but the zoo has a replica that looks exactly like this, with giant vines and trees so green they almost look plastic. It's dark here, and more humid than the bathroom on the hottest summer day during the hottest shower. Oversize ferns with leaves bigger than Peyton's wings sway all *Jurassic Park*–like, and I wouldn't be surprised to see a T. rex thundering through. Birds trill and monkeys chatter over-enthusiastically. What do they have to be so happy about? I wish they would shut up for a second so I can think.

The girl stands over me. "Not to be rude, but do you have any food?"

Finally I get a good look at her. Her eyes shimmer green and gold and brown, and she has thick light eyebrows that arch. Black eyeliner is smudged all over her lids, so I figure she's at least thirteen, if not older. Who knows when girls start wearing makeup? She has a smattering of light brown freckles over her nose and cheekbones. She doesn't smile. She doesn't . . . anything. Her face is expressionless.

"I . . . I don't know," I stammer. I hadn't thought about it, what with running away from a murderous witch and all, but now my stomach growls in agreement. Every bit of the food's back on the ship. Along with my shoes, the comic book, and anything else that could have possibly helped us on this quest.

I fumble with the netsuke on my belt, remembering the monkey with the rice that Obāchan showed me. Is that our food? Is it going to turn into hamburgers? I pop open the monkey's box. The rice sits there.

Nothing happens. I pour a few grains onto my palm.

Inanimate.

The girl is unimpressed. The corners of her mouth turn down. "Well. Guess that was a useless question. Surprise." She turns on her Conversed heel and scampers off, her hands gripping vines and bushes—almost like she's swinging through them—as she makes her way into the thick fern underbrush.

Peyton kicks the ground with his toe, sending up a small cloud of dirt. "You could at least thank us for rescuing you!" he calls after her.

She doesn't turn around. "Yeah, great rescue. Now I get to starve to death more quickly. At least the snow woman fed me once in a while. Thanks a lot." The girl's voice trails through the air as she disappears into the jungle. "If you'd listened to me, we wouldn't be here."

CHAPTER 14

"**C**ome back!" I shout.

She can't be off in the jungle all alone. She's dressed like she was standing in line for a rock concert when she got kidnapped, not prepared for the wilderness.

"Xander, if she wants to go, let her. It's not like we know what we're doing." Peyton examines his scabby wing.

My rash itches like crazy. I wonder if there's a jungle plant I can mash up and put on it. Obāchan always uses aloe for cuts, but I have no idea what its leaves look like. I can't even tell lettuce apart from cabbage. "But she led us out of the cave. I think she knows her way around," I point out. I still have the grains of rice in my hand. I pop the three grains into my mouth without thinking.

Suddenly I'm chewing on three big wads of onigiri. Cold rice balls, filled with chicken. My cheeks puff.

Inu and Peyton stare at me for a moment. Then Peyton nods and holds out his hand. "Dude." Inu barks. I give them each a couple of grains, and soon we're all eating.

I feel much better once I have something in my stomach. I take a deep breath and look toward the broken foliage where the girl disappeared. "Can you fly up and find her? Or a way out of here?"

Peyton wipes a grain of rice off his chin and pops it into his mouth. Hey, it's survival time, not manners time. He spreads out his wings and tries jumping upward, but one wing hits a tree trunk and one hits foliage. "Not enough room. Besides, if I go up there, I might not be able to find you guys again through all these plants."

Woof! Inu charges forward.

"Find her, Inu!" I yell. Not that we trained Inu to be a search-and-rescue dog, but by now I know he understands a lot more than we ever thought he did.

He galumphs through the underbrush.

We follow.

A yellow snake thicker than both my thighs put together slithers in front of us. Python. We all freeze. Even if it's not poisonous, it could choke us to death.

Maybe Peyton has a point. Maybe we should let her be on her own, if that's what she wants. "Okay. If we don't find her in, like, five minutes, we go back to the boat." If we can, that is. I glance behind me. The vegetation we crashed through has sprung back up, and now I can't tell which way we came from. Anyway, do we really want to go through the snow woman's cave again?

An animal chatters overhead. *WOOF, WOOF, WOOF!* Inu barks in response.

"What's the matter, boy?" I look up, but I can't see anything except swaying branches. "It's just a monkey."

"Xander." Peyton shakes my shoulder and points upward. "That's no monkey."

Now, through the leaves, I can spot the girl, way up in the top of a palm tree, her legs wrapped around the trunk. She must have shimmied her way up there to get a coconut.

"I tell you, she's a real Tarzan." Peyton nudges me.

Whack! Whack! Whack! The girl is pounding the coconut hard against the tree, trying, I guess, to crack it. When that doesn't work, she hurls it down. "Stupid green coconuts!"

I leap back, narrowly avoiding getting conked in the head.

"Let's go." Peyton hops in a different direction. "I don't even like coconut."

"I didn't offer you one!" the girl yells down. She leans back, her feet on the trunk, and grabs another coconut, twisting it around and around until it breaks off the tree. "Hey, guys!" She waves at us. "Thank you so much again for rescuing me. Now you just go do whatever you were going to do, and so will I."

"All right," I say in a voice loud enough for her to hear way up there. "I guess we'll enjoy this endless supply of onigiri all by ourselves." I put a rice grain into my mouth and let it puff up into a ball. Then I take it out and hold it up to show her. Her eyes widen. "Let's go, Peyton."

"Finally." Peyton's already moving. "Real nice girl. She should be friends with Lovey."

"Wait!" the girl calls. She scrambles down from her perch, super quick, and leaps into my path. "You found your food?"

I pop the onigiri back into my mouth.

She narrows her eyes as if that sight physically pained her. "Stop teasing me. My stomach's about turned inside out. I'm literally starving to death." Her lower lip falls into a pout.

I munch the rice. "And it's delicious."

"Come on! What do I have to do to get one of those?" She wipes drool from the corner of her mouth.

I hold up the netsuke. "You get us out of this jungle and I'll give you all the rice balls you can eat."

The girl looks from me to Peyton to Inu. The dog sits there and pants, appearing so friendly that she can't help but pat his head. "I guess I could do that."

"Deal?" I hold out my hand.

"Deal." She shakes it firmly.

"All right." I spill a few grains of rice into my palm. "Open your mouth."

She glares at me suspiciously, but I guess she's too hungry to argue. She opens her lips, revealing teeth very white against her pink gums. I'm about to toss the rice into her mouth when she grabs the monkey netsuke out of my hand and shakes the box furiously, pouring a bunch into her maw.

"No!" I say, but it's too late. Rice balls explode in her mouth, expanding her cheeks to their limit, and then pop out of her lips. She almost chokes.

Peyton clucks disapprovingly and crosses his arms. "Serves you right. Didn't your parents teach you any manners?"

"My parents didn't teach me anything." She bends and snatches the sticky rice grains out of the dirt, shoving them into her pockets. Inu tries to eat some, but she pushes his head away. "Those are mine, dog."

"Leaving her behind sounds better all the time," Peyton mutters into my ear.

Probably, I'm about to say. But then I get a big, fat lightbulb over my head. "Hey," I whisper, "she's the monkey!" The monkey from the Momotaro story. It couldn't be more obvious. The climbing. The uncanny speed. Even the rudeness.

She lifts up her upper lip, showing her teeth. "Monkey? Ha. I've been called worse." She wipes her mouth with the back of her hand, then extends her palm to me. It's covered in bits of sticky rice and mud. Ew. I'm about to shake it anyway when Inu saves me by getting between us and licking the rice off. "I'm Jinx."

"I'll say." Peyton crosses his arms.

"It was my great-great-grandmother's nickname. She was a flapper. Al Capone's girlfriend." Jinx wipes Inu's slobber off on her jeans. "My family has a long history of lawlessness. Or at least"— she grins—"being associated with lawless people."

"You say that like you're proud of being associated with mobsters." Peyton's voice deepens in disapproval.

"I'm not *not* proud of it. I didn't choose who came before me. I suppose you did, Mr. Perfect?" She rolls her eyes at him.

Jinx has a point. And Peyton is sounding a lot like his father— not that I'd point this out to him at the moment, in front of a stranger. Instead I squint at her. "Do you really know how to get out of here?"

She looks right and left and up and down. "That depends on where you want to go." She wiggles her fingers at me. "Come on, already. Give me another one. I haven't eaten for days. No joke."

"Wait a second." I close my hand protectively around the monkey netsuke. She's not going to trick me into handing over more food. I've got to find my dad. "I want to go where the oni live. Tell me where that is and I'll give you all the onigiri you want."

"The oni live everywhere on this island. Duh." She eyes my hand, perhaps assessing how to steal the food.

"No, I mean where their, like, headquarters are, or whatever." I don't know how to describe what I'm looking for.

Jinx stares at me disbelievingly. She snorts. "*Baka*. Nobody goes there *on purpose*."

Peyton raises his brows quizzically.

"Baka. That means we're dumb idiots," I say to him. "It's kind of rude, actually."

"Yeah, I know how to get there. But I'm not showing you until I get more rice." She reaches for the netsuke on my belt, yanks at them. "Let me have some."

"Stop!" I try to push her off, but her long fingers snag my belt. She pulls me right to her. She smells like mud and coconuts. I slap her hands and try to turn, but she's too persistent. And strong.

Peyton steps in and shoulders her away from me, sending her crashing into a giant hairy fern. He unfurls his wings and squawks so loudly I have to cover my ears. "Enough, jungle girl!"

Whoa. He really *is* my bodyguard. "You guys, cut it out. Now." I wipe the sweat off my forehead and pat my belt to make sure everything is still there. "Jinx, if you can't play nice, you can't play at all."

Jinx regains her composure. She stands up straight and glares at Peyton. "The little kid better keep his word."

"Of course I'll keep my word!" I say hotly.

Jinx lunges toward me, and Peyton blocks her. She holds up her hands as if she's afraid Peyton's going to hit her. But he's got his arms crossed—he only wants her to leave me alone. I wonder who *has* hit her, made her so scared and mad at everybody. That witch back in the cave?

Then Inu thrusts himself between me and Peyton and Jinx and

barks. *Ruffruffruff.* That's what he does at our house whenever people raise their voices. I always assumed it was because he thought we were playing and he was excited. But now I see that Inu really understands what's going on. He looks at Peyton. *Ruff.* He looks at Jinx. *Ruffruff.* My dog is scolding everyone like he's my grandma.

Jinx sinks to the ground, suddenly looking as exhausted as I feel. "Fine, fine, fine. Truce."

Peyton glances down at Inu and then takes a step back. His wings expand and contract slightly with the rhythm of his hard, angry breathing. He points at Jinx with an index finger that might as well be an ice pick. "Don't you ever touch Xander again. Do you understand?"

Her hands go to her hair, smoothing it back as if she doesn't have a care in the world, but I can see the pulse beating in her neck. "Or what? Do you really think a chicken can take on a monkey?"

"Pheasant!" Peyton spits.

Jinx smiles. "Whatever. I've eaten those, too."

Peyton takes a step toward her again.

Ruff! Inu jumps up on Peyton, putting his paws on his shoulders. *Woof!* He barks right into Peyton's face.

"Ew, your breath smells like the garbage dump." Peyton pushes Inu down. "Okay, boy, I get it." He pets Inu's fluffy head. It's hard to stay mad with Inu around. Inu sticks out his long tongue sideways and thumps his tail.

"Can we please get back to saving my father now?" I move closer to Jinx, but not within reach of her. I'm done trusting this monkey. "Jinx, are you going to show me or not? If not, tell me now and we'll leave you alone."

Jinx lies back in a bush like she decided it's a nice resting place. She crosses her hands over her belly. "Why would you want to go to the oni nest, anyway?"

I gulp. "The oni have my father, Jinx. I have to get him back."

Jinx glares up at me, her eyes turning a very light amber. I realize she's holding back tears. She scrambles to her feet. "You want to see the oni? It's your funeral. I'll get you there. Then we're done."

"Fine by me," I say.

Jinx nods once. She starts walking through the bushes. *Stalking* is a better word. She beats the branches aside with her fists, probably wishing she was hitting me and Peyton instead. The underbrush seems to make room for her, moving to the sides to get out of her way, but it smacks us in the face and chest as it springs back. When I feel something like a hummingbird land on my bloody arm, I look down and see that it's actually a giant mosquito. I wave it off.

Jinx keeps moving. "So, the oni have your father. He must be the Momotaro."

"You know the story of Momotaro?" I hurry to keep up with her.

"Everyone here does." She glances back at me, then stops short. "But if you're his son . . ."

I wince at the disbelief on her face.

Her eyes go to the silver hair on the sides of my face. "I never would have guessed it. Momotaro are warriors. Big and strong. Like him." She jerks her head toward Peyton. "You are—"

"He actually prefers to be called Peach Boy," Peyton interrupts.

I sock him in the arm. But I can't worry about what Jinx thinks about me. I just need her to get me to Dad. "What do you mean, 'everyone here'? Do you live in this jungle?"

"I make it a habit not to tell people things unless they need to know. And you don't need to know." She pulls back her hair and knots it high on her head. The ends are tinged green. Then she starts running again.

I consider telling her that she's supposed to stick with me, because, according to the story, I have three sidekicks. She didn't care about being called a monkey, but I can't say that she's my, like, pet. She might just climb into a tree and disappear forever. "I'd *like* to know, though."

The day's getting hotter. Now I'm sweaty *and* bloody. Jinx doesn't let up her pace. "Originally, I was from Kauai. One of the Hawaiian islands."

"We're in sixth grade. We know where Kauai is." Peyton scowls.

Jinx comes to a halt again. My feet skid in the crumbling red dirt as I try to avoid bumping into her. "How am I supposed to know what you don't know, genius?" She moves her hand in a circle by a leafy fern. Another plant with flat succulent leaves leans toward us, as if she's pulling it forward with an invisible thread. She tears off a leaf and snaps it in two. Clear gel oozes out of the middle.

She grabs my arm and, before I can say anything, turns it over and dabs the gel on the cuts and hives. A coolness slides over the skin and immediately my arm feels better. "I started in Kauai; I ended up here. A place like Kauai, yet not like Kauai."

I flex my fingers. The welts are gone. "Thanks, Jinx."

She ducks her head and, for the first time, smiles a genuine smile at me. Her cheeks turn pink. "You can find the plant all over the place here. It's like aloe, only way stronger. If your throat or stomach hurts, drink it. It'll help."

Peyton squints at her. "And how long have you enjoyed this whacked-out paradise?"

Jinx shrugs, and her dimples disappear. Her hair falls over her face. She closes up like a clamshell. "It doesn't matter."

"What was that thing in the cave?" I ask her. We start moving forward, and again Jinx makes those beating motions with her arms. She's not trampling the plants; they're pulling back for her. Even Peyton's got to admit that jungle travel's a lot easier with her.

"An oni. A *yuki-onna*. A woman made of snow. Lures travelers to their deaths. Mostly men, who are easy to trick." Jinx smiles with amusement. "Eats their souls."

"So how'd *you* get tricked, smarty-pants?" Peyton asks.

I snicker. She glares at him. "Again—you don't need to know.

Anyway, the forest ends soon." She points. "We have to head due south."

This sounds like a pretty good plan. Also, it's the only plan anybody can think of.

"Lead on, monkey girl," Peyton says under his breath.

CHAPTER 15

The sun moves across the top of the jungle and still Jinx keeps pushing forward. Sticky mud pushes up disgustingly between my toes. By now, my vision is blurry, my hair is sticking to my scalp, my lips are cracked, and my face feels like it's melting off. Did one of the netsuke boxes have water? I look in both of them, but there's nothing new to be found. I didn't bring the canteen.

Peyton's breathing so hard it sounds like he's panting, but he keeps looking ahead and doesn't slow. Another nugget of info from a nature show floats to the surface of my brain—birds don't sweat. They kind of pant when they get hot, like dogs. Convenient for him—my shirt's drenched, and the only reason I don't take it off is because I don't want to get sunburned. Or blind anyone with my moon-white belly.

Ahead of us, Inu isn't moving at his usual trot; instead, a paw-dragging trudge, and he's also panting. Jinx seems like she's doing all right—no crankier than she was an hour ago, anyway. Maybe she's used to the jungle climate, being from Kauai and all. Nobody speaks.

I take what my grandma would call a "deep, cleansing breath." Or I try to, at least. The air is so humid it's like breathing in warm soup, which sticks in my throat. I cough. What I really want to do is sit down in the shade for approximately twenty hours and have a good rest. Apparently I'm not meant for outdoor life. I think of my room at home and my video games. Heck, I'd even be happy washing dishes for Obāchan, if it meant I could be inside.

Then again, if I was home, that would mean being back in a room wrecked by the disaster. It would mean that everyone and everything in my town was gone, including my father and Peyton's parents.

Not to mention what it would mean for the rest of the world when the oni attacked them, too.

I'm walking straight into the oni nest—no, I probably don't want to think about that.

A shadow passes overhead, and then a giant splotch of bird poop, neon yellow and green and white, plops down in front of me. Ew. I glance up and see a monstrously huge bird flapping away. I'm pretty sure it's laughing.

How much longer can we keep walking?

I stare at Jinx's back as she leads us to wherever we're going. She's my sidekick, and so is Peyton. They're here to help me. But even with them, how can I fight all the oni? Throwing salt can't be the answer—I don't have enough. I need a sword. Or something. Anything.

I remember the dream I had about my grandfather. *Ojīchan*, I say in my head, *what am I supposed to do?* Obāchan told me I had faith and imagination. But imagination isn't good for much when a real live monster is trying to claw your guts out. I don't know what she meant by faith. Faith in what? I don't have any faith. I don't even have a weapon. That sword in my dream—my grandfather's sword—shouldn't I have that? I'm no expert on heroes and demon fighting, but that weapon seems kind of important. In my frustration, I hit a palm leaf that's sticking out into the path, and it hisses and smacks me back. I jump forward, almost knocking into Peyton. Okay, mental note: leave plants alone.

The trees become more closely packed, their roots gnarled foot-traps. We have to slow down, pick our way over the knotty, ropelike appendages. Abruptly the light dims and the air cools, though there's not a breath of wind. Thank goodness. I inhale and feel the refreshing chill seep into the deepest part of my lungs. I look up, and the sky's completely obscured by leaves again. No birds or creatures chirp. It is as quiet as a baby's nursery at naptime. Ahead there's an especially big tree, with space between its huge, exposed roots that look like two arms waiting to hug me. I want to lie down between them. Usually dark forests are spooky, but this one's as inviting as a pool on a hot day. I stop walking. My eyelids are so heavy I might literally fall asleep on my feet. "Can we rest in here?" I try not to show how tired I am. I put my hands on my hips.

Jinx looks back at me and frowns. "This is not a good place. It's the Sacred Grove."

"Why's it sacred?" I move toward the roots, where I want to lie down. "We won't hurt anything."

"I don't know. It's just really ancient." She purses her lips. "It's like a church. Would you sleep in church?"

The two times a year when my dad takes me to church, I do tend to nod off during the sermon. "Yeah, pretty much."

Peyton yawns loudly and sits down on a root, his wings folding up behind him. "I vote for a rest, too."

Inu leans against Jinx. Guess that means he's siding with her, which makes me reconsider my opinion. But Peyton's already slid down to the ground, and his head's bobbing against his chest.

Jinx wipes sweat off her forehead. "Whatever. I guess it's safe enough. Just don't hurt anything." She sits against a root, too, and Inu throws himself down beside her with a sigh.

"I won't. I'm a regular tree hugger." I examine the massive tree. Its bark is gray-white and only slightly rough, like watercolor paper. It's as wide as three men lying end to end. I stare at the bark, looking for something out of the ordinary. Nothing. I turn and examine the other trees in this copse, too. A soft breeze rustles the leaves and dappled sunlight hits the uppermost branches. They're just regular trees.

Jinx and Inu are already fast asleep, as is Peyton. I sit down against the biggest tree, in between two roots, curling my body up against its trunk.

In a moment, the grove falls away and I'm standing on a mountainside that overlooks an ocean. A regular, non-tsunami ocean. And it's not my mountain, either. I look down at big white waves crashing into rocks, up at pine trees and snow.

"Musashi."

I turn. My grandfather sits on a small boulder. He is older this time, a hump in his back. A jolt goes through me.

"You were at school!" I point at him. "It was you, older!"

He winks. "Suffering through your boring social studies class with you."

I grin. Finally, a grown-up who will admit the truth. Too bad he's an ancestor now and can't back me up in real life. "I'm having trouble, Ojīchan. How do I know what to do?"

"Have you consulted the comic book?" He stretches his legs out in front of him, flexing his feet in his wooden *geta* sandals, wincing as if this action pains him.

"It's back on the ship. But we read it." I stand in front of him, my arms crossed. I'm not going to let him turn into the beast-man this time. This is *my* dream, darn it. "The comic book doesn't say, like, how to kill the beast-man or get my father back. His father's not even missing in the story. It's not the same at all."

"But you created it, Xander Musashi. You know all you need to know." He reaches up and taps my temple with his cold right forefinger. "All you need to do is access it. Like with your computers."

"Well, I don't know how to do that." My nose begins running, and my eyes sting. I look down to stave off tears. "I don't know why nobody will tell me anything."

My grandfather's calves are bare under his kimono, crisscrossed with blue veins and red scars. This man has seen a fight or two. I soften. "Please, can't you help me?"

He laughs, not unkindly. "If I helped you any more, Musashi, I would be having this adventure for you. You must live it yourself."

My nose tingles. I sneeze once, twice. By the third, I'm awake, back in the grove, my face pressed against the tree.

So I still don't know where Momotaro's sword is, or how to vanquish anything. Everything I've done has been through trial and error, not because I know how to access information stored somewhere secret in my brain.

And the sword! I didn't ask about the sword. I punch the tree's bark lightly. Not only would I like to live this adventure, I'd very much like to live through it, *thankyouverymuch.*

I take a few breaths so deep my lungs pinch. The bark smells like lemongrass. I see now that the bark is actually many colors, light greens to grays to green-whites and silver-whites. It looks like a *CraftWorlds* tree, made of thousands of pixels. I stare at the pixels and think about how I'd re-form them into different shapes. Like a tree-colored person.

Then, before my eyes, the pixels of the tree bark actually shimmer and move. Whoa. I take a step back. The squares clump and rearrange themselves into a silvery shape that mirrors my shape, like a light-colored shadow of me.

You have awakened me, a whispery voice says. It might be a man's, or a woman's. A teenage boy's, maybe? Like a dude whose voice is still changing, not too high and not too low.

"Who's there?" My voice sounds out of place and too loud in the grove.

I *am here. You wanted to speak to me.* The tree-shadow thing is talking. I look behind me, but everyone else is still sleeping.

I move so I'm kneeling in front of it, facing it. "I didn't want to talk to anybody," I whisper. "Who are you?"

I am Wakunochi-no-kami, second son of the gods Izanami and Izanagi, who created this place.

Those names sound vaguely familiar. My dad has a book called *The Kojiki,* which is a Japanese legend of creation. Or maybe it's *not* legend—who knows anymore? He used to read it to me when I was little. Izanami and Izanagi, I recall now, were gods who gave birth to the islands of Japan as well as a bunch of other gods. I don't remember this Wakunochi, though. Probably because I was mostly asleep when Dad shared the story with me at bedtime.

You are looking for your father.

Well, I guess a god would know that. I spread out my hands and so does the shadow. It has no face. To my surprise, maybe because I'm still so darn tired, I'm not scared. It's just a tree without eyes or a mouth. "If you're a god, can you help me find him? Or tell me how I'm supposed to do it? Like, how do I fight the oni? I don't even have a sword." I shut my mouth. I sound kind of whiny. Not at all like a hero.

I am a kodama, *a tree spirit, and as such can only stay here.* It raises its hands, which I am definitely not doing. *I can tell you this: you have powers the sword does not. The sword has powers you do not. Together, you have twice as many powers. But the sword will not appear until you earn it.*

"Well, how am I supposed to do enough stuff to earn it, when I don't have the sword to fight with?" I ignore the fact I don't know how to use the sword anyway. It's obviously magical. Once I get it in my hands, I'll probably turn into a crazy good fighter straight out of a video game. That's what always happens.

I'm sick of people (or spirits) talking to me in riddles I can't figure out. Going on about powers they claim I have but I don't. Maybe it's just the fact that I'm super-duper thirsty and tired, but I'm as cranky as a toddler coming down from a sugar high. "Spirit, if you can't leave your tree, what good are you?"

The shadow reaches out of the tree, its arm all see-through pixels, and puts its hand on my forehead. It's as cold as an icepack.

The ground shudders under my knees—only under *me*. The chill seems to pierce my skin and touch my brain. It doesn't hurt, but it doesn't feel good, either. I try to stand up, get away from it, and— yowch!—now *that* hurts, like my head's caught in a vise.

You are not very respectful for a boy without a weapon. Not like a Momotaro should be.

"Sorry!" I yelp, and the cold lessens. "I don't know how a Momotaro *should* be. I'm just me."

The kodama sighs. *That is not an excuse.*

I gulp and try to turn to look at my friends, but I can't move at all. I take a deep breath, and I don't even feel my stomach move. It reminds me of the time I got my tonsils out when I was five—that moment when the doctor sticks the mask over your face and tells you to go to sleep, and you know you have no choice. Okay, now this is getting a little scary. "I thought you were a god. Aren't you a good tree spirit?"

Why do you think this part of the forest has so many trees? the spirit says, sounding almost gleeful. *These were all people once, until they annoyed me.*

Uh-oh. "What did they do?"

They were both impertinent and stupid. There is no crime worse than being so stupid you do not even realize how stupid you are.

I think of Lovey, being racist and mean and too dumb to know it, even when people tell her so. I guess maybe the kodama's right.

I could not let them infect the world. Now, if you prove to be imperti-
nent but smart, I may let you go on your way. Listen.

"Okay," I whisper. I hope I'm up for this. I don't exactly feel at my mental best at this moment. If I mess this up, my friends will turn into trees right where they're sleeping. And my dad will never be able to find me, if he does manage to escape on his own. Who'd think to look in a sacred grove on an island of oni?

The kodama speaks again.

It occurs once in every minute,
Twice in every moment,
And yet never in a hundred thousand years.

I shut my eyes, picturing the words written on a blackboard in front of me. A comet? An eclipse? A dying star? A breath? No, no, no. It has to be something not so obvious.

In my head, I look over the words. The letters.

I can't tell.

Time's up.

I flinch, my heart racing. "You didn't tell me this was timed."

I don't have to tell you anything. This isn't school. It's life.

"I give up!" I yell. And then, suddenly, I see the answer on my mental chalkboard. Of course! It's so obvious. "The letter *m*!" I say, and I can't keep the huge grin off my face. Take that, tree.

But the kodama continues.

It can be said:
To be gold is to be good;
To be stone is to be nothing;
To be glass is to be fragile;
To be cold is to be cruel.
Unmetaphored, what am I?

I raise my voice. "Another one? That's not fair!" I've used up all my brainpower already.

I never said I was fair.

I could swear the shadow smiles.

"That's right. 'Cause you're a tree," I mutter under my breath.

I take another breath. Now I'm sweating again, the moisture leaking down my sides. *Metaphor*—I remember the definition from English class: a figure of speech, a comparison.

If only I had my phone! I could Google this. But no, there's only me and my brain. *Think, Xander,* I command myself.

He's not even in GATE, I hear Mr. Phasis say.

My face goes hotter yet.

You just have to access this information, I hear my grandfather say. *You know this.*

I decide to listen to my grandfather.

I picture something gold, something stone, something glass. What is something that could be all three? My head pounds. I picture my dad, remember how once, when we were already running late to a doctor's appointment, he saw a man with a stalled car in the street and he stopped to help him. Another time, he rounded up a stray dog and put it in his car, even though it tried to bite him.

I lift my head. "You know what people always say about my dad? He's got a heart of gold."

The tree seems to inhale sharply.

I think of my mom, abandoning us, and how other people talk about her. *Poor Xander, no wonder he's weird. His mom's so cold she left them without a word.*

I clear my throat. "Do you know what people say about my mom? Heart of stone."

And I remember asking my grandmother why my dad couldn't forget about my mother after all these years; why he still keeps wearing his wedding ring and won't even glance at another woman. "Because his heart will shatter," she told me. "He has a heart of glass."

I suck in a big breath. "The answer is *heart*."

Instead of being mad, the shadow seems pleased. *Very good, Momotaro.*

I'm so relieved my muscles turn into jelly. "Can we please go now?"

One last.

"No," I groan. "Come on, already. I got two out of two."

He ignores me.

Power and treasure for a prince to hold,
Hard and steep-cheeked, wrapped in red,
Gold and garnet, ripped from a plain
Of bright flowers, wrought—a remnant
Of fire and file, bound in stark beauty
With delicate wire, my grip makes
Warriors weep, my sting threatens
The hand that grasps gold. Studded
With a ring, I ravage heir and heirloom.
To my lord and foes always lovely
And deadly, altering face and form.

Yikes. This one's harder. My brain is sludge. Inside my head, I suddenly hear every teacher I've ever had chorusing at me that I'm slow, that I don't pay attention.

I'm not smart enough for this. I'm two breaths away from getting all of us turned into trees forever. My mind feels like that twenty-year-old car Dad used to have that had trouble starting. He would turn the key over and over, muttering, "Come on, start. Start!" until finally the motor caught. "You always have to rev the engine now," Dad would say, hitting the gas pedal. "Give it as much juice as you can and it won't stop."

"Come on," I whisper, like Dad. "Start. Start!"

My head clears. Just picture the words. *Ripped from a plain of bright flowers? A remnant of fire and file? Power and treasure for a prince. Warriors weep.* The images come together as one. I see King Arthur—he's pulling something from a stone. . . .

"A sword!" I exclaim before I can think twice. Whoops. I close my eyes. Please be right.

Very good. The voice is impressed. Maybe even smiling.

"Do I get the sword now?" That's why he posed that riddle, right?

But the kodama says nothing, just releases me, the shadow disappearing. I shudder and gasp and stumble forward, catching myself on the trunk. Uh-oh—hope that doesn't make it wake again.

Nothing happens.

I sink down into the dirt. Oh my gosh. That was so close. My brain's an engine out of gas now. I hug my knees close to my chest and feel a smile playing on my lips as I think of how I outsmarted the tree.

I wish Mr. Phasis could have seen that. He'd probably think, *Kid outsmarted a plant. Big deal.* I could become boy president of the United States and Mr. Phasis wouldn't be impressed.

On second thought, I don't care about his opinion. Maybe the truth is that all those school tests don't matter quite as much as they think. Maybe what matters is not your score, but how you use the talents you have.

I stretch out my legs and look at my sleeping friends. My body's full of nervous energy again, as if having the confrontation was the equivalent of drinking a caffeinated soda. "Hey, you guys."

My companions stir. Peyton lets out a blood-curdling yawn-squawk. All of us jump. "Well, that was refreshing!" Peyton stands. "Ready to get this party started?"

Ruff. Inu rises and shakes, sending bits of fur, sticks, and dirt flying.

Jinx stretches, then grabs her stomach. "Oooh. You know, I could do a lot better if I had a little bit of something-something in my tummy."

I shake out a rice grain for her. "Here."

She pops it into her mouth with a grin. "Thanks."

Inu's at my feet, pawing the netsuke. *Woof.*

"I won't leave you out." I give him one, too.

I check around the tree trunks, expecting the sword to pop up as my reward. But there's nothing.

Well, at least I didn't turn into a tree.

"Come on, you guys." Jinx is on her feet and moving again.

"Jinx," I grab her arm, "why'd you let us stop here? That tree's a kodama."

She yanks her arm away. "I know. The God Tree. But he's been asleep for two thousand years." Then she leans toward me, curiosity written all over her face. "Why? Did you see something?"

"He talked to me. I guess I woke him up." I shrug.

"A tree talked to you?" Peyton half opens his wings and leaps forward to land next to me. "Oh man. Sorry I missed it."

Jinx opens her mouth as if she wants to ask about the God Tree, but I don't say anything more. I don't want her or Peyton to know that I was almost impertinent enough to get us all turned into vegetation.

I change the subject fast. "That was a neat trick. The long hop." I point at Peyton's wings. "Those things come in handy."

"What?" Peyton looks behind him at his feathers. "Oh yeah. I hope I get to keep these. Think of how well I'll be able to play basketball."

"Ha." I feel a small twinge of envy in my chest. "Your dad will be happy."

Peyton's face darkens. "My dad will sign me up for pole vault, too."

"My dad would just cut them off of me." Jinx taps my arm. "Another rice, please?"

I give her one and study her face, trying to figure out if she's joking or not. My stomach flips. Something tells me she's not. I kind of want to give her a hug, but I think that would feel about as nice as hugging a blackberry bush.

Peyton frowns and helps himself to a grain of rice. "Your dad doesn't like you to be different, huh?"

"No. He doesn't like me to be better than him." Jinx shoves the rice into her mouth. "Let's get out of here."

CHAPTER 16

We leave the God Tree copse, and the forest canopy begins opening up overhead again. I hear a *shoosh*ing noise. Water! Thank goodness. The plants underfoot give way to sticky red mud, and we begin making our way down a steep embankment. The running water sounds closer. We navigate through the last little thicket of trees, and I see heaven: a big, clear, wide expanse of river. All of us break into a sprint.

"You can drink it!" Jinx kneels on the bank, cups her hands in the water, and slurps it down. "I've had it plenty of times."

Inu's already lapping it up, so I know it's got to be good. Inu never drinks bad water, unlike a lot of dogs. I drink, too, then wade in up to my waist. It feels so good to wash off all the sweat and jungle grime.

"Wait!" I back up quickly, peering into the water. A school of small purple-silver fish, with golden beaks like parakeets, swims by. "What if there are piranhas?"

"Nah. I swim here all the time." Jinx kicks off her shoes and splashes in. "I have to warn you, though: none of the fish are good to eat. Those purple ones taste like tile grout."

I raise my eyebrows. "How many times have you eaten tile grout?"

Jinx smiles at me. "You can eat it and it won't kill you."

"The fish, or tile grout?" Peyton mutters. He dips his face into the water.

I do the same, opening my mouth to let the cold water rush in. Ahhh. Nothing ever tasted so good. I duck my head all the way underneath.

"Come on." Jinx starts walking downstream. "If we follow this river, it'll take us to where we need to go." She glances at the sky. "And we should try to get there before dark."

"There?" I ask. "Where's there?"

"Where your father is, dum-dum."

I bristle at the name, but now I think she's joking around. "But where is that, exactly?"

"You want its satellite coordinates or something? I don't know."

"Have you been there before?" Peyton asks, catching up to her.

"I know where it is," she says evasively.

I stop moving. "Why won't you give us a straight answer?"

She presses her mouth into a thin line. "I just don't like telling you my personal business, okay?"

Peyton and I look at each other.

She points at us in turn. "See? That. It's because of stuff like that. If I tell you things, you two are going to use it against me somehow. I don't know you well enough to trust you."

Inu barks and whines. Jinx pats his head. "I trust you, Inu. Of course I do."

I close my eyes. *Give it time*, my father's voice says in my head. *Trust builds over time.* "Okay, fine, Jinx. You don't have to tell us if you were there before. But do you know how much farther it is?"

She starts wading again. "Not much."

"That's specific," Peyton huffs.

We start following in her wake. This is better than making our way through a steamy, bug-filled jungle or slogging through slimy mud. The sand beneath my feet is silty and soft. Inu splatters us as he lopes and leaps through the water. Jinx laughs and he chases her. She splashes him.

Could she be having fun? Peyton and I look at each other. He points to Jinx, like *What do you think of her?* I shrug. Maybe she's okay after all. For the first time all day, I relax a tiny bit.

In fact, all in all, I have to say this quest is going pretty darn well. I mean, there was that thing with the snow woman—but we got my monkey sidekick out of that deal.

I push my shoulders back. Maybe I'm actually as smart as my

father says I am. Maybe I'm stronger than I thought I was. Wings or no wings. I smile.

Peyton kicks some water at me. "What's that big old grin for?"

I kick water back at him. "Nothing. Just thinking about how awesome I am."

He stretches his wings and spins, sending a wave flying at me.

I shake my dripping head. "Now you're in for it!" I leap at him, catching him off guard, and tackle him into the water. We play-wrestle. The water feels great. Inu jumps on us, barking happily. Jinx doesn't join in, but stands off to one side, watching with a big, old eye roll, like she thinks we're two little boys. That's okay. She's not ruining our fun. We mess around for a few minutes.

Then I hear the sound of branches snapping. I turn my head to look at the bank. Oddly, Inu seems oblivious. I see two black eyes peering out at me.

I stop moving and hold my hands up to the shrieking Peyton and barking Inu. "Guys, shut up!"

"What?" Jinx turns to look where I'm looking. "I don't hear anything."

But I do. Something's there. Watching us. I move toward the bank.

A tiny red bird hops out of the growth, chirping. I relax.

But then, suddenly, the sunlight dims and I sense something else, this time from the sky. An undulating black cloud has formed over us. Thunderhead?

Jinx's eyes widen. "Move!"

We start running, but it's like we're in slow-motion, since we're in the water. The cloud is following us. "Stalker cloud!" I say.

"What's the worry?" Peyton slows to a walk. "It'll just be a little water, and we're already wet."

The cloud rumbles, and I raise my face, ready for the rain. "But if there's lightning, we have to get out of the water."

"We're fine," Peyton says confidently.

"Not fine. I heard thunder!" I start sloshing toward the bank.

"It's not a storm," Jinx says. She quickens her pace. "Stay in the water, Xander. And move faster." The rumbling intensifies. Jinx looks up, eyes wide. "Cover your face!" She drops into a squat and covers her ears with her hands. She shuts her eyes and buries her face in her knees.

Inu whines and dives into the water. All the way in—I've never seen him do that before. Peyton jumps in, too, his wings folded tight. What's the matter with them?

The cloud opens. Tiny black dots hit my skin. It's not rain at all. The pebblelike things don't hurt. I pinch one between my fingers and it squishes, leaving a red trail behind.

"Hey, guys, it's okay, they're harmless," I try to say, but as I open my mouth, I inhale a bunch of the black things, and the moment they hit the inside of my cheeks, they start moving around. Bugs! Panicked, I spit and spit, but they won't come out. They're digging into my flesh. It feels like a dentist is poking me with a sharp tool.

I fumble open the octopus netsuke box and throw some salt inside my mouth. I can feel the things shudder, then stop. I spit again, and a huge black-and-red glob plops onto the dirt in front of me. "Blecch!" It's like I ate a big wad of dirt.

The cloud dissipates, leaving the sky clear again. Jinx blinks her eyes open and wipes at them. Inu gets up and shakes, tossing black dots all over the place. Peyton stands, unfurls his wings, then flaps them. More black specks fly through the air, landing like a handful of pebbles thrown in the water.

"Oni eggs. They burrow into wet flesh." Jinx wrinkles her nose as she surveys me. "You have stuff"—she points with one jagged-nailed finger—"around your mouth."

I wipe my face with the back of my hand, then wash off the trail of saliva and blood in the water. "What kind of oni egg? Like, all kinds? Is that how they reproduce?" I think of Inu's flea medicine, which kills flea eggs before they hatch. If we could get to all the oni before they were born, we wouldn't have to fight them.

"No. Not all of them." Jinx frowns and stares hard at me, her hazel eyes boring into mine.

I flush. "What?"

She shakes her head, as if waking up from a spell. "Sorry. It's just that I still can't believe you're from the Momotaro line. Except for your hair. They're usually so strong. It must be because you're half-white. Your blood is diluted."

Ouch. Heat rises into my cheeks. I turn away from her and watch Inu slurp up water like nothing happened. I'm so angry I can't trust myself to say anything civil.

"Hey, I'm mixed, too," she continues. "If I weren't, I'd be stronger. I'm sorry. It's just a fact."

Argh. She just keeps getting better and better. I swivel back and point at her. "Jinx, your mouth."

She touches it. "What?"

"Stop it from moving."

"Yeah, Jinx, it would be nice if you could go for an entire hour without insulting us." Peyton plucks eggs from between his feathers.

I turn toward Peyton. "Are you all right?"

He nods once. The skin on his face is bright red, his nose is peeling, and his hair is sticking up even more than usual. "I'm thinking about flying ahead, seeing what's up." He lowers his voice and glares in Jinx's direction. "We're out of the jungle now. Do you want to ditch her?"

"Thinking seriously about it," I mutter. Jinx stands behind us, scratching Inu's head in the exact spot he likes it, between his ears. His wagging tail churns up the water. He likes her.

Doubt tugs at me. Inu has never liked anyone who wasn't nice.

Besides, Jinx is supposed to be my monkey. Momotaro relied on all three of his friends. They were his team. And seriously, we'd be stuck in the jungle still, or maybe even snow-woman food, if Jinx hadn't helped us out. I look at Peyton, and I know he knows what I'm thinking. That's the beauty of being friends with somebody forever. He nods once, his face relaxing in agreement with me.

"It's not much farther." Jinx points ahead to where the river flows into a small tributary off to the right. Straight ahead, the water disappears into a thick forest again. It looks like the tributary leads to cleared land.

However, we can't get there without crossing a big patch of water.

I look at Peyton. He shakes his head. "It's too far to swim. We need a boat."

"BRB." Jinx walks out of the water and disappears into the thick underbrush on the bank.

"What's that mean?" I ask Peyton.

"Be right back. Internet-speak." Peyton kicks at the mud. "What kind of person uses that in real life?"

"A crazy one?" I offer.

Jinx emerges from the tree line, dragging something behind her. A giant piece of palm-tree husk. It's curved and about five feet long, and it sort of looks like a shallow, small canoe. A leaky canoe you'd fall out of, that is. She drags it to the water. "We're going to need another," she pants.

"That's watertight?" I say doubtfully. Peyton and I exchange a look and a smirk. I mean, not to brag, but I've watched enough survival television to know this thing couldn't make it across a puddle, much less a river.

"Fine, Mr. Outdoorsy McDoorsman. You come up with a better idea. Or you can just swim by yourself." She shoots daggers at me from her eyes, daring a response.

We shuffle our feet. Um, build a raft out of branches? But these branches are all either way too flimsy or too big to work with without axes and saws. Nothing else comes to mind. "I can't think of anything. Must be because I have mixed blood."

Jinx sniffs disapprovingly.

Peyton shrugs. "I got nothing, either. Except flying. And I can't carry all of you."

"You could carry us over one at a time," I suggest.

"Do you want to rescue your father in this century? We need to go down the river. This will be tons faster." Jinx jerks her head toward the palm trees. "Go get another one of these. Please."

"Drill sergeant much?" Peyton mutters. "It's like hanging out with my dad."

"Hey. Apparently it's the only way to get you guys to listen." Jinx allows herself a small, satisfied smile.

Anything to get us all to my dad faster. Peyton and I walk into the bushes where she went and discover a bunch of bark at the base of a massive palm tree. Hopefully it's not another God Tree, but it doesn't seem to need these pieces anymore.

Some of the husks have huge moldy holes or are too small. We poke around until we find a good large one, plus two smaller ones to use as paddles, and drag the canoe into the water.

Inu's already sitting in the other one. It bobs gently up and down, and Jinx's pushing it out into the water. Suddenly I don't want Inu with Jinx. What if she wants her own animal companion and takes off with him?

"I'll ride with you, Jinx." I slosh to the boat. "Peyton, you go with Inu."

"You sure?" Peyton says.

"You can fly," I say quietly. "So you can come get me if you need to. And you can help Inu out."

We fist-bump. "Just push her out if you need to," Peyton whispers.

"I swim better than any of you clowns," Jinx says.

I guess her hearing's pretty good, too.

We slowly paddle across the river to the offshoot. Peyton sits in the back of his canoe, rowing alone like it's no big deal, his Halloween costume muscles flexing, swooshing his way past us. Inu barks twice, playfully.

We drift lazily along an eddy. It's not 100 percent comfortable, because a bit of water sloshes in the bottom of our makeshift canoes, but it's a lot easier than walking. I look up at the sky. No more black clouds. The sky's got that purplish tinge instead of blue. I wonder if we're on the same planet anymore. Maybe there's a different moon here.

A green bird swoops in a lazy figure eight overhead. It's bigger than an eagle, but nowhere near the size of Peyton. A giant macaw, maybe? Except its tail is long and skinny.

My dad liked to bird-watch. Since our house backs up to protected forest land, we see lots of different kinds of birds just from
our back deck. I used to sit out there with him sometimes, looking
through the binoculars.

"Look at that beak and those claws," my father would point out.

"Bird of prey?" I would say. "Black back, white belly—peregrine
falcon?"

"Yes," my father would say.

Now I try to get a better look at the bird, but it's too high up. I
point and yell to Peyton, "See any relatives?"

"Ha-ha!" he shouts back.

The green bird approaches us. Its wings make virtually no
sound—that means it's a predator, because they don't want anything
to hear them coming. It circles down, down, down toward the water.

I sit upright, suddenly worried. "Uh, Jinx? Do you know what
kind of bird that is?"

Jinx glances at it and stiffens, her eyes going wide. "Be still."

I look over at Peyton and Inu, but they're drifting away at this
point. I hope they notice this thing, too.

As it gets closer, I see that its tail is not feathery, but covered
in hair, and undulating like a serpent's. But it's the face that has my
heart hammering. It looks like a small ogre's face, with a little squat
nose and eyes like a person's. Its mouth is fairly human-looking, too,
except that the lips form a pyramid, like a beak.

I don't have to be told to sit completely still. I couldn't move if I wanted to. The bird creature swoops lower and lower. Its eyes are a light shade of white-blue. The little nose twitches, its nostrils opening and closing as it sniffs.

Then it opens its pyramid mouth and lets out a cry: *"Itsumade!"*

"It's talking!" I flinch involuntarily. "What's it saying?"

A thin plume of blue flame flares and disappears just as quickly. I stiffen, hoping it won't catch the canoe on fire. The air from its beating wings ruffles my hair. If it gets too close, surely it'll feel our body heat. I can hear its rasping breath rattling in its throat, and suddenly I know that it's about to shoot flame again. I duck and simultaneously stick the oar into the water and push. *Go.* I imagine the boat zooming away from the bird just as it sends out another *whoosh* of fire. I feel heat on the back of my neck.

To my surprise, the oar pushes strongly into the water and we careen at a forty-five degree angle away from the bird. *Yes!* I do a fist pump in my head. My arms are getting stronger. I moved the boat all by myself. I feel powerful enough to pick up the boat and carry it to wherever we need to go.

I sneak a glance upward. The bird thing climbs into the sky again, and I let myself relax a little. "Oh my gosh, Jinx. What was that thing?"

Jinx lets out a big breath, and I realize she's trembling, too. "Itsumade. Creepy things."

"It looked like a human!" I wrinkle my nose. "Humanish, anyway."

Jinx grimaces. "A lot of oni are part human. Or used to be human."

I shudder.

She gives me what she probably thinks is a reassuring smile. "Don't worry. You usually have to die before you become something like that."

"Great." I set my gaze on the water but peer up at her from under my eyelids. "Did you see how I pushed the boat away from the bird?"

"What do you want, a gold star?" Jinx leans over the side of the boat, clears her throat, then hawks a huge loogie right into the river. The spitball swirls rapidly in the water, bouncing about like a pinball in a machine. "The current's getting rough and crazy. It wasn't you."

"Oh. Thanks." She's so pleasant. I bet if Jinx went to a little kid's birthday party, she'd go around popping all the balloons and cackling. I look for Peyton and Inu and spot them on the other side of the river.

I hear the sound of what I think is a hard rainfall up ahead. I try to look at the sky, but now there's a copse of trees in front of us and it's difficult to tell what's going on. "Do you hear that? What is it? A storm?"

Jinx frowns and squints. She scratches her armpit absentmindedly, and I giggle. "I think that's just a little bit of rapids. But don't worry. The trees will slow us down."

Now we reach the trees growing straight up out of the water in the middle of the river. A big one with enough branches to black out the sky and millions of roots reaching into the water dominates the copse. The roots look like knotted snakes diving into the darkness. For the first time, I can't see the river bottom.

A root tickles the raft. But it's no root. It pops out from the water, making me gasp. It grabs the side of our canoe with a sucking sound. Octopus?

Jinx smacks it with her paddle and the root lets go and disappears under water. "Xander! Come on, you have to be ready."

I stick my paddle experimentally into the root mass. The roots make a grab for it, and I yank it out. "I'm not used to stuff like this. I don't know how you are." She must have been on this island for a really long time.

Jinx shrugs. "I just am."

"Is it a kodama?" I'm pretty much going to be paranoid about trees for the rest of my existence on planet Earth.

Jinx tilts her head at me, and the sun reflects off her freckles like they're a constellation of golden stars. "I don't know. Why don't you see if you can wake this one up, too?"

But I don't have to answer, because the boats start moving. Really fast.

"Oh no." Jinx sticks her branch in the water and starts paddling. "Help me!"

I try to obey, but the water grabs my paddle and washes it right out of my hands. Wow. This river suddenly went from couch-potato-lazy to Olympic-active.

ARROOOOOOO! Inu howls from far away on the other side of the river. They're stuck on a pile of rocks.

"Peyton!" I scream.

Peyton waves and shouts, "We're okay! Meet you downriver!"

"Okay!" I shout back.

Jinx slows our boat a little bit with her branch. "What'd he say?"

"I could hear him like he was next to me. Couldn't you? He said he'll meet us downriver." I look around for a branch to use as a paddle, but there's nothing.

"Huh. If you say so. You have some good hearing." Beads of sweat stand out on Jinx's forehead. We bump into a massive pile of logs and debris, a small island of the stuff, slowing our trajectory to a crawl. Jinx looks relieved. "Okay. Hopefully we'll be good now."

I hear water rushing around us. A fish (or possibly something I don't want to think about) swimming to our left. Wind rustling leaves.

Suddenly I remember: all those times I eavesdropped on the adults. Hearing the sea dragon swim underneath the ship. I smack my thigh with my hand. "Hey, I *do* have good hearing!"

Jinx kind of shakes her head at me. "Thanks, Captain Obvious. It's not like I didn't *just* say that."

"I mean, it wasn't always good. I mean, I think it's been getting better." I sit up straight. "I think that's my power, Jinx—hearing."

She wrinkles her nose. "Unless we need to spy on people, Xander, that's sort of a limited skill. So I really hope you have something else to fall back on."

Me, too. But I don't respond, because just then a jet of water hits us from a weird angle. The canoe dislodges from the debris and starts spinning down the river like we're on one of those water rides. Except this one isn't on a track. We pick up speed. I hold on tight to the sides, unable to do anything else. Through a veil of water I see Jinx doing the same. Water begins filling the bottom of the boat, and I can feel us going lower, lower, lower. Sticks that were floating on the surface are jerked under by the force of the current, then tumbled and borne away faster than I can blink. We're going to sink. "Jinx! What do we do?"

"I don't know!" She shakes her head, her hair flinging all over the place and whipping me across my eyes. I raise my hand to brush it away.

And then the bottom falls out of everything.

CHAPTER 17

White water churns all around me, pushing, crushing. I tumble head over heels, my body useless. I can't tell which way is up. I see blue and white both above and below. *Let me off! Make it stop!* I yell in my head, the way I did when I rode the world's tallest roller coaster at Magic Mountain. But all I can do is hold my breath and wait for it to stop.

Suddenly, everything's quiet. I've gone deaf.

I'm standing on the shore of a large pond or a smallish lake. Soft white sand comes up between my toes. My clothes are dry. I look around. Leafy trees, then pale dunes border the area. Ahead of me, across the water, is a waterfall twice as tall as my house.

And I'm watching Jinx and me falling down it, limbs flopping as if we are rag dolls.

I don't have time to wonder how this is happening. The other Xander and Jinx splash limply into the pond and bob up. They lie there motionless, floating facedown. Oh no—they're not going to make it. My stomach sinks.

The water needs to push them to shore.

Slowly, they begin to move.

Faster. I watch the current give them one last little push toward the beach. The water is shallow there. I don't actually know if it is, but I want it to be.

Turn your head. Cough up the water. All the water, out of the lungs. Now.

A shock of cold comes over me, and I'm back in my body, hacking up a huge stream of river water. My lungs burn worse than they did when we had to run a mile in PE. It *is* shallow here, and I crawl onto dry land, little pebbles cutting into my hands.

Ahead of me I see Jinx lying on her side, her face out of the water. I manage to stumble to my feet, put my arms under her armpits, and drag her onto the white sand. "Jinx?" I shake her. She hacks up water without opening her eyes, keeps on breathing.

I glance back at the waterfall we just came down. I don't know how on earth we survived. Was I having an out-of-body experience just then, or was I dreaming? Did I really tell my body what to do?

Maybe I *can* affect reality, somehow. Just like I can program a computer game. My stomach does one excited flip. "Jinx!" I whisper.

Not because I want to whisper, but because that's all I can manage. I cough up some more water. "Hey, Jinx, I saved us! Wake up! You're fine."

Jinx doesn't move. I picture her waking up, and both of us being as healthy as two kids who did not just fall over a waterfall. I imagine myself floating up into the air, Superman-style, and flying us out of here on invisible wings like I'm Peyton. . . .

Nothing happens.

I lie down beside her. "Jinx," I try again, but she doesn't respond. Where are Peyton and Inu? Peyton *can* fly. He would have saved both of them. They're fine. They've got to be. He'll be showing up any minute now.

The sand feels as warm as a blanket. Sometimes sand gets too hot to touch, but this is so soft and I'm so tired. I have to close my eyes. All this trying-to-be-a-hero stuff is getting to me.

I don't know how much time passes before somebody nudges my ribs. "Jinx?" I ask sleepily as I open my eyes.

Above me stands a turtle boy. A somewhat human-looking creature nearly six feet tall, with arms and legs extending out of a green shell. He cocks his head and considers me with bulbous, wet black eyes. An olive-green third eyelid slides over in a blink.

I blink, too, thinking I'm dreaming again. "Teenage Mutant Ninja Turtle?" He sort of looks like one, except his hands and feet are webbed, and he has a shock of short, sleek black hair. Instead of a normal mouth, he's got a sharp beak. His face reminds me more of a chimpanzee than a turtle, though, and his skin is covered in sleek greenish-brown scales.

"*Kappa!*" Jinx croaks from someplace next to me. I turn my head. She's prone on the beach, her arms and legs tied behind her with dirty rope. "Kappa."

"Kappa?" I repeat dumbly. I don't know what a kappa is. Some kind of Greek fraternity? Like Delta Gamma Kappa?

The turtle boy pushes me roughly onto my back, then sits on my legs. Owwww. That does not feel good. My shins pop. "Get off!" I try to crawl away, but I'm pinned. The turtle boy says nothing, just sets about tying my wrists together with an itchy rope. Then my ankles. I try to fight back, but I might as well be fighting an ogre. He's like a trillion times stronger than me. He opens my octopus netsuke box, looks inside, and tosses it aside. He takes off my belt with the other netsuke and carries it to a dead, branchless oak tree with a black jagged gash in the middle of its trunk. He throws my stuff into the hole.

Half of Jinx's face is covered with sand. "Leave me here. I'll catch up."

I kind of have to admire her optimism. She might be sort of a jerk, but at least she's a confident one. "I doubt either of us is going anywhere anytime soon," I say.

The kappa speaks. "*Zurripty ʒung ʒoo!*" He gags Jinx with a cloth and ties it behind her head. Then he bends over and examines me, patting my pockets for more loot. His neck is crooked at a funny angle. The top of his head has a bald spot, which is indented like a bowl, and filled with something that looks like thick water. Clear Jell-O? He's holding his head carefully, as if he doesn't want the stuff to spill. The liquid smells like a thousand rotting anchovies. A couple of gnats buzz above it.

I wrinkle my nose. What is that? His brain?

The kappa throws another rope over a tree branch and ties the end clumsily around my feet. Then he yanks.

I go upside down. My heart pounds in my ears as the blood rushes to my head. "Stop!" I bellow. "Let me down."

The kappa makes a snickering noise in the back of his throat. He pushes me, and I swing wildly back and forth. "Stoooppp!" I yell. "Please, I'm not going to hurt you."

"No." He laughs again from deep in his chest and shoves me again. "Dis fun," he says in English.

So he understands me. And obviously he's bored, since he thinks swinging me around is so great. I bet he probably doesn't get that many people falling over his waterfall. As I sway back and forth, I grow so dizzy I feel like I'm about to pass out and my neck is going to snap clean off my torso. "Let me down! Look, I'm a lot of fun. We can be friends." I'm babbling without thinking. Friends? With a monster? Not likely.

"No friendly." He pushes me some more, clicking his tongue.

"If you eat me, you'll just be bored again." He spins in my vision.

Jinx flops around like a strangling fish. Maybe she can wriggle away, somehow, while I distract him.

The kappa sits down on the beach. "I keep. Swing, swing. Then eat, by and by."

Ugh. The prospect of my neck snapping seems better than swinging upside down for who knows how long. I come up with something different. "Let me make you an offer."

"Offer?" A fat pink tongue appears, and he licks off his beak.

I squish my eyes shut. I imagine fighting him, and before I can stop myself, I say, "Let's have a wrestling match. If I beat you, you free us. If you beat me, well, then you can eat me or whatever. But let the girl go either way."

"MPPPHHH!" Jinx sputters incoherently, rolling helpless along the shore. "HWETOWJ!"

I know exactly what she's saying. *You're going to die, fool.*

I kind of agree with her.

The kappa appears to consider my offer for a while. A supernatural creature against a small boy. Easy peasy. My stomach is churning, and my neck is throbbing. Maybe that's why I made such a stupid proposition.

But, hey, we're both still alive, and that means something.

The kappa gives me an extra-hard push, and I swing around wildly, feeling like I'm a yo-yo on the end of a string. "Yup yup," he says at last. He snaps the rope around my ankles with his dagger-sharp claws, and I fall onto my back. Ouch. I roll over and crawl on my elbows toward Jinx.

"TWETWOJ!" She's incomprehensible with the gag in her mouth. She shakes her head, sort of.

The kappa puts his foot on my back, knocking me to the ground. "No girl. You." He unties the rope around my wrists, and I stagger to my feet, rubbing my sore skin, waiting for the world to right itself. Oh no. How am I going to do this?

Without further hesitation, the kappa lunges for my upper body. Automatically, I drop down to the sand, onto my hands, in a push-up position. The kappa misses and falls, all the time trying to keep his head level. A bit of his liquid spills, and he lets out a little moan. He goes still until the sloshing stops.

Hmmm. That water-gel is very, very important to him. I scramble to my feet. All I have to do is get him to tip that bowl head.

The kappa lurches up and makes a high-pitched squawk, something between a monkey's scream and a bird of prey's caw. I prepare to dive away again, but then he feints to the right and moves left, jumping forward. This time, I'm not so lucky, and he tackles my legs. We both fall into the sand.

But I wiggle out of his grasp, turn around, and jump on his back. I wrap my arms around his neck and try to jostle the liquid. The kappa's neck is like a tree trunk, immovable. With an angry snarl, he flips over, pinning me beneath his shell.

I can't breathe. But we're at an impasse. He can't move, because he'll spill his head juice, and I'm trapped.

He rolls off me, freeing my arms. His scaly beak opens. "Heee, heee," he laughs, his breath like a liquid fart coating my face.

I stretch out one arm and scoop up a big handful of sand. Then I reach up and plop it into the cavity on his head.

The kappa lets out a shriek and backs away.

I stand, scoop up another handful, and throw it in there. It sops up the liquid, turning it into mud.

The kappa screams again. He gets down on all fours and heads into the water, diving, disappearing beyond the waterfall.

I run over to Jinx and work the gag out of her mouth.

"The kappa always keep their word, and they love making bargains." She coughs, her voice hoarse. "How'd you know?"

"I didn't." I shrug and try to loosen the ties around her wrists, but the knots are too tight. "I just figured anybody who plays with his food that much can't be very hungry."

"Please hurry." Jinx grimaces. Blood is seeping out from her wrists under the rope.

I can't get the knots out. I remember the tree with my stuff stashed in it. Maybe there are more things in there—like a knife. "Wait a second." I run over to it. On the way, I see the octopus netsuke and pick it up.

Inside the tree, just like I'd hoped, there's big pile of junk the kappa probably stole from people. An old orange wool cloak,

moth-eaten and scratchy. I toss that aside. A black velvet bag holding something that clacks. I open it up and throw it to the side. Bones. I don't want to know what kind.

My belt, with the netsuke still attached. I buckle that around myself.

"Hurry up!" Jinx yells.

"Hang on." Something gold peeks out. I reach down. A big, fat cuff bracelet, engraved with intertwining circles. It's not the kind of thing my grandmother would ever wear, but maybe it's gold and it's valuable. You never know. It's not going to do the kappa any good, anyway. I stick it on my own wrist for now.

Finally, I see something that might be a blade, resting against the very back of the tree and partially covered by a ripped pair of pants. Gingerly, I pull out the metallic thing.

It's a sword.

A samurai sword.

The polished steel blade is slightly curved, about three feet long. Diamond-sharp on one side, dull on the other. I heft it up, expecting it to be heavy and bulky, clumsy. But it's much lighter than I thought it would be. The hilt rests as naturally in my hands as a video game controller.

White enameled peaches shine out from the black enameled hilt. Japanese characters gleam on the blade.

夢主

I gasp. It's my grandfather's sword.

The sword from the story.

A wave of happiness fountains up from my stomach to my face. The kodama. I earned it. "Thanks, God Tree," I whisper. I hold the sword over my head.

It whistles as I swing it through the air, cutting Jinx free.

Her eyes grow large. "The Sword of Yumenushi!" She sits up, rubs her reddened wrists. "You really *are* Momotaro." And now she looks . . . kind of admiring. Like for the first time she's thinking *Maybe he* is *a hero.*

I put the sword in the sand and try to look as heroic as possible. Shoulders back, feet planted. But my legs still feel like they're going to collapse. I hold out a hand to her and she actually takes it, pulling herself up.

"Thanks." She brushes sand off her knees and smiles up at me. When she smiles, her face changes into something almost human. Kind. When she doesn't smile, her natural expression looks like she's about to shove you off a cliff.

Jinx turns to the tree and shoves at a net full of dried purple fish. "Ugh! Why couldn't he catch a good kind?" Her T-shirt's torn a little. I can see blue-black bruises running down her back, but there don't seem to be any other injuries on her. My back feels fine—she must have had a harder fall than I did.

"Are you all right, Jinx? You look a little beat-up."

"What are you talking about? I'm better than ever." She smiles again, but this time her face doesn't transform as much. "Let's get moving."

"Are you joking? What about Peyton and Inu?" I glare at Jinx, who seems totally oblivious and unconcerned as she scavenges for items we can use. She finds a rather brown banana and, faster than I can blink, peels it and scarfs it down. I glare harder.

She swallows. "Oh, sorry. Did you want some?"

"No." I stride to the water and look up toward the waterfall. "I want to wait for Peyton and Inu. They'll come over the water-fall, too." They should have been here a long time ago. We should have stayed in the same boat, stuck together. I can't do this without them. Yes, I managed to trick the kappa, but that was just blind luck. What kind of creatures are Peyton and Inu encountering? Are they all right?

"There are different ways to get here. Peyton can fly, remember? He could even carry Inu for a short distance. He'll find us." Jinx stands next to me, her hands on her hips. A breeze blows her dread-locked hair into my face and I step away. "Besides, we can't climb back up the waterfall to look for them. We have to hike out." She turns away from the water and begins walking. "And we have to find shelter before dark."

Can Peyton carry Inu for more than a minute? I'm not sure. We've both been getting stronger, though, so maybe . . . He has to. I swallow, watching the waterfall for another few seconds. Jinx, I grudgingly agree, is right.

I find the sword's worn black enamel scabbard in the tree trunk, put the sword in it, and stick it through my belt like I saw my grandfather wearing it in my dream. It's too long, though, and the end drags on the ground. How am I going to carry this?

Jinx shakes her head. "Do you want me to wear that for you? I'm a little taller. And you know, some samurai had people who carried their swords for them."

I grip my grandfather's sword. Okay, that might seem like a fairly reasonable idea, but a part of me wants to hang on to it. "Um, no thanks. I'll manage."

"Are you thinking I'll steal it?" Jinx looks straight into my eyes.

"Of course not." I shrug. Yes, I do kind of think she might steal it.

"Well, I don't want it. Wait a second." Jinx runs to the tree trunk and rummages until she finds a long leather rope. She crisscrosses it over my shoulders and around my torso, tying it into an expert square knot near my armpit. She loops the scabbard through this, diagonally across my back. "How's that? Try to walk."

I take a few steps. This is a lot better. The scabbard hits the back of my upper thigh and comes up high across my right shoulder. "Thanks, Jinx."

She gives me one of her genuine smiles again. "Welcome."

I can't believe the sword is actually in my possession. *The Sword of Yumenushi.* Is that someone's name? I wait for my mind to provide the answer, but it doesn't oblige. Why can't my brain do what it's supposed to? Or at least be consistent about what it does or doesn't do? "Hey, Jinx, what does *Yumenushi* mean, anyway?"

Jinx is already at the top of a white-blue sand dune bordering the beach. "If you're the real Momotaro, you don't need anyone to tell you."

I blow out a big breath. Hot and cold, that's Jinx. "Thanks for your help."

She doesn't even get my sarcasm. "Quit thanking me left and right, and let's get going." Jinx disappears over the dune.

As I run to catch up with her, the sword taps the back of my thighs. I really need to grow taller soon. Otherwise, though, carrying the sword is not so bad. I would never admit this to the others, but its weight feels as comforting as the blanket I slept with when I was a baby.

CHAPTER 18

run as fast as I can up the dune to catch up with Jinx. It's not easy, with my feet sinking into the hot, pale blue sand. And, like I said, hot. "Yeouch, yeouch, yeouch!"

"Down here." Jinx waits for me on the downslope. "The sand isn't hot on this side."

"Easy for you to say." I look enviously at her Converse.

She points. "Come on. We have to cross this desert."

I raise my head. Yes, this *is* a desert, a wide expanse of blue sand for as far as I can see. Not a plant or animal in sight. The sky seems low, a misty lavender here, with darker violet clouds combed across the horizon. I flex my blistered toes. "Desert. That's just great." I don't know how much more of this I can take. I mean, the most physical activity I normally get is walking downstairs to get a snack. Muscle fibers I didn't know I had are burning. "Hey, at least there aren't any scorpions in this desert. Right?" My voice squeaks on the last word, and I clear my throat to hide it.

"No, no scorpions. Are you kidding?" Jinx waves her hand dismissively.

"Phew." I grin. Good news for my bare feet.

"An oni would eat a scorpion in, like, two seconds. Scorpions could never survive here." She walks the rest of the way down the dune.

Fantastic. I follow her. "And how big did you say this desert is?"

"Pretty small. It's maybe a two-day journey." Jinx slogs through. With each step she sinks up to her ankle.

I stop short. "Two days?! You call this *small*? It's the biggest desert I've ever seen! There's no end to it." I wipe sweat off my face. It seems like days since we were in the waterfall. Hasn't Jinx seen every desert survival movie, ever? Eventually we're going to be crawling along on our hands and knees, searching for an oasis. But this time we started at the oasis, so I guess we'll just die of thirst. We have no water with us. And how are we going to meet up with Peyton and Inu? Can Peyton really carry Inu over this entire desert until they find us?

"Or maybe it was seven days," Jinx says thoughtfully. "I'm not really sure. I don't always pay attention to time when I'm alone." She shrugs. "Anyway, I know the *general* direction of where we need to go." Jinx drops into a resting squat and contorts her face in a huge yawn. "Okay, we can stop for one minute. But that's it. Sheesh. I've never known anyone who stops as much as you. Can I have another rice ball?"

I put my hands on my hips. "No, you can't have another rice ball. You don't know where you're going, do you?" My voice shakes. I shouldn't have trusted her to be a guide. She's only in it for the food.

She shrugs. "I know enough. Look how far we've come."

"Yeah. All the way down a waterfall!"

She stands up and thrusts her finger in my face. It's encrusted with dirt and sand, the nail bitten down to the quick. "That was all you. You made the boat go into the rapids when that bird came around."

"I was saving us."

Jinx shakes her head. "Whatever. You panicked."

"If I hadn't done that, we'd be barbecue meat right now." I turn around. "I'm going back to the water."

Calm, Xander.

It's my grandfather's voice. I jump, startled, then go still.

Calm? I argue with my grandfather in my head. *How can I be calm when it's the blind leading the blind around here?*

Now I can only hear the sound of the wind moving across the sand, a soft *shoosh*ing noise.

I take a moment. Calm. Yeah, okay.

Bickering with Jinx isn't going to save my father. Or my friends. Or the world.

I swear I can feel my grandfather patting my back. Nah, I must be imagining that.

Jinx begins moving forward. "If you don't want to follow, just go on back to the pond. There *probably* aren't any more kappa living there. They don't like to share their space. Of course, a new one could always come along. It is a prime location for fishing, and they're pretty lazy when it comes to that stuff."

I stand there for a moment, then follow her.

After a minute, I figure out that Jinx is right. My feet are okay.

This is one strange desert. The air is much cooler here, more like on a fall day than a hot summer afternoon, maybe because it's getting late. The sand feels pleasantly cool on my toes. I pick up a handful. Cold, like sun hasn't touched it for a week. I close my fingers around it as if I'm squeezing clay. When I do this, some of the sand heats into teeny charcoals. I drop it quickly.

Jinx talks over her shoulder. "After this, we're not far from oni territory at all."

"I thought this whole place was oni territory. It's all monster island up in here." I wave my hand around.

"True. But you know, not every single oni is bad." She looks at me from under her eyelashes. "Some who live here aren't, like, demons. Everyone here is a *yōkai*, a supernatural creature. There are thousands of kinds of yōkai. Oni are just one type. Some yōkai even bring good luck."

Like the snow woman, or the bird thing, or the oni eggs, or the tree gods? "Huh," I say doubtfully.

"Oni types like to live together, in packs. We're heading to what I call 'oni central.' "

"Great," I say under my breath.

Jinx flashes me a quick smile. "Wait a second." I pause. She adjusts the sword harness, shortening it. "The sword's really too big for you."

"Yeah, yeah, yeah." I don't need to be reminded of how small I am. "I can handle it."

"I really wouldn't mind carrying it for you." Her voice is hopeful.

There she goes, asking again. The thought makes me feel panicky, like the time when a really grimy kid with dirt and sticky Popsicle juice all over his fingers asked to borrow my favorite comic. "I already said no," I say, a bit more crankily than I intended. Nobody except me is touching this sword. I might not have wings, but at least I have a weapon. My grandfather's weapon. No offense, but of course I'm not going to let her use it.

I glance up at the sun, try to predict how many hours of light we have left. I can't. "What happens when it gets dark?"

She flashes me her quick smile again. "Let's just say that most oni are nocturnal and they don't stay in oni central then."

I decide to believe her.

Though we have no landmarks to guide us, Jinx's march is as determined as a soldier's. I'm actually grateful she's pushing me so hard, because otherwise I'm pretty sure I'd be lying facedown in the sand, never to move. Not that I'd admit how tired I am again, and get another lecture.

The sand might not be hot, but it's rough. The soles of my feet feel as if I've been walking over sandpaper for the last two hours. I lift up my right foot. A fat red blister has formed on the ball.

Every time I want to quit, I think of my father. It's only been a day or so, but I feel like I haven't seen him for five years. A cold cannonball lurches in my stomach when I imagine that I might never see him again.

It's the same feeling I had when my mother left. For so long, I kept expecting her to walk right through the front door and say, "I'm back. I'm here to stay. I'm sorry." Even after my grandmother came and put our household in order and I had spent more of my life without my mother than with her, I still hoped that Mom would come back.

Eventually that cannonball shrank down to something more like the size of a BB pellet. But it remained there, lodged in my intestines forever.

I don't want that cannonball-size feeling sticking around with me again.

I shake away the thought and search the sky, hoping to see Peyton gliding overhead. Nothing. Not even a cloud. In fact, I can't even tell where the sun is. It's like the light is filtered. Twilight. The sun's almost gone for the night.

"Look." Jinx speeds up. A glint of silver metal is sticking out from a dune ahead of us. As we get closer I can make out that it's a passenger jet—a big one, its wing and top visible. The rest is buried.

I run up to it, rub a dull window, and peer inside, half expecting to see a plane full of skeletons. But it's empty.

I turn to Jinx. "Where'd the, um . . . bodies go?"

"Where do you think?" Jinx splays her palm over the glass. "Oni don't joke around."

I recall my comic book. In the first part, Momotaro saved the maidens from getting eaten by the oni. Is my father now in some oni's stomach? "I wish there was a way to get to my father faster."

"Well, if we hadn't gone down the waterfall, the river would have been a straight shot to the volcano." Jinx shrugs. "But we did go down the waterfall, so now we're here, and there's no use in worrying about what we can't do, is there?"

A little jolt goes through me. Jinx is right. However, I don't answer her, because I still don't want to admit that she's right about anything.

The horizon is turning into velvety shades of purple and red, like long swaths of fabric piled on top of each other. A frigid wind kicks up, blasting sand into our faces with a ghostly whistle. I shiver. Are there any oni about? I haven't even seen a flying one during our forced march. The air's smoky and thick, and it stinks like a room full of farting people who had beans and old eggs for dinner. I gag. "Do you smell that?"

"Oh, I thought that was you." Jinx smirks.

I clap my hands together weakly. "Good one."

"Look over there." Jinx points, and I face that direction, but she grabs my shoulders and turns me around.

"That is not the way you were pointing." I shrug her mitts off me. "What am I looking at?"

In the distance, it looks as though the landscape is finally different. I think I can make out hillsides covered with low, brushy vegetation. And beyond that I can see a taller, craggy range jutting up, its rough black ridges outlined in an orange-red glow like melted sun. Gray smoke, blacker than the shadows we cast on the sand, spews up in a rhythmic *pop-pop-pop*.

"That's where the oni are," Jinx says flatly.

"Inside a live volcano?" I dig my feet into the sand. "Um, isn't that dangerous?"

Jinx flutters her lashes. "Did you think fighting demons would be *safe*?" She spreads out her hands. "We have to stop here for the night."

"No, we can't. We should push on. I don't care if it's dark." Why doesn't she see that we need to rescue Dad as soon as possible? We've wasted too much time already.

Jinx pulls at the handle on the airplane door. "We need shelter. You can't help your father if you're dead, can you?" The handle doesn't budge. "Ugh. It's rusted shut. Help me."

I balk. "Wait. You want me to sleep in the airplane? What if there are skeletons in it?"

She turns her head from side to side. "Do you see a better place, genius?"

I shrug. A distant cry, like a weedwhacker mixed with the howl of an injured animal, makes me jump. Goose bumps raise on my flesh. "What was that?"

Jinx pulls at the door, putting one foot on the body of the plane and leaning back with all her might. "That is the reason we need to get the heck inside this plane."

The shriek sounds again. Then, *"Itsumade!"*

"It's the itsumade!" The monster bird we saw back on the river. I sort of push her aside. "Let me try." The handle is as rusted shut as she'd said, meaning that it doesn't move at all. Not even a tiny little jiggle. We're in trouble. "I hope Peyton and Inu found shelter."

"They're in a better position than we are. I'm sure Peyton could find a much better place." Jinx pushes me aside now. "Get this thing open! Aren't you good for anything, Momotaro?"

Hot annoyance lances through me. I take out my sword and stick the point into the crack by the handle, trying to jimmy it open. It doesn't move, of course. Jinx lets out a long sputter of annoyance.

"Hush," I order. "I need to think."

"Don't tell me to hush. Let me try." She grabs the sword with both her hands and tries to muscle me out of the way, elbowing me in the ribs. Instinctively, I bring up my knee and bop her on the side of her thigh.

"Ouch." Jinx holds her leg, her face contorting in pain, baring all her teeth. "Xander! That hit my nerve."

I reach out to her, but she moves away. "I'm sorry. I didn't mean to."

"You really hurt me. Like really, really, really." Jinx sinks down next to the plane, looking away from me in injured silence.

My rib throbs. "You weren't gentle with me, either. Maybe you could, I don't know, respect what I ask of you."

Jinx snorts. "Whatever, 'Momotaro.' " She does air quotes with her fingers. She's not *that* hurt.

I take a deep breath and ignore her. I stare at the airplane door hard, like it's that God Tree whose pixels shifted. Of course, nothing happens. I try the handle again for good measure.

What my grandfather said in my last dream about the comic book floats back to me. *You created it. You know all you need to know.*

But I don't remember creating the comic or the drawing of Lovey. I must not have been awake at all.

Could that have something to do with it? Being asleep?

I don't talk myself out of my idea. I stick the sword down into the sand and relax against it. I close my eyes.

My breathing slows.

The light changes, as if the sun's come up. Jinx is nowhere to be seen. The sun's hot now, and I touch the plane, expecting the metal to burn me. Instead, it's as soft as butter.

"Xander!" Jinx's voice, sharp as the sword blade, jolts me back to reality. "Are you actually *falling asleep* right now? What's wrong with you? We need to get inside the stupid plane!"

"Jinx!" Frustrated, I kick a little sand in her direction. "I was almost there! I almost solved it!"

"By sleeping? Yeah, sure." Her disbelieving, disdainful expression tells me she doesn't take me seriously at all.

"Don't you understand? I *have* to be asleep." The truth of these words rings through me like I'm the Liberty Bell (before it got the big crack in it). I take a huge breath as I figure this out. "I was asleep when I created the comic book. I was asleep when I helped you with the kappa. I'm asleep when I talk to my grandfather. I have to be *asleep* to be Momotaro."

Jinx puts her hands on her hips and doesn't blink for what seems like three hundred years. I stare right back at her. Then she breaks her gaze and laughs. A big, hearty one from her gut. "If this is true, Xander, you are the truly the most useless Momotaro I ever heard of." She stands up and shakes off the sand. "How can you fight demons while you're unconscious?"

I don't respond. Instead, I pick up the sword and jam it back into the plane. Jinx inhales in sharp surprise as I push the sword through the now-soft metal. I draw the sword downward, and the door clicks open.

"And *that's* how I'm Momotaro, Jinx." My mouth turns up in a smug smile. "Ha-ha. In your face! You never think I can do anything, do you?" I go tingly all over. I feel like I'm on the verge of figuring out how to use my powers. My heart is pounding as if someone with a giant million-dollar check just showed up on my doorstep. "Have a little faith, for Pete's sake."

Faith and imagination, someone's voice whispers.

Jinx touches the plane wonderingly with her fingertips. "You got me, Xander. You really got me." Her tone is more than halfway to admiring. "How'd you do that? Did you picture it first? Just— imagine it?"

I shrug. I don't fully understand how I did it. I kind of did something like this when I got Jinx out of the acid, but I sure wasn't asleep then. How do I control this power without actually being unconscious? "Basically."

"Can I see the sword now?" She still doesn't quite believe me. Fine. I let her have the sword, ready to tackle her if she tries to run off with it.

She hefts it in her hands. "It's not as heavy as I thought."

"It's heavy enough." I hold out my hand. "Give it back."

Jinx stabs at the plane, but the sword bounces off with a metallic twang and smacks her face. "Ow." She rubs her jaw. "That hurt my teeth."

I grab the sword from her. I want to try something new, something while I'm totally awake. Without thinking it through, I grip the sword in both hands, the blade pointing down, and carve a big *X* into the body of the plane. "Oh!" I grin and put my palm on the *X*. "See? I did that while I was awake!" The *X* is a good half inch deep and the color of bricks.

Jinx rolls her eyes. "Good job. Now the oni have a big old red *X* to tell them exactly where we are."

Oh. I deflate immediately. Yeah, not such a great thing.

She taps at it. "Fix this."

"Okay, I'll try." I shut my eyes, picture the *X* being smoothed out, and then take my sword and use the blade like it's an ice scraper. It makes only a minor scratch. Panicked, I try to turn the *X* into something else—a blotch, anything. Nope.

I can't believe I've messed this up. A royal screwup. Good going, Xander. Can't I do anything right?

Desperately I try to imagine another way to fix it, but now my mind's shooting down all my ideas. Nothing will work.

Another spine-rattling squawk infiltrates my eardrums, louder still. I hunch over.

Jinx yanks on my arm. "Forget this business."

We duck inside.

CHAPTER 19

The air inside of the plane is stale, as if it hasn't had any new oxygen in a decade. Which is probably true.

We creep toward the cockpit. It's pretty dark, because the moon hasn't risen yet. For all I know, there isn't even a moon in oni central. Outside, the wind whistles over the metallic shell.

Finally my eyes adjust. No skeletons. Just suitcases stuck in the overhead bins, some on the floor, more on the seats. All is still, thank goodness.

I put my hands on the seat backs as I make my way forward, as if I'll fall otherwise, even though the plane's not moving. I don't want to trip on any creepy-crawlies. My head almost hits the ceiling, and the seats seem too close together. "At least we can sit in first class." My voice echoes through the chamber.

"Yeah. Finally, some leg room." Jinx stops short so suddenly that I bump into her. "Hey. I wonder if there's any food in here."

My stomach jumps in revolt. "Ew. If there was, it'd be way too old. Rotten and moldy."

"Only one way to tell." She hunches down like a monkey and scampers toward the galley. The darkness and the close quarters don't bother her at all. In a second, she's banging open cabinets and drawers.

A distant boom shakes the jet. I hold on to the seat backs. "What was that?" I call to Jinx.

"Just the volcano burping." She emerges with a little flashlight and tosses it to me.

I grip it like I'm holding a cross against vampires. "Thanks."

I shine the light around the cabin. No oni hiding out. At least, not as far as I can tell. The suitcases and bags are unopened.

"But don't use the light too much. Something might see it." Jinx hands me a bag. "Chips."

I shine the light on the expiration date. "Um, five years ago. Don't eat these."

Jinx is already crunching away. "Too late."

I turn off the flashlight and open my netsuke box. "How about a rice ball?"

She flops down in one of the big first-class seats. "Nah. I'm kind of tired of those."

"Me, too, but they beat expired chips." I pop a grain into my mouth and chow down as it expands into a full rice ball. Some kind of veggie filling—not my favorite, but better than nothing. I remove the sword in its sheath from the harness on my back and sit down across the aisle from her.

Jinx tosses her empty bag onto the floor. "Let's just get some sleep."

I think, uncomfortably, of that big red *X* marking the plane. "Shouldn't we keep watch or something?"

"Do what you want." Jinx turns away from me. "We'll hear if something tries to break in. Probably."

"I'll take first watch, then." I remind myself that *I* am the Momotaro, not Jinx. She's opinionated, but I'm kind of supposed to be the leader. I move to the window seat and look outside.

Nothing but blackness. Black sky, black desert. No shadows moving around—to my relief.

I really, really hope Peyton and Inu are okay.

I shut my eyes and try to imagine them safe and warm someplace. Maybe in a big tree. A tree that's a regular tree, not a monster-type tree.

And Dad. My dad is safe and warm, too. I imagine him behind his desk at home, sipping tea out of his *Star Trek* mug with Mr. Spock painted on it, books cracked open and papers over every surface. He looks thinner than I remember, and a bit grayer, but it is my father. He scribbles furiously on a legal pad, writing long columns of Japanese characters.

So, all these years, was he really researching how to defeat the oni? What did he find? Why didn't he share his knowledge with me? It seems like he should have started training me when I was, oh, three years old.

In his study, I see the Momotaro comic on his desk. I'm there in the room with him. "Dad?" I run over, grip his arm. My hand passes through him. He keeps on working.

This is a dream. Again. Darn it.

I look over his shoulder and read what he's writing. Suddenly the Japanese characters, which have always appeared to be chicken scratches to me, move and form words I can recognize.

He is here, Xander. He is here. Be careful.

"Here?" I look around the study. "Who's here?" But my father still can't see me, doesn't seem to realize I'm standing right next to him.

He sighs and swivels his chair to gaze out his window. I do, too.

The Pacific Ocean ripples in a vast sapphire expanse. The same as the day we left.

"Oh no," I breathe. "Dad, what happened?"

I glance back at Dad. His chair is empty.

And I realize then that he was the ghost, not me.

The ocean is still covering California, and my father's not rescued. I've failed. I'm going to fail.

"Dad!" I shout. I sit up, grab the headrest in front of me. I'm on the plane. Phew. It was only a dream—another extremely intense dream.

Who's here?

A sense of unease shakes me around the ribs. Nobody's here. We're alone. I'm just nervous about this adventure. Nothing more. It's not real. I hope, after all this is over, I can actually get a good night's sleep for once.

Speaking of which, I wonder if Jinx is asleep. I was supposed to be on guard. Shoot.

There's some light coming in through the windows now— enough to show me that Jinx's seat is empty. I turn on the flashlight and shine it down the length of the plane. No Jinx. I see that the door's open a crack. I make my way outside.

"Jinx?" I whisper into the wind.

I hear movement on top of the plane, near the embedded nose.

She is perched on top, staring at the sky.

I can see why.

The sky is no longer black. It is lined with lemon-yellow crackled clouds that are punctured with orange-colored holes. Through these holes stream funnels of crimson light that plunge straight down to the horizon. From there, light bounces back up and zigzags across the sky in shades of deep blue and royal purple. The colors shift and change, fading in out, as if some celestial being is controlling this really awesome light show.

I sit next to Jinx. "Wow," I breathe.

She sniffles. "I thought you were asleep."

I glance at her. Her face is sopping wet with tears. She catches my eye and turns away, embarrassed. Well, I don't like it when people see me crying, either. I pretend like she's not. "I woke up. Thanks for taking my shift."

"No problem."

"Is this like the aurora borealis or something?" I've never been far north enough to see the northern lights.

"Not really. It's all the weird gases from the volcano and the oni and their energy." Jinx gulps audibly. "You wouldn't happen to have a tissue, would you?"

"Nope."

"Drat." She uses the hem of her T-shirt to wipe her nose. "Oh well. It's already dirty, right?"

"Yeah." Now I steal another look at her. Her upper left arm has some kind of mark around it, like a rope burn. I touch it gently—the flesh is indented. "Oh my gosh, Jinx, what happened?"

"Eh. No biggie. I hurt myself opening the door." She laughs. "Some clumsy monkey I am."

I wonder how that injury could have happened by opening a door. But maybe it was even simpler and she feels dumb about it. Like the time I was running to get my popcorn out of the microwave and tripped on a rug and split my forehead open on a table edge. I told my grandmother I was running because I thought the microwave was on fire.

I shiver, rocking back and forth on my bare feet. "It's cold out here. Want to go back in?"

"Just wait." She points at the sky.

The colors swirl together now, all separate bands, undulating back and forth and up and down from the ground. They swell into a big sphere, and then, like a miniature multicolored sun, they finally melt into one another until all becomes black once more.

I lean back on my hands. "That was awesome."

"Yeah. Now we should get inside." She starts to scramble down, but winces with a sharp inhale.

I shine the flashlight on her wound. The mark looks like a combination deep bruise and light burn. "Ouch, Jinx. That's bad."

"Yeah. But really, I'm okay." She shoots me a smile that I can tell is fake.

I have an idea. "I'll be right back." I slide off the plane and run back inside to the galley. I open cupboards until I find it. Sure enough, there's a big white box with a red cross on the side. I open it, take out a roll of gauze, and go back out to Jinx. "Let's wrap it. It'll feel better." I hold up the gauze.

"Yeah, yeah." She grabs the gauze from me and begins wrapping her own arm. "I can do it faster by myself."

I let her. Just when I think we're starting to become friends, she proves me wrong.

Suddenly the gauze drops from her fingers. She bends to pick it up and it falls again, then flies upward like a demented moth and wraps itself around her head.

"Xander!" She claws at the cotton. "Help!" The gauze flies around and around her face as if it's possessed.

I rip at the gauze. It doesn't feel like cotton now; it feels as substantial and muscular as a snake. Oh no. My sword's inside the plane.

Determined not to let it hurt Jinx, I grab the end of the gauze and jump off the top of the aircraft, hoping it'll come with me.

Instead, Jinx falls down with it still wrapped around her.

Whoops.

We land in the sand, Jinx on her back, and me beside her in a crouch. She sticks her hands in between her neck and the gauze, between her mouth and the gauze, leaving herself some breathing space.

Nothing's working. I race inside to get my sword, wishing I hadn't been sitting all the way up by the cockpit.

Then I hear that inhuman, *un-animal* shriek.

"Itsumade!"

Oh crud.

I grab my sword and run back out.

The demon bird is hovering over Jinx, who is still wrestling with the possessed gauze. The bird swoops down and lets out a puff of fire.

CHAPTER 20

leap toward the bird, my sword swinging before I can even think
about what I'm doing.

I'm too late.

As I leap, the fire catches the gauze and, like a candlewick, it
goes up in flames. *Poof.*

I scream and pierce the bird's chest with the sword.

The demon bird falls over.

"Jinx!" I fall to my knees, sure that she's gone.

Her face is covered in black ash. My heart sinks.

Then she coughs and spits and wipes her face. "Ugh. Really? An
ittan-momen. I swear, we have the worst luck."

"You're okay!" I clap my hand on her shoulder. "You're not
burned?"

"No. The itsumade just got the ittan-momen. That oni actually saved my life."

"Ittan-momen?"

"That, believe it or not, is cotton that tries to suffocate you." Jinx stands, brushes sand off her legs. I must be giving her a stupid, open-mouthed look, because she laughs in spite of herself. "You should see the expression on your face."

I shake my head. "But why did the itsumade help? I didn't know—I thought it was burning you alive." My heart skips. "Was I not supposed to kill it?"

"No, you had to." She points to it, lying limp on the ground. "*Itsumade*—the word it screams—means *How much longer?*" She walks over to it, begins scooping handfuls of sand over its body. "These things were people who died in a famine, thousands of years ago, in ancient Japan. They never got put to rest properly, and they turned into these nasty critters."

"Oh." That seems particularly horrible.

"All it wanted was a resting place." She pushes more sand on top of it. "And you gave it one."

I help her bury the monster.

"You're not freaked out?" Jinx asks.

I don't stop working, digging into the sand up to my elbows. "I'm mostly sorry for it. Poor oni bird who used to be a person thousands of years ago."

Jinx sits back on her haunches, panting from the effort. "You know what, Xander? You're not as bad of a Momotaro as I thought."

That's probably the biggest compliment she's ever paid anyone in her whole life. "Thanks, Jinx." I throw more sand on the bird. "I appreciate it."

"And, Jinx," she imitates my voice, "you're not as bad of a monkey as I thought. That's what you're *supposed* to say. Sheesh."

I nod at her. "Good monkey."

At dawn, we get up for real and Jinx pokes around in the galley again. "Oatmeal packets and Coke." She waves them in the air. "Breakfast of champions."

Coke seems safe enough. Would that expire, ever? I pop open the can and take a cautious sip. If I don't look at any expiration dates, I won't freak myself out. It tastes mostly like Coke—kind of syrupy, but not too bad.

I glance outside. The sky's a clear purple. Somehow I'm getting used to that color. "Is it cold again?"

"It's always a bit cold around here. I'll be right back." Jinx goes outside, carrying a bag of something. I figure she wants to do her business and needs privacy. I tried to use the bathroom on the plane, but opening that door turned out to be not such a good idea. Talk about stinky.

But then Jinx raps on the window and motions for me to follow her. When I get out there, she's got a rock in each hand. She strikes them together over a metal cup with a small amount of syrup-colored liquid in it. "What are you doing?" I ask.

"Making us a hot breakfast." She taps and taps some more until, finally, a little spark comes off the rock and the liquid whooshes into a full-blown fire. "Jet fuel. It burns fast and hot."

She sets another cup on top of the fire and fills it with water from a bottle. When the water's boiling, she wraps the cup with a towel, takes it off the flame, then pours the instant oatmeal into it. She presents it to me with a little bow. "For you." She hands me a plastic spoon, too.

"Thank you." I bow back, feeling a little guilty, like I'm not pulling my weight. Jinx isn't so bad. Look how helpful she's being.

"My mother always said there's nothing like a hot breakfast to shore up the soul on a tough day." Jinx sits cross-legged in the sand, waiting for another cup of water to heat.

I take a spoonful of the oatmeal. Peaches-and-cream flavor, my favorite. Even the dehydrated peaches taste like heaven. The warmth goes into my core and down to my numb toes. I gobble it all down. "Your mother was right." This is the first time Jinx has mentioned her mother. I squint at her in the bright morning light. "Do you live with your mom?"

"Not anymore." Jinx concentrates on stirring her oatmeal and won't meet my eyes. That's all she wanted to say, I guess.

"I miss my dad and grandmother," I offer into the silence.

She frowns, blows on her cereal. "Haven't you ever been away from home before?"

"Yeah. For camp."

"Then what's the big deal?" She tips the cup into her mouth.

"You mean besides the fact that my dad is being held hostage by a contingent of monsters?" I let out a muffled belch and consider saying *Excuse me*, but when I see Jinx scooping the last bits of oatmeal into her mouth with her fingers, I decide she doesn't care. "I just want to get home, is all. Have things get back to normal."

"What's normal?" Jinx peers at me with curiosity, as if she really wants to know.

"Hanging out with Peyton. Playing video games. Sleeping in my own bed. All that good stuff." I remember the feel of Inu next to me as I slept on my bed, wrapped in an old quilt my mother's mother made a long time ago, and tears spring into my eyes. I turn before Jinx can spot them.

"Sounds about as exciting as a bag of rocks." Jinx wipes her mouth with the back of her hand. "I have news for you, my friend. You're Momotoro. You're never going to be normal again." She stands up and kicks sand onto the fire. It takes at least a bucketful before the flame finally goes out.

CHAPTER 21

We set off away from the plane right after we finish breakfast. Jinx takes the airline bag she found and packs it with water bottles, oatmeal, and more of those handy metal containers. The sun's up, but it hasn't heated the desert yet. Icy fingers of wind tickle my ribs.

You're never going to be normal again. The phrase repeats itself in my head as I put one foot in front of the other. It used to be that my biggest worry was keeping chip crumbs off my keyboard. No more of that. I am the Momotaro. Saver of worlds.

A sour taste rises in my throat. Am I really ready for this? It doesn't matter anymore—I'm already here, and unless a Momotaro can time-travel, I have to keep moving forward.

The temperature rises as we hike all day through the sand,

stopping only occasionally to rest and eat rice balls under the purple sky. Jinx folds us paper hats from magazines she found in the plane, and these keep our heads nice and shaded.

It's late afternoon when the ground shakes, making the dunes roll like the ocean. I drop into a crouch, my sword clattering behind me. "What is that?"

Jinx freezes, her eyes going wide. "Uh-oh."

"Uh-oh? What's uh-oh?" The dune we're walking on shudders. Then it rises, and the sand swirls around me. I can't see.

"Jinx?" I reach out for her and grab hold of something, but I'm not sure what.

The sand falls away as I'm lifted by a rising piece of land. The air clears, and I can now see treetops below me. Where am I? I try to walk. The ground is squishy and crisscrossed with shallow ridges. It smells like a dirty rest-stop bathroom.

"Xander!" Jinx calls. She sounds far away.

Suddenly I'm looking into an enormous blue eye the size of a semitruck's tire. "Hello, boy," a deep voice rumbles in Japanese. "How did you enter the land of oni?"

I glance down again and realize I'm standing in the palm of a hand. I jump up, but that's a bad idea, because he's still lifting me.

Jinx waves and shouts up to me, "It's a *daidarabotchi*. A giant."

"Really? I thought it was a midget." Great. Another monster. "What do I do?"

What I thought were plain old sand dunes are now gone. The

giant was taking a nap under the sand, and the dunes were his knees and belly and whatnot. He must be fifty feet tall. Not something I want to fall off of.

"I don't know!" Jinx yells back. "Try talking to him."

Dude. Talk? That won't work. The hand moves and I crouch for balance, trying to hang on. "Please don't eat me."

The giant chuckles. "I don't eat. I collect."

"Collect?" I squeak.

He holds me at arm's length and now I can see his whole face. Humanlike. A wide nose with flared nostrils, and nose hair so long I can see it waving with his breath. But his skin's orange and, of course, he's not human at all.

"A half-Asian boy," he says in a voice that sounds like a jet engine. "Very rare in these parts. I don't have one." He holds up his other hand. In it he's got a shaft of steel, deadly sharp on one end, between his tree-trunk fingers. It's a huge pin. He makes a *tsk*ing noise. "Now, try not to wiggle. It will only hurt for a moment, but it hurts worse if you move." He pinches me between his forefinger and thumb. The piles of dirt under his nails are bigger than me. The piece of metal comes at me like an arrow.

He's going to stick me with that pin, like a butterfly collector, and put me on a wall someplace. I scream. Without thinking, I unsheath my grandfather's sword and jab it, hard, under his fingernail.

His shout's like a bomb going off. *"ITAI! ITAI!"* *It hurts!* "I told you not to squirm." He drops the pin and shakes the hand that held it. His grip around me loosens.

Jinx appears at the giant's shoulder. How did she get up there? She looks like a gnat compared to him. She motions me to come toward her. To crawl across his huge arm.

I gulp. Don't look down.

I put my sword away and start crawling. The hairs on his arm are like a black forest. A stinky black forest. A huge louse scuttles by, the size of a small terrier, and I shriek.

"Where did you go?" The giant examines his arm.

"Here." Jinx kicks him in the Adam's apple.

"Ouch!" He claps his hand to his throat and drops me in the process. It's like falling off the side of a mountain.

Somebody catches me. Somebody with golden wings. "Peyton!" I shout.

"Don't you know you're not supposed to wake a sleeping giant?" Peyton grips me under my arms. Jinx clings to his back, like Yoda did to Luke. Her face is about two inches away from mine.

Peyton flies for a minute, to grassy hills farther away from the oni volcano. Hopefully these are giant-free. He sets me down next to my dog.

Inu's whole body wriggles with glee. He jumps up and hugs me, licking my face. I laugh and scratch his head, his chest, his sides. "Inu! Hey! Did you miss me, boy? Huh? I missed you."

Woof, woof! Inu barks, then whines. I pet him some more.

"Okay, boy, down," I tell him at last. Inu goes over to Jinx and repeats his greeting with her. She giggles with delight. I turn to Peyton and give him a half hug. I swear, he's bigger than I remember. His hand dwarfs mine. "How did you find us?"

Peyton shrugs, smooths down his shock of hair. "It wasn't hard. A giant man suddenly stood up in a desert. I could see him from a mile away."

I squint at him. "Did your voice get deeper?"

"Maybe," he says, and, yeah, it's definitely deeper. He sounds like a television announcer. He strokes his chin. "Look. I even have real stubble."

"No way." I'm getting on my tiptoes to admire his growing beard when every hair on my body stands straight up, like I'm about to be hit by lightning. Peyton and I both tense. What's going on?

Inu leaves Jinx and starts growling, his ruff poofing out around his neck.

"Xander," a deep voice says from behind me.

I turn slowly. But I know who it is before I see him.

"Welcome to the land of oni. We've been waiting for you."

The beast monster man stands there. He looks about two million times worse in real life than he did in my dreams or in any drawing. He has bulging muscles, and the muscles seem to have muscles of their own. A long monkeylike tail, reddish brown, swishes impatiently, and his knifelike scales gleam. He smells like a sandwich somebody forgot to throw away a week ago. His coal black eyes focus on me.

That giant was a beacon for more than one person.

Or thing.

Salt. I need my salt.

The beast-man grabs my wrist. I'm like a toddler fighting Superman. "No salt," he hisses.

I try to reach for my sword, but he crushes the fingers in my other hand, too. *Inu, Jinx, help.*

Jinx leaps on the thing's back, her nails clawing his eyes. He lets go of me, reaches behind him, and throws Jinx off like she's nothing. My shaking hands grab my octopus netsuke and open the box for the salt.

Inu goes after the beast, snarling like I've never heard him snarl before, his jaws opening wide and going for the thing's neck. He makes contact and the beast tries to get Inu off, but my dog won't let go. I didn't know Inu had this in him.

The beast screams. The tail whips around and slashes at Inu. My dog falls down with a wail.

I throw the salt at the oni—only a few grains hit. He shrugs them off with a growl. I jump forward, my sword in my hands, and swing it through the air. The beast-man blocks it with his tail, but the blade penetrates the scales and slices through his flesh. The end of his tail wiggles on the ground like a cut worm. The monster hisses, then gets on all fours, and runs away over the hills.

I fall to my knees, panting, my blood on fire. "Yes!" I pump my fist. "Oh my gosh. It worked. It actually worked." I let out a big sigh of relief.

Jinx glances at the darkening sky. "Now let's get to shelter before it's totally dark."

"Oh no," Peyton breathes behind me. "Inu."

Inu, my best friend since I was a baby, lies limp on the ground. He weakly thumps his tail. Gashes wider than my hand gape open on his neck and along his ribs.

For a second, I can't believe my eyes. Then I see his blood pumping out and know it's all too real. "Nooo!" I throw myself on my dog, over his soft furry body. I feel his heart racing. "No, no, no." He doesn't deserve this. He only wanted to protect me.

Jinx gets up from where she landed. Breathing hard, she staggers over to us. "Inu! Not Inu." She begins crying hysterically. "Inu. It wasn't supposed to be Inu."

"It could be any of us," Peyton says.

"I don't care that Momotaro is supposed to have a dog. I should have left him with Obāchan." I stroke his neck. My dog's brown eyes look up at me sadly. They say, *I forgive you, Xander.*

But I'll never, ever forgive myself. I bite my tongue to keep from screaming. A sob escapes. "I'm sorry, Inu."

I wish this was all a bad dream.

Jinx touches my shoulder with a hand wet with her tears. "Come on. I know where to go to get help."

CHAPTER 22

Peyton cradles Inu in his arms. I'm glad all over again that Peyton's so strong. We run like there's still a giant chasing us, following Jinx as she goes deep into the hilly terrain, Peyton breathing hard.

Suddenly she drops right, heading down between boulders taller than a man. "Unnngh!" With all her weight, she pushes aside a large rock, and there's an opening. A cave.

I pause. "There's not another yuki-onna in there, is there?"

"No. This is Tanuki's lair." She looks back at me. "Come on. He'll help us."

"*Tanuki?* What's a tanuki?" The name tugs at my memory. I'm sure my grandmother said something about tanuki at one point.

"Don't worry." She disappears into the dark.

237

We duck to enter.

Inside it's warm, protected from the wind that's whistling outside. A couple of candles, set in nooks above the ground, light the low, wide space. I half expect it to be a hobbit-style hidey-hole with furniture and a food cellar, but there's nothing like that. Instead, thick piles of hay are scattered over the stone ground, like chairs.

In one nest toward the back sits a raccoon. Or badger. Or dog. I'm not exactly sure. I stop moving. It looks up and lifts its brownish-black snout. A row of needlelike teeth comes at me.

"Watch out!" I grab Jinx by the arm and hurl her back through the cave opening. Unfortunately, I'm not that strong, and Jinx outweighs me by at least a dozen pounds, so she sort of just stumbles to a stop right outside. "Run! We're in a badger den!" I've watched enough Animal Planet to know that badgers are mean little critters. So are raccoons. Especially when cornered. Their teeth and claws can do a lot of damage. And this animal is some kind of crazy oni badger, as tall as my waist. A badger on steroids.

I take my sword out and point it at the badger. "Stay back."

The badger hisses, then coughs. "Um. Excuse me." It moves toward the opening on its hind legs, while shading its eyes with one clawed paw. It is wearing a child-size blue-and-white kimono, printed with lotus blossoms. "My, my. I shouldn't have coffee so late. It disagrees with me." It bows low from the waist. "Jinx, I haven't seen you in a long time." Then, to me, "Please, little boy, I do you no harm. I am your humble servant. Come inside."

"Xander,"—Jinx dusts herself off—"this is Tanuki. He's not a badger. He's a . . ." She cocks her head. "Like a raccoon dog. Another type of yōkai, Xander. A helpful one. Tanuki, we have an injured dog. He needs your medicine."

"Set him down." Tanuki waddles closer to us.

Peyton carefully places Inu on a mound of clean-looking hay. Tanuki peers at Inu, touches the wounds. Inu whimpers.

Tanuki looks concerned. "Oh my. Oh yes." He reaches into his kimono sleeve and takes out a fabric envelope. From this, he removes white tissue paper. He licks it and applies it to Inu's wounds.

He's *licking* tissue? "What good is a piece of toilet paper going to do?" I shout. "My dog is dying! He needs stitches, not your spit! Which, by the way, is totally unhygienic."

"Shush." Jinx puts her hand on my arm. "Watch."

The tissue paper sticks to Inu's wounds. But it does more than that. Within seconds, it acts like a new piece of skin, stopping the blood, filling in the gashes. Inu relaxes. "It will take some time. All night," Tanuki says. "The cuts are very deep."

I fall to my knees and throw my arms around Tanuki. "Thank you."

"Ah. Yes." Tanuki pats my back awkwardly. "No problem. See? I am a good tanuki. It is true there are some bad tanuki. But also many good ones." He struggles to his feet. He wears a pair of straw sandals with long laces that wrap around his legs.

"Come more inside. Sit." Tanuki bows again and bobs his head.

"Take off your packs, make yourself at home. Have dried fish and *matcha*."

"Don't mind if I do." Peyton helps himself to the dried fish jerky that's sitting in a shallow woven basket, popping a strip into his mouth. "Mmmm. Salty."

I hesitate. Should I take off my sword? I do remember reading someplace that it's kind of impolite to bring a weapon into a friendly house. Or was that a Viking thing only?

Jinx reads my mind. "It's okay," she says softly. "You can leave it." I place the sword on the floor just inside the cave opening. Obāchan would be proud of my good manners.

We walk farther into the cave, down a narrow hallway. Peyton carries Inu and tries not to knock over the knickknacks Tanuki has on shelves all over the walls. They look like broken plastic toys—a headless baby doll, partially melted toy soldiers. Junk, really. But I guess it's not junk to Tanuki.

He bustles away and returns with a tray carrying a white mug that says WORLD'S BEST MOM in pink letters, a plain brown mug, a brass goblet, and a plastic kid's tumbler printed with an American flag. They are all filled with a frothy green liquid, like a milk shake you'd see on St. Patrick's Day. I bow to him in thanks.

Jinx settles into a mound of hay and accepts the kid-size tumbler. "Thanks for saving my life, Xander." She lifts her glass toward me. "Cheers."

Peyton selects the plain mug and I have no choice but to take WORLD'S BEST MOM. I peer into the mug and sniff. It smells like sugar. "What is it?"

"My great-great-great-grandfather's matcha posset recipe. Very good for warming up bones." Tanuki takes a big gulp. "Try it."

"It's like a creamy milk drink, mixed with green tea," Jinx explains. "Kind of like that green tea latte they make at Starbucks."

"Bah! Starbucks!" Tanuki waves his claw and looks fierce. "Do not speak of Starbucks in my house!"

"Sorry." Jinx holds up both hands in surrender.

Tanuki takes another swig from his cup. "Starbucks. No match for Tanuki's posset."

I try a sip. A warm sensation moves from my throat to my stomach, all the way down to my toes. My muscles go limp. "It *is* good." Tanuki beams at me. I take a bigger gulp. This time I swallow a lot of air, and I belch, loud and very long. My cheeks burn. "Pardon me."

Tanuki raises his cup. "Compliments to the chef! I accept it." He makes a strange, high-pitched trilling noise. It takes me a second to realize he's laughing.

Peyton downs the entire contents of his mug in one gulp. "Oh man. That's good stuff." He sinks to the floor near Inu, his wings looking large and out of place in such a small space. Big bags line the undersides of his eyes. Poor guy probably didn't find a plane to sleep in like we did.

"Drink up!" Tanuki says approvingly. "There is more where that come from."

Something moves at the back of the cave. "Are you guys having fun without me?" a squeaky voice asks. "That's not fair."

"Oh, dear." Tanuki shakes his head and knocks back another drink. "Karakasa, while you are up, would you mind getting us a refill?"

A folded umbrella walks into the light. Wait—what, now? A walking umbrella? I blink. It's tall and made out of paper and bamboo. Yes, definitely an umbrella. Two large, round white eyes peer at me from near the top. I don't see a mouth, though—maybe that's down below, on the handle. I shake my head. I must have fallen asleep again. I mean, in the past day I've seen plenty of strange creatures, but a walking, talking umbrella? Who would even *imagine* something so weird?

Peyton shakes his head, too. "Dude," he whispers, "this drink . . . is it just me, or am I seeing things?"

Jinx leans over. "Karakasa is a *tsukumogami*. Those are objects that come to life when they turn one hundred years old. For some reason, there are a lot of umbrellas."

Long bamboo skewers unfold from the umbrella—its arms. Spindly toothpick fingers grab Tanuki's goblet. "The Japanese take very good care of their parasols. They last for generations." I still don't see how it's talking. It walks to the back of the cave and pours more drink into the goblet.

When it returns, I say, "Nice to meet you. I'm Xander." I watch it carefully, looking for its mouth.

"I know." Karakasa bows, sloshing drops of the green drink out of the goblet. "We are honored to have a Momotaro in our midst." It points to my head. "The silver hair. You cannot hide anymore."

I grin. "I wouldn't say I was hiding. I just didn't know I was a Momotaro before."

"Oh, you were hiding. Believe me." The umbrella winks at me.

"Try not to spill." Tanuki holds out one lazy paw for his refilled goblet.

"Don't forget about me!" a low voice says from somewhere under Tanuki.

He sticks his legs out. "I did forget. My *bakezōri*."

The sandals strapped to Tanuki's feet wiggle on their own, and two black eyes—one on each shoe—roll up toward me. "It is a true pleasure to meet you, Xander. Would that I could be on *your* feet instead of on this stinky tanuki's. But, alas, I am made too small."

I swallow. The room spins a little bit.

"Nice to meet you," I say hoarsely, really hoping I don't have to shake the sandals' hands, which I think would be the laces winding around Tanuki's legs. That would be awkward.

Two more animal forms appear in the cave entrance. Like Tanuki, they are furry and four-legged, but they walk upright. I hear a meow, like cats do when they want food, loud and obnoxious. "We heard there was a party."

"You can't make matcha and not invite us. We all smelled it," another adds.

I've given up being surprised. I have another sip of the matcha and wait to see who else appears. My eyelids feel heavy.

Tanuki doesn't bother getting up. He points to each visitor in turn. "Bakeneko, the good-luck cat, and Kitsune, the clever field fox."

A huge shorthaired cat, nearly the size of Inu, all white with a black patch on its head that makes it look like it's wearing a widow's peak toupee, comes in. Its tail is ridiculously long, but then, the cat is ridiculously large. Its tail swishes as it bows to me. I catch a glimpse of long, sharp claws.

Bakeneko looks very familiar. Then I realize I've seen it as a statue and figurine in stores. It's supposed to bring prosperity by waving at customers.

The other animal is a red fox. As it bows, it changes into a Japanese man wearing sort of furry shorts. He's still got a feathery fox tail. Kitsune sees me staring at it. "That's why I stay here on oni island," he says. "I just can't get rid of this tail."

I have a thought. "What about Peyton?" I ask Jinx. "Is he some mythological creature, too, now that he has wings?"

She screws up her mouth. "If I had to say, I'd say a *tengu*. A man-bird."

"Man-bird! Man-bird!" Peyton holds his mug aloft, sloshing some liquid out. He stands up and beats his chest with a fist. "That's right. I'm a MAN. No boy-bird around here." He hiccups.

The umbrella and the fox titter. "The man-bird had best slow down on the matcha," the fox sneers.

"Peyton." I make a motion for him to sit down. "Dude, relax."

"*You* relax." Peyton points at me. "Have some more of this delicious drink." He gets up to refill his cup.

I sip some more. My insides feel pleasantly warm, my fingertips tingly. "Do you think I'll turn into an animal, too?" I put one hand around the golden bracelet from the kappa on my wrist. If I did transform, this thing might fall off. Or become too small. Depending on what I turned into.

Jinx wrinkles her nose at me. "Does Momotaro turn into an animal in your comic book?"

"No. But that doesn't mean it can't happen. We didn't see a castle, either, or maidens washing away blood. Just maidens causing blood to spill." I wipe my mouth with my hand. Somehow I'm dribbling liquid. Since when did I get so sloppy? "And I'm not adopted, either. It doesn't have to be exactly the same." I consider the comic book some more. "I mean, Momotaro made pictures of his battles. But I didn't. Not ever. So that's not helpful." I squint at Jinx, who seems a bit blurry in this low light. "But we found you because you're my monkey friend. It's fate, Jinx."

She stares at the floor like she expects a bag of treasure to pop out of it. "I don't really believe in fate."

"You don't believe in fate. But you believe in all this?" I sweep my hand around the room. "Come on."

Jinx looks up at me. "Are we friends?"

Weird question. I try to answer it honestly. "I saved you from the kappa. You saved me from the giant. You saved my dog. Yes, I would say we're friends. Why?"

She shrugs and her gaze falls to the floor. She seems exhausted all of a sudden.

"Where *are* your parents, anyway?" I ask, still curious. Do they know Jinx is roaming oni backcountry in filthy clothes and a ton of eyeliner? Did she run away from home? Does anybody at all care about her? "You never answered before. Are they back on Kauai? I want to know." My fingers and legs tingle in a nice, warm way.

Jinx doesn't answer, just sips at her drink. Peyton returns and sits on the floor, stretching out next to Inu and putting one hand on his ribs. "He's doing better," he reports.

"Good." Jinx eats some more dried fish. She sniffles. "Good."

The umbrella comes around with the plastic pitcher and refills my mug. Suddenly I'm really thirsty, and I swallow almost the whole thing in three big gulps. I set the mug on the floor. "So answer my question. Tell us about Jinx."

Jinx sips her drink slowly, keeping her eyes averted. Her shoulders slump forward. "It's a boring story."

"Tell me." My words sound all squishy, like my tongue has stopped working. "I wanna know the whole thing." I nudge her leg with my foot.

Now she looks up at me, straight into my eyes. "I'm a princess. My parents are the fabulously wealthy emperors of a small Asian kingdom. They wanted me to marry some gross weirdo to unite two kingdoms, so I ran away."

I blink at her. Call me crazy, but I'm pretty sure she's making this up. "Jinx, you don't have to be, like, ashamed or anything. I don't care about your background. My mother ran off and left us when I was little." I shrug. "Her loss. We don't know if she's dead or alive. She never even sent a postcard." A wave of self-pity sweeps over me. My mother doesn't know if I'm dead or alive, either. Doesn't she care?

"My dad wants to make me into his mini-me," Peyton says from where he's now prone on the floor. "I don't want to go to military school." His words sound like fruit in a blender, all whirred together. "He's not gonna make me!"

"That's right! He can't make you! You tell him so!" I raise my fist at Peyton, but his eyes are closed now.

"Parents can make you do anything," Jinx says, shifting uncomfortably on her pile of hay. "We're just kids."

"We're not just kids," I scoff. I point at Peyton, then myself. "Wings! Momotaro!"

A sound like a small train going by comes from the floor. Peyton has passed out like he just finished Thanksgiving dinner. He's stretched out next to Inu, and both are snoring loudly.

"That was mighty harsh of your mother to leave like that." Jinx shifts her eyes away again, as if looking at me is physically painful. She takes a big gulp of the drink. Wetness appears at the outer corners of her eyes, but it's gone almost as soon as it appears.

"Your parents don't want you, either, do they?" I ask softly. "That's how you ended up with that snow monster."

She shrugs. "I haven't exactly been Princess Sunshine. I can't blame them." She waves at the air. "Hey, doesn't matter now, right?"

But clearly it *does* matter to her. Jinx is all broken inside. The way she acts, like she doesn't care, is just a mask. I wish I could make her feel better. Something tells me Jinx is a lot worse off than I am. "You can't be that bad," I say. "You're a kid. Parents are supposed to stick with their kids. It's their fault, not yours."

She doesn't glance at me. Just bites down on her lower lip until she draws blood that trickles down her chin.

"Jinx, stop it." I put my hand on her arm. This is the part where I'm probably supposed to hug her, since we're friends and all, but the thought makes me feel even weirder than this drink does. Instead, I take the bracelet off and nudge her arm with it. "Hey. This kappa bracelet." I swallow. Now my words sound fuzzy. I poke her harder. "Have it."

She glances down at the solid-gold cuff. "You don't want to give me that."

"Yesshhhh. Yessssh, I do." I push her with it. "Takes it." My ability to speak English has apparently vanished.

"I said I don't want it." She smacks the bracelet out of my hand, sending it clattering across the floor. The room goes still. The creatures stop chattering and stare. Jinx stands up, upsetting my mug, spilling the drink. Her breathing comes hard as she leans in toward me. "Listen, you little speck of dirt, I'm not taking your stinking butt-ugly bracelet, and I am not your stinking monkey. Got that?" Jinx's hands ball into fists.

"What's your problema? I'm just being nice. Something you are highly unfamiliar with." I put the mug upright. Tanuki scrambles forward with a cloth to sop up the liquid. "Calm down."

"I *am* calm!" Jinx's face wrinkles into a scowl. "I don't need your charity, you weak little half-breed."

My head gets so hot my earwax melts. "No wonder your parents didn't want you!"

Jinx's face goes still; she's as expressionless as a statue again. "That's right," she says quietly. "You're exactly right, for once." She walks away, disappearing into the cave's darkness.

I feel bad. Maybe I went too far. But I wasn't the one who spilled a drink and threw a bracelet. I was just trying to be nice. What did she think was going to happen? I inhale deeply. Dad never would have said something as hurtful as that, no matter how nasty somebody acted to him. He would have been all Zen and said something like, "Jinx, I'm sorry you're having a rough day." But he's a forty-five-year-old professor. I'm just a twelve-year-old boy. It's her fault, not mine.

I help Tanuki clean up, mopping up the drink with rags that I hope aren't actually living creatures. "Sorry, Tanuki."

"No worries." He stands upright again. "I am glad you are helping her, Momotaro-san. That girl has been through a lot."

I straighten, feeling sick to my stomach. "I doubt I'm helping her much."

Kitsune turns back into fox form and curls up in a C-shape, settling his tail over his paws. The umbrella sets a shallow bowl of matcha in front of him. "So he's it?" the fox says, his voice sounding exactly like a fox's should. Wily. "The Momotaro without magical powers? Ha. Tanuki, all the animals from far and wide will be coming to your house to see this spectacle."

All the creatures laugh heartily.

"I will lock the door when I run out of matcha." Tanuki smiles— or *seems* to smile with his snout. "Rest now, while you can, little hero."

I burrow into my pile of hay. The umbrella refills my drink, and I empty it again. I feel so sad all of a sudden. Yes, I'm nothing special. Yes, I'm not a Momotaro. Yes, I'm just a big garden-variety jerk who made an orphan girl cry.

Tanuki pulls hay over me like a blanket.

I try to sit up, but my head spins. I feel numb all over, kind of like I'm not even in my body. "Doesthismatchahavealcoholinit?" My words slur. I manage, "Myobāchanwillnotbehappywithyou."

"I'm sorry," Jinx whispers from somewhere in the cave. "I'm sorry."

But my eyes are closed, and I could just be dreaming it.

Ojīchan stands over me, shaking me with both hands. I open my eyes a little wider. I can see straight through him. It's not the buff, young version. It's the pale old man from the bus stop, here in the cave. If I were at home, I'd be a little freaked out. But here I just say, "Hey! What's up?"

"Wake up!" Ojīchan says, his voice like a far-off echo. "Get up, Xander. Hurry!"

I try to rouse myself, but I can't move. I'm too deep asleep. Too comfortable.

"Later," I mumble, and everything goes dark again.

CHAPTER 23

W hen I do wake up, it's to the worst smell ever. Worse than a pail of dirty diapers left for three weeks in the sun. Worse than the Easter eggs I didn't find behind the couch for a month. Worse than a garbage dump in a sewer full of cow waste.

I half wish I could stay asleep so I wouldn't have to smell this awfulness anymore. Daylight hits my face, and, reluctantly, I wake up one hundred percent. I'm moving. But my legs aren't moving.

My face is banging against something slimy.

I open my eyes all the way.

The ground is above my head. Then I see two moving human-oid legs. They're red and black and blue-gray—and raw-looking. Not exactly like raw meat you'd find at the grocery store. More like somebody's wearing a costume made out of old random carcasses they found on the side of the road.

This carrion thing is carrying me over its shoulder.

"STOP!" I yell. I have to take a big breath to do it, and I almost pass out because the smell enters my lungs. My stomach retches and I'm sick all over the thing's back and legs. But the creature doesn't even pause, or say "Ew," or anything.

You know it's bad when barf improves the smell.

"He needs a rest," a girl's voice says. I recognize it as Jinx's.

The thing grunts, but stops and lowers me to the ground.

I splay out on my back, looking up. The monster makes a low, guttural sound and stares back at me with beady red-black bird eyes set into its rotting flesh. Zombie? I try to wiggle away, but I can't. The ground's too hard, too sharp under me.

"The best thing you can do is relax." Jinx kneels over me, but I can't see her face because the sun's behind her. Her hair hides her expression. The sky is full of black smoke. I'd rather inhale smoke than the monster smell.

"Jinx, what is this thing?" It looks like a swamp monster. A dead one. "What happened?"

"Shush." She smooths the hair back out of my face. "We were hoping you'd stay asleep during this part."

I don't understand. Not a bit. I scoot backward again, and the monster grunts and grabs me around my ankle, his long bony fingers closing slimily over me. I'm covered in disgusting, rotten warm green goo. "Where are Peyton and Inu?"

She doesn't answer. I look around. A second monster stands behind us.

On his back, like a crazy Santa, he's carrying a mesh bag containing my dog and my best friend. They are unconscious, but alive—I see their sides moving. "Peyton! Inu!" I try to yell, but my voice is barely a whisper. I clear my throat and try again. "You guys okay?" My head is pounding with the worst headache ever. Ow.

"Don't fight it, Xander." Jinx stands up and gestures to the creature. My sword's strung around her waist, along with both my netsuke.

The beast picks me up and throws me over its shoulder like a sack of potatoes, continuing on its galumphing up-and-down walk. Oof. That did not make my stomach feel good. What's going on?

Then I know.

Jinx.

Jinx betrayed me.

I turn my head and try to breathe shallowly through my nose so I don't gag again. "Are you one of them?"

She doesn't answer.

"What are you?" I shout.

"This is my real shape." Her voice is as dry and hopeless as that desert we crossed.

"I trusted you!" Angry tears spring to my eyes and I don't care.

Actually, the tears help my eyes feel better—they're stinging from the goop. "I *saved* you."

"I know it doesn't seem like it, but I'm helping you." Her voice sounds determined.

"How?" I pound on the beast's back, but it's useless.

"We're taking you back to your ship, Xander."

"What? What about my father?" I try to look at her, but all I can see is a blur.

She doesn't answer.

"My father!" I flail around again, sending bits of slime all over the place. "Take me to him. Not to the ship."

"Xander." Her voice is quiet. "You're no match for those oni. You need to grow up some more. If your father had to choose between his life and yours, whose do you think he'd pick?"

A terrible scream starts in the soles of my feet and travels up through the top of my head. I scream without words, louder than an ambulance siren. The thing carrying me grunts and lets me slide to the ground so it can double over and put its hands to its ears. Good.

I push myself up and stand in front of Jinx, whose mouth hangs open. Rage makes me shake uncontrollably and I have to concentrate to still myself. "That's not your choice to make, Jinx."

"It is." She grabs me by the shoulders. "Having one Momotaro alive is better than having two dead ones. He's sparing you. Don't you get that?"

"Who?" I break free of her grip. The slimy dead-meat creature grabs me yet again and throws me over its shoulder. This time, it ties me down with something even slimier. "Jinx, this isn't right!"

"It *is*, Xander." Her voice sounds calm now. "Tanuki and I knew you wouldn't leave on your own, so we had to do it this way. I'm sorry. But I know your father would agree."

I close my eyes, feeling my forehead bumping against the creature. The thing is, I remember my father telling me to stay in the house, no matter what. It's true that he wouldn't want me here. He knew I was too wimpy to try something like this. And of course my father would rather die himself than have me die, too.

But that doesn't mean I don't want to find him. How could I live with myself if I made it this far and didn't even try to rescue him?

"You don't know what you're talking about." My voice is as strong as a piece of granite.

She doesn't answer.

The sun bakes the slime on my back dry. I'm almost used to the smell. I guess you really can get used to anything.

Even though crazy yoga people spend all their time on their heads, upside down, it will actually make you pass out if you do it too long. So that's what happens—I black out. And really, that's better.

No dreams of grandfather this time. No nothing. I'm just out, and when I come to again, it's because of the heat.

I'm lying on something hard and hot. My neck has an awful knot in it, and the rest of me aches. I blink slowly. The surface I'm on feels and looks like super-hard black glass. Volcanic rock.

Bright sunlight creeps in through white smoke. I sit up slowly, trying to take everything in. I'm in the middle of a valley.

Jinx said she was taking me to the ship. This isn't the ship. Where are we?

It's a volcanic crater. A circle of mountains surrounds a city that was built in the center. It's abandoned now, though. Husks of houses, shops, factories—they're all here. Rusted-out cars parked next to crumbling sidewalks. Dry yellow grass and bushes sticking out through cracks everywhere. White smoke belches up from crevices in the flat landscape.

A large circular gap surrounds the entire clearing where we now stand. A ring of fire. It's keeping the other wild oni out, I guess, and us inside.

Everywhere, dark shadows scurry and glide among the ruins. I can't tell what the creatures are. Rats, or dogs, maybe? Some walk upright, some close to the ground. But when I see them, tiny hairs I didn't even know I had stand on end.

Run! my body screams. I'm not tied up. I get to my feet and look around with my blurry eyes for Peyton and Inu. There's a fog of volcanic ash that makes everything appear to be happening in black and white, with only a little bit of faded color. I don't see them, or anyone else, just the oni. I'll go find my friends. I take a tentative step forward, and the ground seems to quiver like a water bed.

I put my hands on my thighs, trying to get my bearings. I take a deep breath and get ready.

But before I go anywhere, I hear her voice. "Xander."

I turn to see Jinx lying in the black ashy dirt. Her eyes are almost swollen shut, her face blue and purple. Dozens of scratches mar her face and arms, and dark ash has mingled with her blood, making her look like a burned-out log. Her lower lip is split open and oozing. Somebody's beaten her up.

Even though she's the one who had that yucky-smelling oni bring me here, my gut instinct is to want to get her some ice. "What happened?"

She looks at the ground. A tear splashes down her face.

She makes a noise that sounds like a choked-off word.

"What?" I say. "Tell me."

She makes another strangled, garbled noise, like somebody stabbed her in the back with a rusty knife. Then big, deep sobs erupt.

"Stop!" I say in my sternest tone, hoping to jolt her out of her crying paralysis. "Get up and help me, Jinx."

She blubbers, sucking up snot and blowing it out. Ew. "I can't," she says finally. "Ican'tIcan'tIcan't."

"Yes, you can." I make my voice sound as nice as I possibly can. "Jinx, come on. Help me, and I'll help you."

"I'm sorry," she whispers. "I'm so sorry, Xander."

A foot kicks her in the side, and the girl winces. *Sorry never helped anything, Jinx*, a deep voice says. *Forgiveness means it's already too late. Better not to make a mistake in the first place.*

I look up. Next to Jinx stands the beast-man.

I gasp and, like a little bug trying to run away from a foot that's about to squish it, try to scrabble away. But my body won't do what I want. I am frozen.

When he sees me looking at him, his thin lips break into a smile over the jagged teeth. I shiver involuntarily.

He takes a step closer to me and sticks his tongue out. The three little snakes at the tip dance and hiss over my face. I shut my eyes. Their tongues tickle my lashes, my eyebrows.

I try to back up and yell and punch him all at once, but my body won't do what I tell it. I reach for my sword, and there's nothing at my back. That's right—I don't have it anymore. My muscles go slack and I fall to my knees, my heart thumping.

The tail swishes back and forth as the deep voice speaks. *Momotaro. Jinx told me so much about you.* His mouth doesn't move. The voice purrs low and loud in my head.

I look at Jinx. "You know him?"

A chuckle. *Better than you think, Xander.*

She doesn't answer, just squishes her eyes shut.

The beast-man puts his arm around her. *Don't be shy, Jinx. Acknowledge your father.*

I try to swallow, but my mouth's so dry there's nothing to go down. "This is your father? An oni?"

Not a beast-man, Xander, the thing says in my head. *A satori. Sort of like your Bigfoot. You should have studied with your father. He must be disappointed to have such a lazy son.*

Jinx's shoulders slump, and her voice sounds funny when she speaks, because of her swollen lip. "He told me he would help you get back to the ship, Xander."

"Yeah, right." Volcanic ash tickles my throat, making me cough. I manage to produce enough saliva to spit into the dirt. Rude, I know, but sometimes you have to be rude to survive. "I should have listened to Peyton. We should have left you behind."

She doesn't answer, just closes her eyes. But something prevents me from being too mad at her. It is weird that she got beat up instead of me. . . . Something's not right.

The beast-man chuckles. *What Jinx failed to realize was that not all oni keep their word as readily as the kappa. Even if an oni is your own father.*

I look at broken Jinx, who is crying and bloody, and this awful thing who is her father. Who abandoned her and forced her to live in a jungle. Who beat her so horribly. Suddenly I'm not mad at her anymore.

Because I understand.

We all want to believe our parents will do the right thing. Just like I've always hoped against hope that my mother will come home someday. Jinx wanted to believe her father would keep his word.

She's just a kid. Like me. Only, I've got a father and a grandmother who care about me, and faithful friends like Peyton and Inu. She has nothing. Nobody.

I stare up at the beast-man and instead of fear, I feel something else.

Resolve.

I draw my head up and square my shoulders.

Let us go, I say, strong in my head. *Let us go and I won't harm you.*

The beast-man's eyes widen for a moment. Then he throws back his head and laughs. "Oh, look, it thinks it can fight. How adorable." He speaks aloud this time, and Jinx stares at me. He gestures around him. "Will you let all of us go, then, noble Momotaro? For we all stand and fight as one."

I look beyond him. Things are moving in the ruins.

Those creatures I saw before are not rats or dogs. They're monsters. Oni.

Thousands of them.

They're in the sky, too.

Creatures of all shapes and sizes weave and bob above us on leathery wings. Blobs of flesh. Swords with legs. Troll-like things. It's like every scary fairy-tale monster I know—and a lot I've never imagined—has come to life.

I swear, every hair on my arm stands on end. I feel the overwhelming need to run away. But I still can't move.

"Dude," I hear a voice—a real voice that I recognize—whisper. Peyton!

I can't locate him immediately. The voice seems to be coming from outer space. Then I spot him, a few dozen yards to my right.

He's trussed up in a rope net that is hanging from a giant, ancient tree. His wings look mashed. Inu dangles in another bag next to him.

They are suspended above a smoking, hissing gray pit. I'm pretty sure we're on top of the active volcano.

Inu manages one pitiful little woof.

"Peyton!" I shout. "Inu!"

Peyton lifts his head. A long, deep gash extends from his hairline, across his eyebrow and cheekbone, all the way to his left nostril. The whites of his eyes are crisscrossed with red, so bad that the damage is visible from this distance. His skin is a mottled purple. "Don't come any closer." His eyes look down into the smoky pit.

I follow his gaze.

The deep pit is filled with rice.

In the middle of the rice, buried up to his neck, is my father.

CHAPTER 24

My father's face is turned upward, his eyes closed. He is missing his glasses. His skin is an icy blue, his mouth slack and open.

"Dad!" I have to get to him. My muscles twitch but do nothing more.

We move as one, the beast-man says, and all those things in the air suddenly pause and shift. They coagulate into a giant sphere, like swarming bees. Pointing toward me. *It is over, Xander.*

He is correct. I'm done. I shut my eyes and brace myself for the onslaught. *Good-bye, everybody. Sorry I failed you.*

Iie! My grandfather's voice shouts in my ear, shoving at me from the inside. *You will not give up.*

Like a snap of the fingers, it comes to me, what I must do. *Move,*

I command my muscles, and I get up and start running. I think I hear the beast-man laughing, but I don't care. Let him try to catch me. Nobody can stop me.

I jump in to save my father.

"Don't!" Peyton says hoarsely.

Too late. My feet plummet in, the rice giving way, and it feels like I'm dropping into water. Except I can't stay afloat. I keep on sinking and sinking.

I manage to find and grab my father's shoulders. He doesn't move. He's stiff and cold. Grayish vapors rise mistily around him.

I wrap my arms around his neck, stick my head above the rice. I put my cheek against his and feel just the faintest little bit of air *whoosh* out of his nose. I keep imagining. I keep hoping. "Dad!" I yell again, and shake him. Nothing happens. It's like trying to shake a huge tree.

Hot tears fall out of my eyes onto his neck where they turn into powdery ice. That's how cold he is.

"Please," I whisper. "Please don't be dead."

He descends with me as the rice pulls us under. I try to climb back up, to save us, but there's nothing to grab on to. My fingers comb through the rice.

The grains swallow my dad completely. I'm next. I tilt my head back. Up above, the beast-man looks down at me triumphantly, his tongue pulsing in and out of his mouth. And above him I see Peyton, strung up and immobile in his big webby net, his eyes huge and horrified. *Sorry you had to watch this*, I say silently. Then I sink.

Rice swallows my neck, starts filling my ears. I cough and try to hold my breath, but it's no use. Rice goes up through my nose, into my lungs, and presses into my eyelids. And then everything goes black.

I'm dizzy. I stand up slowly, expecting to spit out rice, but my mouth and my nostrils are clear.

Where am I? Am I dead? Everything looks fuzzy. I try to breathe deep and slow. To not panic. It's one of the hardest things I've ever had to do.

Four walls, a wooden floor, windows come into focus. My house. I'm in my house! I want to cry from relief.

I look around, dazed, at a familiar scene. Dad and Inu are sitting on the couch. Peyton sits in the armchair at one end—no wings in sight—and Obāchan's in the kitchen, bustling around. She has cleaned everything up. There's no evidence that an earthquake or tsunami ever hit. It's dim in here, though. Why doesn't Obāchan have any lights on? I crane my head up at where the ceiling lights are—or where they should be. Nothing there but black sky. The roof's not finished yet, I guess.

Maybe it was all just a strange bad dream. Caused by eating too much of Obāchan's chicken and Flamin' Hot Cheetos. Or maybe I passed out during the earthquake, and I'm only waking up now. "Hey." I test out my voice. It sounds normal. "Hey," I say again, louder, getting the cobwebs out.

The others don't respond right away. I sit in the armchair opposite Peyton, my heart rate slowing. I did imagine it all. There was no tsunami, no boat, no wings, no demons, no Momotaro. Life is back to normal—heck, it never even changed.

What a relief.

But, though I shouldn't, I feel more than a little bit disappointed.

I'm just plain old ordinary Xander after all.

Dad strokes Inu's furry head. There's no sign of the dog's injuries. "I'm glad you've come around." His voice is super calm, even for Dad.

Peyton stretches in his chair. He's wearing a baseball cap backward. "Hey, dude," he says. He tosses a baseball up and down in his hand. "Took you long enough to get here. Want to play some *CraftWorlds?*"

Obāchan comes in, wiping her hands with a dishtowel. "I'm so happy you're home." She kind of laughs then. It doesn't sound quite right. Not like her.

The hairs on my arms stand up again. This is wrong.

I examine the scene more closely, and then I'm absolutely sure. You know how I know it's wrong?

Obāchan *always* tells Peyton to take off his hat when he comes inside. There's *zero* percent chance Obāchan wouldn't have marched over there and yanked it off his head. He'd be sporting serious, matted-down hat hair.

"This isn't right." I move backward. "Not right at all."

Obāchan and Inu and Peyton and Dad all look at me, and their eyes are blank. They're here, but not *here* here. Like those wax figures of celebrities that look *almost* lifelike, but not quite. Or an animatronic figure. I've seen mice that look like they have more soul than these fakers.

I back up a little.

They all start walking toward me, and it's like one of those zombie movies, the way they lift their limbs oh-so-slowly. I wouldn't be surprised if they tried to eat my brains.

"Xander," Obāchan says.

"Xander," Dad says.

"Xander," Peyton says.

"Xander," Inu says.

Inu?

No way I'm believing my senses this time.

The floor shivers and slants, sliding the zombie imposters away from me. That gives me a little time.

I turn and run for the front door, but I hear something on the other side that makes me stop in my tracks. Some creature, scratching at the wood. I look to my right and left; there's nowhere to go. Then the door swings open abruptly, the bell chiming its hollow ding-dong.

Lovey stands on my front porch. Her blond hair is gone and (I want to wash my eyeballs with bleach), she's got no clothes on— because she's completely covered with reddish ape hair. It both looks like her and doesn't look like her at all. But I recognize her anyway.

She smiles at me with feral eyes and big yellow teeth. "Hey there, Xander."

I back away, but not too far, because my fake family is gaining on me. "Are you *joking* right now, Lovey?" Ugh. She might just be a figment of my imagination, but I still don't want to deal with the likes of her right now.

"Even when you were hiding from your true self, you knew what I was." She puts her right index finger in the space between my collarbones and draws it down my chest.

"A horrible, horrible person?" I flinch away.

"A satori. Well, good for you, Mr. Momotaro."

"Xander," Inu whispers, getting closer.

"It's bad enough that you bug me at school. Now you gotta bug me in my dreams, too?" I try to sidestep Lovey. How do I get rid of her? Shove her? I reach for my salt container, hoping it's here with me in this dream world, but my belt is empty.

During the pause, she grabs my shirt collar with both hands and yanks me toward her. "Don't go, Xander. You know, I only ever bothered you because I liked you."

I let out a burst of laughter. "I'm sorry, but it's never going to work out between us." I smack at her hands, but she tightens her grip and draws me closer. Is she trying to kiss me? I turn my face away as best I can.

The white plaster walls start turning pink and grow thick with swampy moisture that drips down.

This house is a mouth. Attached to who-knows-what. I need out of here, *now*.

Desperately I look over Lovey's shoulder. It's pitch-black outside. We're floating in nothingness. Outer space, with no stars and no sun. My lungs shrivel as the oxygen-less, subfreezing air hits them.

I'm going to jump out there and find my real live, breathing father. My father is waiting for me. I can feel him.

"That way lies death," Lovey whispers, her breath no better than her looks.

"Every way lies death. What's one more?" I thrust my arm between her hands, grab her right thumb, and twist it back as far as I can. She yelps and releases me.

I wrest away from her and leap straight through the door. Into blackness.

CHAPTER 25

For a second, I think I've died for real this time. Coldness surrounds me, as if I've jumped into a vat of ice cubes. My insides feel like I just drank a jumbo-size Slurpee.

Everything goes numb. There is nothing but blackness all around me. Time stops. I have no sense of floating or falling. I'm just standing still, unable to move or feel or see.

I'm frozen. And alone, a speck of something smaller than dust in all the galaxies in the universe. I will never find anyone again.

I remember the Momotaro comic, how he dreamed of a cold and dark land.

I'm there. I'm here. This is what Momotaro saw.

My heart has a tight cage around it, squeezing until I know it will burst.

If I could move, I'd be clawing at the air like a drowning, desperate rat. *Make it stop!* I shout in my head, but nobody hears.

Is this what it will be like forever? Me and this unending darkness?

My mind relaxes. *Accept this fate,* something whispers. *Being in nothingness is easier than trying to keep fighting, Xander.*

I jolt back to myself. *No, no, no.*

This isn't the end. I force my brain to calm down. To think without trying too hard. To just know what I need to do, instinctively.

Dad! Peyton, Inu, Jinx!

Something invisible pushes away from me, but not far enough.

Mom! I scream inside, with every single one of my cells, and I feel longing and love and pain stronger than what I felt when Inu was injured, or when Dad went missing. The little BB of hurt I've been carrying for years expands into a cannonball again, filling me from the top of my head down to my feet.

Whatever force is holding me shatters like a soft snowball thrown against brick, and then there's wind, and I'm falling. Freefalling, like I'm on a roller coaster without a seat belt on and I can't see if there's even a ground to hit.

Without effort, I picture a harness around me, a parachute better than the one I made when I was little and wanted to jump off the roof. Instantly, something yanks on my shoulders. Sure enough, there are ropes holding me tight. Saving me.

Light rises up around me, like spotlights on a stage. I land on my feet, squinting and blinking until my eyes adjust. I hear a tapping, like somebody typing on a keyboard.

I'm back at school. Mr. Stedman sits at the computer.

"Did your father punish you the way you deserve?" Mr. Stedman smiles cruelly. "With a belt, I should hope. Useless boy." The slightest flicker of tongue peeks out from between his lips. His black eyes shimmer under the fluorescent lights.

I stand in the middle of the rows of desks and look squarely into those eyes, though there are no irises to focus on. It's like looking at an empty space. I'm still shaking-scared, but it doesn't matter. All that matters is helping my dad and my friends. "Tell me your name, beast-man."

"Gozu." The monster man smiles and allows his arms to redden and flicker back into slimy scales. He grows in height and width, like Bruce Banner turning into the Hulk, and now I'm staring up at him. I come up to maybe his upper leg someplace, as though I'm a toddler.

I was mistaken. How am I ever going to beat him?

"What do you want with me?" I glance around the room, looking for escape or weapons. The windows outside are black, as they were at my "house."

Gozu's tongue flickers in and out. "I'm here to take you into the underworld, Xander."

"Aren't we already there?" School being the oni underworld

would actually be the least surprising thing that's happened during this whole adventure.

Gozu chuckles softly. "Where your ship landed is merely the dwelling place for oni, Xander. Where oni assume physical form. There is also a place where we wait. Where we are still demons, but without bodies. You have no idea what the true underworld is like. This is a vacation spot in comparison. Wait until you meet Ozuno."

My entire body tenses, as though some Momotaro gene inside me recognizes the name. "Who is that?"

"The oni king," Gozu says simply. He walks toward me. "All I had to do was get you to voluntarily leave your body. Make you vulnerable. And now you are mine to take. Defenseless and weak." He shakes his head. "It was so easy. Stupid, pitiful Momotaros. Forever enslaved to us. You will do our bidding, and we will take over the whole earth." He smiles, an action more sinister than the worst dictator's frown, and suddenly I feel very, very sorry for Jinx.

"You're not the king, then?" I back up.

"No. And glad of it." He laughs. "I'm getting paid handsomely."

So Gozu's a bounty hunter. "What do you even need with money? You're a demon."

He shimmers and turns into Mr. Stedman again. "We can turn into whoever we want. Even a social studies teacher."

Mr. Stedman with his sorry comb-over. I start laughing. I laugh so hard I have to lean against a wall.

"This is not a laughing matter!" Gozu/Stedman says. With a scowl he turns back into the oni.

I shake my head. "You're showing me you can turn into any human in the world, and you pick *that* guy? What a waste. How about an interesting person, like George Washington or somebody?"

Gozu shimmers and turns into my father. My father with black eyes. "How about him?" He strides toward me. "I'll choke the laughter out of your scrawny neck while I'm in your father's form." His hands go up.

I should be afraid, but I'm not. He can't hurt me. Not now. I'm not in my body, just as I wasn't when I was in the waterfall or talking to my grandfather in my dream.

My mind is my land. Not Gozu's. "Go ahead and try. I'd like to see how forgiving Ozuno is when you fail."

Gozu growls and reverts back to his oni form.

I leap away to the other side of the room, look around for something to throw at him. The textbooks on the shelves say *World History*, same as in our class. I pick one up and open it.

Empty.

For some reason this freaks me out the most. A blank history book.

I remember all the times over the past week I stared at page 150. All about climate change.

The text appears on the pages.

I feel heat next to my arm. Gozu.

I jump up onto a desk and skip over the tops across the room, like I'm running over stepping stones, back to the other side.

I made those words appear, just by picturing them. My heart pounds. This is my talent.

I can do things. With my imagination. Somewhere in my head lives this thing—this *being* of its own, almost—that creates. That comic book. The samurai in the video game. Me swimming to Peyton. Turning acid into gel. Telling my real self what to do when I was in the waterfall. Exiting the house through space. Putting the words in the book.

I just don't completely understand how to control it.

Before, I did things while I was unconscious. Now I've done a few things while I was awake—but how?

I hold out my hand and imagine the weight of my sword in it. The cool scabbard. Coming to me from where they are keeping it, like a trained falcon flying to my hand.

Gozu whips his tail around and smacks me sideways, catching me under the ribs. *Oof!* I fall to the floor, the wind knocked out of me. "You're wrong. I *can* hurt you here."

No sword appears. I look at the textbooks, and I make something else happen.

The books fly off the shelves at Gozu, striking him hard, so fast that he's buried. Now there's just a big pile of books on the floor.

I run for the door. My hand closes around the knob. Sticky, just like in real life. My mind sure remembers a lot of little stuff.

Hands clamp around my neck, lifting me up and up. My legs dangle off the ground. I flail and hit at his arms and kick at his chest, but it does no good. He shakes me like Inu does with his chew toys.

I pry one of his fingers up enough to get a little air. "Hunhhh." My larynx is getting crushed.

"Come, Xander," the demon hisses. The snake tongue darts out. "Time to meet your new master."

The classroom dissolves. We're in the middle of freezing-cold nothing again. My body floats up, perpendicular to Gozu's. My head gets light. I might be about to die for real. *Sorry, Dad*, I think. *Sorry, Ojīchan.* I feel my mind drift, like it does when I'm about to fall asleep.

And, oh, sleep will feel so good.

My heartbeat slows, fades. Here I go.

Then my father and my grandfather appear in my mind. Solid and real. I look at them through bleary eyes. I'm having a waking dream within a dream.

Unlock yourself, Xander, my father says, so quiet it's like he's only saying it in my head. Which he is.

Faith.

Gozu's hands squeeze my neck harder.

Imagination.

Whose voice am I hearing? I don't recognize it.

Remember the Momotaro comic. Everything you need is in it.

The voice is mine.

Oh.

Momotaro was an artist. Like me, when I draw or make things— what do I do? How do I do it?

I pause for a moment, and then I know. The answer is that I just *do*, without questioning or thinking or doubt.

When I create, when I draw my pictures or I'm programming my computer games, I'm in what my father calls the Zone. The place where my imagination bubbles up without stopping. Where hours can pass and it seems like minutes.

Where I'm in a beautiful waking dream.

I don't need to be totally unconscious.

I need to let my imagination do its work. Be free, without worrying or trying to make it happen.

I take a deep breath. My mind paints a picture, as easily as remembering a memory. *Don't force it.*

The darkness disappears.

My home. The first fresh powder of the year. I stand outside the house, in the trees. Thinking about getting my skis out so I can go down our little hill.

My feet go back down where they belong. Gozu loses his grip and makes a disbelieving noise deep in his throat. He repositions his hands around my throat, but I've already taken a breath.

It begins to snow. I stick out my tongue and taste it, already knowing what it will be. It's what I want it to be.

Salt.

Purifying salt. It's all around us.

I stare into Gozu's face. His snake tongue jumps out and touches my nose, but the little snakes are crying for help now. His legs begin to burn and melt.

He glares and shakes me again. The snow-salt stops. My neck crackles like popcorn, and blinding pain lances through my skull. Ow.

The landscape fades out as if night's falling fast. Darkness is returning. Coldness tingles through my fingertips.

In front of me, Inu and Peyton and Dad all stare at me, buried by the snow. Melting in it like they're oni, their eyes dripping gooey messes. *You've failed us,* they whisper.

I'm afraid again. The fear grips my heart harder than Gozu's gripping my neck.

Dad, Ojīchan, I call in my head. Nobody appears.

Come on, Xander Musashi, I say in my head. *Come on. You did it once. You can do it again.*

I shut my eyes, and now I don't picture anything. I just feel it instead.

I breathe in and out. The air, so fresh and cold, stings my lungs pleasantly. Christmas coming soon, the first day of winter break. I smile. I feel my family waiting for me inside the house. I can sense their presence, even if I can't see them and in reality they're way far away.

I'm bringing all of us home.

My hands warm and I open my eyes. Light beats back the night, filling every shadow and icy hidden spot. But the light's not coming from the sun.

It's coming from me. From my fingertips and my belly button and maybe even my eyes.

I'm filling up the darkness.

Gozu lets go of me. I drop to the ground, but I don't fall. He staggers back. I raise my hands and the white light hisses against the slime of his skin. Dissolves him like a marshmallow held too long over the fire.

And then I shout the phrase I shouted in my dream once before. I know what it means now. *"Anata ni wa nani mo nai!"*

You are nothing!

Gozu screams and, just as suddenly as he appeared, vanishes back into the blank void where he lives.

Into nothingness.

CHAPTER 26

At the edge of the forest, Dad stands, watching. The proudest smile I've ever seen stretches across his face. It's as if I won the presidential election, got straight As, and remembered to make my bed, all at once.

Then this world falls away, starting with the sky, like building blocks tumbling over.

I'm back in the mountain of rice with my dad. But our heads are above the rice.

"Xander," he whispers hoarsely. The blue drains from his face, the pinkness seeps back in, and he looks human again. He manages a weak smile. "Your grandmother sent you?"

I nod. "We have to get out." I struggle to keep my face tilted, to get enough air within the rice.

I hear the sound of a scuffle above us. A monkeylike shape crawls over a branch, to Peyton and Inu. A sword flashes, cutting through the ropes, carefully, one by one. Inu and Peyton fall to the ground, and then I can't see them anymore.

"Are you okay?" I yell. "Get out of here, Peyton! Take Inu and fly!"

Some creature like a demon pterodactyl plummets through the air toward the tree, squawking, claws bared.

Jinx stands upright on the gnarled branch. "Xander! Heads up!" she shouts.

She throws the sword, my sword, through the air like a spear. Right at my face, and I can't move out of the way. I gasp.

The sword slices into the rice, right next to me.

The pterodactyl thing screams and snatches Jinx up.

"Jinx!" I call hoarsely. But I can't do a thing from here. I watch as the bird creature carries Jinx away in its claws, her terrified face a stark white against its dark feathers.

"Grab the sword," Dad says, his voice still weak. "We can use it."

I don't know how the sword is going to help us now, but I dig in the rice until I can feel its hilt. I grip it and pull it partway out, and Dad puts his hands over mine.

He shuts his eyes and his lips move, but I can't tell what he's saying. He drives the blade toward the bottom of the pit. The sword moves through the rice like a rocket, and we're jerked down with it, our bodies turning upside down.

And then, by the time I take another breath, we're outside the rice pit, under the tree where Peyton and Inu were hanging. They're nowhere in sight now.

I blink, dizzy at being suddenly upright, still holding on to the sword with my father.

"How'd you do that?"

Dad lets go of the sword. He smiles at me, the way he does when I've learned something he's been trying to teach me. "You'll find out soon enough." Then he staggers backward, and I grab his shoulders and help him sit on the ground.

Around us, the ring of fire blazes and crackles. It separates us from the masses of oni trying to get at us from the other side, which I'm both glad and sorry for—glad because it's protecting us, sorry because it's pinning us between the pit and the tree and freedom.

"We have to get out of here!" I say to Dad. "But how can we go through the fire?"

He shakes his head. Without his glasses, he looks odd. "We can't get around all of them."

"Then what do we do?" Now that my dad's okay, I expect him to take over. Be the real Momotaro.

He shakes his head again, and he hacks wetly from deep in his chest, gasping for breath. "I don't know."

I look around for the salt netsuke and find it near the edge of the pit. Maybe we can throw salt up at them until they're gone. I'm not sure. A piercing desperation slices through my chest. I try to feel like

I did with Gozu, full of love and hope. It's definitely not working. "Dad," I whisper, "how do I make it work again?"

"Make what work?"

"My Momotaro power! Imagination! Picturing stuff and making it real?"

Dad wrinkles his brow. "Is that how you defeated them? That's new."

My heart sinks. So he doesn't know how to do this. "Yeah, that's how I defeated Gozu when we were unconscious. But what about now?"

"I don't know, Xander." Dad sounds defeated. He leans against the tree trunk. This is the worst I've ever seen him. Even worse than when Mom left. Maybe being stuck in the rice messed up his head. "You must be in internal harmony to access all your powers."

Well, harmony's definitely not happening right now. Instead, all I feel is useless panic. Like I want to flail around like a trapped chicken. We're going to have to give up.

My stomach twists like knotted earbud cords. Now there will be no Momotaro at all. The oni will win. California will stay under-water. "Dad, come on. We have to do this. I have to figure this out."

My father just coughs again. He's too weak from his ordeal.

What can I do?

Just then, a whooshing sound makes me look up. Peyton lands crookedly in front of me, holding Inu. His wings look pretty dirty and messed up. "Xander, what are you doing having all the fun while

we were trussed up in that tree?" He puts Inu down and turns to Dad with a big grin. "Mr. Miyamoto! Wow. When you get captured, you really get captured. Are you okay?"

Dad nods weakly. "I've felt better in my life. But it doesn't matter—we've got to get you boys out of here."

Inu yelps and rushes my father, but he seems to know that he shouldn't jump on Dad just yet. Instead, he settles for licking Dad's hands and rubbing against his legs like a cat.

"Inu, my boy, I've missed you, too." Dad scratches Inu's chest.

I grab Peyton's arm. "Did you see Jinx?"

Peyton's eyes shine in the fire. He shakes his plumed head. "I saw that bird flying off with her after she saved us. But I was on the ground and I couldn't help her."

Dad glances at Peyton, then does a double take. He rubs his eyes. "You have wings," he whispers. Then he grins. "I used to have a friend like you. Ha. All this time and I didn't know you were going to be Xander's pheasant." He breaks into a cough again and this time spits up a big wad of rice. "Life is full of surprises."

I wonder what happened to his friend? Now's not the time to ask.

"Listen," Dad says, "the only way out is up."

We look at the fire ring and then upward. "Okay, so what's the plan?" I ask.

My father coughs. "Peyton, you must take Xander right now. Get out of here and fly to the boat. Quick. Go back home."

"What about you and Inu?" Peyton asks.

Dad puts his hand on the dog's ruff, and Inu sits. "You can't take all of us, Peyton. You must take Xander."

Peyton's silent for a moment, looking from my father to the dog to me.

Oh no. I hold up my hand. "I'm not leaving anybody behind. Not ever again."

My father ignores my outburst. "Please, Peyton. I have to stay here and defeat the oni who created the tsunami and put me here. Otherwise California will remain underwater. The needs of the people are greater than the life of one person." He straightens up and, for a second, appears to be my same-old father. "Now that I'm out of the rice, I can fight. Don't worry about me, Xander. I'll meet you back home."

"No, you won't!" I point at him. "You're not strong enough to fight, Dad. You're coming with me. At once."

"Hey." Peyton's voice is scratchy and sorrowful in my ear. "Come on, Xander. You know your father's right." He puts his arms around me, under my armpits. "We have to do this." He hoists me up.

"Put me down!" I scream. I drop to my knees, out of Peyton's grasp. "I'm not going anywhere." I can come up with a better idea. Where's my grand imagination now? All I can think of is how much I hurt, and how much I don't want to lose my father and my dog all over again.

Inu curls up next to my father and barks twice, sharply, at me. *Go, Xander.*

Dad's color is draining again. He looks so pale. I have to get him out of here or he might die for real, oni or no oni. How can he possibly fight? "You must, Xander. You must live on. You will be needed again later."

The oni screech and holler as they try to penetrate the flames. Sooner or later one of them will jump or fly through.

My eyes fill with tears, washing away the ash from the volcanoes and the fire ring. "Then what good was all this? I came to rescue you." Jinx was right—my father was willing to sacrifice himself for me.

Inu thumps his tail and whines. He barks sharply.

Peyton's chin juts out. I recognize that expression—I've seen it on him when he's pitching a losing game and he's putting up one last good fight. "We don't have a choice." He puts his arms around me and begins flapping his wings.

"No!" I scream, reaching out my arms. "Inu! Dad!"

But Peyton's already beginning to lift me into the air.

I squeeze my eyes shut. I imagine the forest where I saw Ojīchan. See him standing in the center. He nods at me.

I'm Momotaro. The peach boy warrior.

Half-breed weakling, I hear the bounty hunter say in my ear.

I open my eyes and look down at the scene below.

Maybe I'm not weak because I'm half. Maybe my mixed blood

gives me an advantage over the other Momotaro. After all, every single one of my ancestors eventually got defeated.

Maybe being different is good, like my grandma hoped.

"Go back down," I say to Peyton. Command him. I sound like I'm a policeman or something. "I have a plan."

CHAPTER 27

P eyton lands back on the ground and I kneel by Dad. "Come
on. Put your arm around my neck. Hurry!"

"Xander." Dad's voice booms like the old days. "Leave."

"I'm the Momotaro now." I sound just as stern as he does.
Somewhat to my surprise, Dad puts his arm around me, maybe
because he's too exhausted to fight anymore. He can barely stand.
I put my hand on Inu, and Peyton grabs my shoulder. I imagine
that big ball of light coming out of me again like it did with Gozu.
It will envelop everything like an explosion. All the oni will be
destroyed.

Nothing happens.

I squeeze my eyes shut and imagine it again. Ball of light! Work, powers, work! I try not to try too hard, but of course that makes me seize up like machinery in need of oil. Argh.

Suddenly I hear a girl screaming. Jinx. She's on the other side of the flames, with the oni. She's trying to fight them off with a big stick, practically a tree trunk, but there are too many. She falls on her back.

I leap over to where she is, leaving Peyton to hold up Dad. Jinx's whole body appears a wavy red through the fire. "Jinx, wait! I'll help you!"

"Get out of here!" she yells. "Go home!"

It reminds me of when I first saw her, through that ring of acid.

The acid.

Of course!

I take out the sword and thrust it through the flame.

The hilt heats under my hand as if I'm putting my palm on a hot stove. My skin smokes. I shout and almost drop the sword. No. Hold on. I'm not leaving without my whole crew. I have to get all of us to the ship.

My hand stops hurting. The flesh is the color of steel, the same color as my sword, as if the weapon is an extension of me. Or I'm an extension of it. Maybe I'm going to be like Captain Hook now, only with a blade for a hand.

Go home, I think. I don't know how, but I have faith that something will happen. Something that I make happen.

A breach appears in the red-orange fire. A dark oval.

A doorway. A portal.

"You did it!" Dad's eyes light up. He glances at me. "You go first, Xander. I'll hold the sword."

"No." I won't let him try to get left behind again. "Go!" I bark at Peyton and Inu.

"How do you know we won't just burst into flame when we go through?" Peyton says.

"I just made a doorway appear in a wall of flame. I'm pretty sure you can trust me." I jerk my head toward the portal. "Have some faith!" Just like my grandmother said.

Inu jumps through. Peyton stops arguing and follows.

"You go, Xander." My father's still insisting.

"Dad, sheesh. Now who's not listening?" I have no choice. I shove my dad through the portal with my free hand.

To my left, Jinx crawls away from the hissing and growling oni. "I'll be fine, Xander!" One claws at her experimentally, like a lion playing with its prey, ripping at her arm. Then it throws her, limp as a piece of meat, right next to me.

"I thought you'd stopped lying!" I shout.

She struggles to rise, manages to get up on her hands and knees.

The doorway's closing, turning back into a solid wall of flame. My hand starts to feel like it's melting. I reach through the fire and grab Jinx by the wrist as quickly as I can. If it hurts, I can't feel the pain yet. With every bit of strength I have left, I yank her through the fire and push her through the shrinking doorway.

A phalanx of oni lunge for me. At the last possible second, I jump through the door.

They disappear as if a curtain's been drawn.

It feels like I've jumped down a set of stairs.

I land on my ship's deck.

CHAPTER 28

I should have died at least six times today, I think. I lie on the deck for a minute, grateful for the blue sky, the faces of my friends and family. The fact that I'm still breathing.

Then Inu nudges my cheek, and I stroke him between the eyes and scratch his woolly chest until he drools all over me. "Inu!" I chastise, but not really, because I'm so happy we're here.

"Xander." My father helps me sit up, hugs me, Inu leaning against both of us at once. Now Dad feels warmer, more normal. "Thank you."

I hug him back hard. "Dad, I'm mad at you."

He rocks me back and forth like I'm a little kid. For once, I don't mind. "Why's that?"

"You didn't tell me about any of this stuff before! For the first time in my life, you had something I wanted to learn." I let go of him to give him my best mock-glare.

He laughs, tries to push up his nonexistent glasses. "Xander, I don't know if you know this, but you happen to be very stubborn. I gave you stories. You enjoyed them when you were younger—like when you made the comic. These days, though, you tell me you'd rather play video games. I offer to teach, and you wander off into your own daydream world. I can only force-feed a person so much. You have to *want* to learn."

"Yeah, yeah, yeah." It's true. Of course it's true. And honestly, even though I'm rolling my eyes, it feels really good to be lectured again. I hug my dad again.

He touches my hair with one too-thin hand. "And I see your Momotaro hair has come in."

"Oh yeah. At the sides." My hand goes up to my temple self-consciously.

"No. Look." Dad takes my sword and holds the polished blade before my face, like a mirror.

All of my hair is as shiny silver as a brand-new quarter, gleaming in the sun.

I wrinkle my nose. "Great. Now I look old, like you."

"Thanks a lot." Dad pretends to be huffy. "It is a mark of honor."

I touch it—it feels the same as always. "If you say so . . ."

"You'll get used to it." Dad smiles at me.

Peyton's reflection appears behind my head. "Hey. I can see myself in your hair, dude! I'll never need a mirror again!"

"Guess that means you'll be spending most of your time staring at it." I turn and Peyton gives me a fist bump. "Everything all in one piece?"

He pats his torso. "Eh. It feels like I might have left a piece of my liver back there, but other than that, I'm good."

Peyton sits down on the deck, directly in front of me. "Ahhhhhh. Never thought a wooden floor would feel like a featherbed. It's just good to sit down." He smiles at me, leaning back on his palms. He looks like he just emerged from a coal mine; he's completely covered in black soot.

I probably don't look much better. "Are your wings okay?" I ask him. I touch one. They look broken, or smaller.

Dad bends a wing gently. "They're disappearing."

Peyton widens his eyes. "Disappearing? No! I *like* having wings! And flying. Oh man—I'd be so the king of basketball."

Dad shrugs. "Sorry, Peyton. No wings in our mortal home."

"Where's home?" Jinx's voice pipes up from the other side of the deck. If Peyton looks bad, she looks worse. Even worse than she did before. Her arms are crisscrossed with deep scratches and cuts that might need stitches. One of her eyes is totally swollen shut.

"I'd hate to see the other guy." I point to her wounds.

She laughs shortly and then puts on her tough-girl expression. "Yeah, that oni bird might be missing a couple of eyes. Oh well, that's what happens when you hold me against my will. It's not pretty."

"Jinx." Dad's face breaks into another grin. "My girl." He hurries across the deck. "Are you all right?"

"You know her?" I ask. *My girl? What?*

Jinx shrinks away from him, holding up her hands like a boxer. "Don't touch me! I don't know you."

Dad takes a step back. "Jinx," he says slowly, "you are the daughter of my wife's best friend. Your mother was maid-of-honor at our wedding."

"That must've been before she met my father," Jinx says shortly.

I say to Dad, "You know her father's an oni."

"It's not her fault who her father is. Remember how these oni can disguise themselves."

I think about Lovey and Mr. Stedman. Are they real people, or oni? Maybe they won't be at school after break! A guy can always hope.

But I seriously doubt my life is going to be any easier now. As Jinx said, I'm Momotaro. I'm never going to be normal again.

Dad bends toward Jinx. "You look just like your mother. Except your hair's lighter."

"My mother thought my father was the lead singer of her favorite cover band." Jinx points at her Misfits T-shirt as she walks in my direction. "After she married him she discovered he had, like, a slight anger-management issue."

"Understatement of the year." I grin.

Jinx grimaces slightly. "Well, my mother has her own problems.

She ended up leaving me with him. She still doesn't know the truth about him. Heck, I didn't know the truth, either, until two years ago."

Now she's next to me, blinking hard. "I'm sorry, Xander. I really thought Gozu would keep his promise this time." Her face is as twisted as a wax paper wrapper on a piece of saltwater taffy.

I can't be too mad at her. Who knows what horrible things her oni dad did to her? Making her live in oni country would be bad enough. He probably also made her hang out with the stinky carrion oni.

Besides, she helped us. A lot. She led us out of the cave. Healed my arm. Took us to the river. Found us the plane to sleep in. Saved Inu. Cut Peyton and Inu down from the tree. Told me to use the fire.

She's not that easy to get along with, but maybe that's okay sometimes. In her own awkward, bitter way, Jinx pushed me to be better. To try harder. To not give up, all so I could prove her wrong.

I hold out my hand to her. "No hard feelings?"

Her face breaks into a grin. I swear, she either looks as mad as a Disney villain, or her smile makes you smile. "None." She shakes my hand firmly.

"Uh, I have some hard feelings," Peyton calls. "Right over here."

"Dude. You'll get over them." I wave him off.

Dad gives me a friendly slap on the back. "You're a good man, Xander. Just like I knew."

A warm feeling washes over me. Pride, I guess.

"You'll come home with us," Dad tells Jinx. "We will take care of you until we find your mother."

Jinx shrugs. "Good luck with that. I'm pretty sure she doesn't want to be found."

He touches her shoulder. "You never know, Jinx. You never know."

Peyton stands up. "They're gone. They're really, really gone." He turns around, his whole body slumping, to show us. Yes, his wings have disappeared.

"But you're still super buff," I point out. "At least you have that. And big muscles are a lot cooler than silver hair."

Peyton straightens his spine. The hair on his head sticks up even bigger now, as if it grew a couple of inches, too. "That's right. Call me Unstoppable now. Can that be my nickname?"

"I thought Birdbrain was your nickname." Jinx offers him a little smile, like an olive branch.

Peyton snorts. "Birdbrain, Monkey Girl, and Peach Boy. Yes. Lamest superhero names ever!" He holds out his hand for a fist bump, and Jinx returns it. Inu lets out a happy bark, and at that moment, I know we're all going to be okay.

"Now I have to do one more thing. I hope it won't scare you. Though I doubt, at this point, anything will." Dad unbuttons one of the side pockets in his cargo pants. He takes out a small ivory whistle, shaped like a catfish, with whiskers and all. He jerks his head toward the galley. "Pull up anchor and go down below."

"Why?" I ask.

"You'll see." He wraps a length of rope around his waist and secures it to the cabin. "Xander, you can stay here if you like."

The others go below, and Jinx closes the hatch. The ship drifts out toward the open ocean. Away from volcanoes and snow women and oni.

Dad wraps rope around my waist, too, and then he hands me the whistle.

I blow it.

It sounds like I'm blowing it underwater, or it's filled with water. I try it again. "Is it working?"

Dad nods and takes it back. "Careful. Not too much."

"Nothing happened." I look over the ship's rail.

Something big and white swims up under the water. Bigger than the biggest whale I've ever seen or imagined.

A round *O* of a mouth peeks out, surrounded by whiskers as long as Christmas trees. It's a giant catfish.

"Namazu," Dad whispers.

It looks at Dad with its great rolling eyes. It seems to be waiting. Dad nods at it. *"Saki ni ike."* *Go ahead*.

It dives under and then begins swimming around us.

Faster and faster and faster, in circles that start out big and then get gradually smaller.

The ship spins.

We're being pulled into a whirlpool.

Dad grips my hand and smiles at me. Oddly. I'm not scared at all. Not with Dad by my side.

"Tadaima," I say softly. Because we're going home.

CHAPTER 29

We sail in as close as we can, then swim to shore. Not a bad thing, considering how stinky we are at this point. And the swim seems like a piece of cake this time. It's harder for Dad, who's still weak. Once he emerges from the waves, panting from the exertion, he looks at me and says one word: "Home."

Home looks the same as when we left. There's still a new beach, and our house is still kind of wrecked. I'm relieved to be here in one piece, but my stomach shudders. How are things going to get back to normal? I hope Obāchan's okay. But if anyone could survive the apocalypse, she could.

It's twilight. In the distance, a half-moon hangs in the sky, and crickets are chirping. I guess it's about seven thirty; the days are getting longer as we get closer to summer. It's not too hot and not too cold, the kind of temperature where you could wear either shorts or jeans.

"How long have we been gone?" Peyton stands up and scratches his head. His wings are completely gone now. There are just two small welts on his back, as if he's healing from a couple of scratches. He rolls his shoulders, and I know he's remembering his wings.

"It's still the same night as our chicken dinner," Dad answers. "Time moves slower here."

"How long were you with the oni?" I ask him. "I mean, how long did it feel like?"

He shakes his head. "Too long, Xan. Too long. Let's go up to the house." But first Dad turns to face the water. He closes his eyes, puts his hands together, and bows, the way they do in Japan. "Good-bye, ocean." Dad waves at it. "Go back to where you belong."

I turn to take one last look at the ship.

It's gone.

The sea rapidly shrinks, the water pulling back from shore until the pine trees that were underneath stand up again. As far as I can see, there's a forest of fluffy pipe cleaners.

Hallelujah! I'll never dis this town again for as long as I live.

We walk up to the house, Inu bounding and barking ahead of us. My sword bounces against my back. "Do you want this thing back?" I ask my father.

"No, you earned it. I'm the mentor now, Xan. Not the true

Momotaro." He ruffles my hair. "Your grandfather would be so proud of you."

"What does it mean? The Sword of . . . what was it, Jinx?" I swivel my head to look at her.

She pushes her hair out of her face. "The Sword of Yumenushi."

Dad nods. "Loosely translated, it means *Dreamer of a Dream*."

"Dreamer of a Dream," I repeat. I have to say, that fits. "That's what I do."

"Indeed." Dad laughs. "But your training's only just begun."

I inhale. "Well, it can't be a whole lot worse than what we just went through, can it?"

Dad smiles but doesn't answer.

"I'm thinking that's a *Yes, it can be worse*, then. Fan-tastic." I jostle him playfully and he jostles me back.

Peyton moans. "All I want is a bag of hamburgers and a Dr Pepper Double Gulp."

Jinx puts her hand on her stomach in empathy. "Can it be from In-N-Out Burger? I haven't had In-N-Out in forever."

"Good idea!" Peyton holds out his fist for Jinx to bump. "Milk shakes, too!"

Jinx hesitates, then holds out her fist for Peyton. He taps it gently.

"That can be arranged." Dad puts his arm around Jinx's shoulders.

A black SUV rumbles up the driveway. It's Peyton's dad. Mr. Phasis gets out of the car almost before it stops. We all freeze.

"Peyton!" Mr. Phasis slams the car door. "Where have you been? You skipped practice and didn't breathe a word to anyone. The coach was worried sick, and so were we."

Peyton sucks in a breath, lets it out again.

I want to answer for my friend, tell Mr. Phasis, *Do you know what we have* just done? But my father puts his hand on my shoulder, whispers in my ear, "This is up to Peyton, Xander."

Mr. Phasis's impressive eyebrows furrow together. "Son, I'm speaking to you. Get over here right now. Hello, Akira. Sorry about this. I hope he was no trouble."

"Peyton is always a pleasure to have around," my father answers serenely. "He helped us tremendously."

Mr. Phasis peers more closely at us, at our filthy clothes. "What were you guys doing? Yard work?"

"Yes." Peyton finds his voice. It's loud and strong, stronger than I've ever heard it in the presence of his father. "Dad, I did skip practice. Xander's dad needed me. I'm sorry I didn't let the coach and Mom know."

Mr. Phasis bobs his head. Hmmm. I never noticed it, but he looks like a bird, too, sort of. He opens the car door. "We'll finish talking about this at home, Peyton. Get in."

Peyton holds up his hand. "But I have something to tell you first."

Mr. Phasis pulls back his head. "I just said, we'll talk at home."

"No!" Peyton's hands ball into fists. "No. I . . . I need you to listen to me right now, or I'm not going anywhere."

Mr. Phasis waits, his small bird eyes round and surprised.

My friend spreads out his hands. "I'm not you."

Mr. Phasis shakes his head, puzzled. "I know you're not me."

"No." Peyton takes a step forward. "No, you don't. I am not you and I'll never be you. I don't like playing sports every waking second of my life. I don't want to be in the military."

Mr. Phasis blinks, and he seems to sag a little. "You never said—"

"You never let me talk!" Peyton reaches his father. He's nearly the same height. "It's always *Yes, sir* and *No, sir* and *How can I help you, sir?* You literally never want to hear what I have to say!" Peyton's voice breaks. "I just want you to listen to me for once."

"I'm listening," Peyton's father says quietly, and something in his face softens. "Let's go on home, son, and we can talk all you like. I promise I'm listening."

Peyton nods once, tightly. He turns and waves at us and we wave back.

Jinx was right. We're home, but we're not the same as we were before.

Peyton's dad backs the car down the driveway, and we turn to our house.

CHAPTER 30

Inu sprints up the back deck stairs, bellowing.

"Obāchan!" I yell. I break into a run. "I got Dad!" I expect her to come out on the porch, or at least look out the window like usual, but she doesn't.

Woof, woof! Inu gallops into the house and I hear Obāchan's surprised, delighted laugh.

"Down, Inu!" my grandmother commands. "Stay down. Sit."

I run up the stairs, Jinx right behind me, and Dad pulling up the rear.

We go inside. Inu's wagging his tail so hard his whole body's wiggling. He jumps back and forth and side to side, barking, whining, licking someone's face. Not my grandmother's face.

There's a woman here, in blue jeans, with a blue scarf tied around her head, and a dust-cloth in her hand. A house cleaner, I guess. But now the house doesn't look like there was ever an earthquake. The damage must have disappeared, like the ocean did.

Inu's jumping up on her, more excited than I've ever seen him. She laughs, a sound like glass bells, and pushes him down. "Sit, boy."

To my amazement, he sits. I wonder why Inu likes this stranger so much. She wipes the dog slobber off her cheeks with the cloth.

"Tadaima!" Dad says.

The cleaning woman straightens up and removes the cloth so we can see her face. When she looks at my father, she takes on a funny expression. Hope and fear mixed together. *"Okaeri,"* she says.

What? She speaks Japanese?

She seems familiar to me. Her cheeks are a ruddy red, like a ripening apple, with a smattering of freckles. Her hair is curly and reddish blond. Her eyes, the color of glaciers with some green mixed in, brim with tears.

"Akira." She breathes my father's name and leans against the table for strength.

Dad lets out a cry and runs to her. He hugs her hard, as though he never wants to let go. "Shea," he says. Then, shockingly, he dips her and kisses her. Right on the mouth. Jinx makes a gagging noise. But I freeze.

I want to run away, too, but I also want to stay, and I want to cry and yell and laugh, all at the same time.

I recognize her now.

My mother has come home.

Coming in Spring 2017

XANDER AND THE DREAM THIEF